TELL NO TALES

HIDDEN NORFOLK - BOOK 4

J M DALGLIESH

EXCLUSIVE OFFER

TELL NO TALES

PROLOGUE

THE TOWN WAS SO different from what she had been led to expect. This town… on the coast, with a beach running as far as the eye could see; usually bathed in sunshine. In many ways, it was a lot like home. But it wasn't home and now it never could be. The beach was predominantly made up of stones and while the skies were powder blue and the sun shone, she couldn't feel the warmth on her skin.

The cold cut to her core and she shivered. Drawing her coat ever more tightly around her she hunkered into it, casting a glance up the street. A few people were visible milling about around the greengrocer and getting ahead with their plans for the day. They paid her no heed as she sat on the bench in silence. Her coat was thick, heavy, but still she felt the chill. Apparently, it was normal for the time of year albeit a little on the cold side. The winter seemed to last so long here, as if it would never end. She could hear a song playing from a radio inside the nearby butcher's shop. She'd heard it many times recently, performed by two brothers who sang about losing the feeling of love. It was popular and struck a chord with her.

Just a short while ago there seemed to be immense hope for the future, such promise of better days to come.

A fresh start.

But that was then. For a brief moment she contemplated how much her life had changed in such a short period. How it came to pass was clear. However, what the future would hold she didn't know and dared not think about. The low rumble announced the approaching bus rounding the corner and a quick glance at the town clock saw it was right on time, as she was told it would be. Standing up, she reached down and looped her fingers around the handle of the weathered, brown leather suitcase at her feet containing all that she owned in the world.

The bus came to a stop alongside her, the noise from the engine growling as the door flipped open. She cast one last glance to either side of her, up and down the street, before hefting the suitcase onto the bus and clambering aboard. Several of the passengers eyed her as she took her seat but no one spoke. Placing the case at her feet, she slid across to sit beside the window. The bus pulled away from the kerb, jolting her backwards in her seat.

The conductor came to her, bracing himself against the seat in front as the bus lurched forward, and she purchased her ticket. His gaze lingered on her, longer than she felt necessary, as he handed over the slip of coloured paper and she averted her eyes from his. For a moment she thought he knew. *They all knew.* But he walked away without a word. The bus took the next turn and the sea came into view. The white caps of the breakers stood out in the bright sunshine, the light shimmering on the water. It was magical, bringing forth memories from her childhood just a few short years ago. She ached for it now.

This place wasn't magical.

She felt her eyes beginning to water and steeled herself, fighting back against the tide of emotion. This was the way it had to be. There was no other choice, that was clear. A lady, sitting across the aisle caught her eye. She was elderly with a kindly face. She smiled and it was returned. Rummaging through her handbag, the passenger produced a handkerchief and offered it across the aisle.

"Don't worry. It's clean," she said.

Accepting the cotton square with a brief smile and a nod, she then recoiled and looked away, fearful of drawing attention to herself. Wiping her eyes, she made to return the fabric but the lady was already out of her seat and moving to the door as the bus arrived at the next stop.

Soon enough, they were on the move again and, after a few more stops, the town was rapidly disappearing from view behind them. She felt a flutter of fear in her chest and reached into her coat pocket, her fingers curling around the tight bundle of notes within.

Where she went from here would be God's will... if not His judgement.

CHAPTER ONE

SCANNING the shop fronts of the town gave rise to a warm familiarity as Tom Janssen took the sharp turn to the right, avoiding the pedestrians stepping from the narrow pavement as they sought to pass slower moving people going about their day. Sheringham was quite a different proposition to the town he remembered from his adolescence. Back then, he often found himself bored with life in the seaside town. In his youth, the traditional career paths open to the locals, that of working the sea or the surrounding land, struggled to remain relevant as society sought to embrace modernity. Arguably, it became something of a generational divide with those caught between the two camps struggling to see their place in a rapidly changing world.

Today, the town was a far cry from what he remembered. Now, the local economy was very much tourism-driven, fuelling employment with cafés, restaurants and entertainments. There was still space for the traditions, evidenced by the skiff pulled up onto the slipway where he drew the car to a standstill. There were more efficient places to land a haul these days than in the heart of Sheringham but even so, here, the fishermen still worked just as they had done for centuries whilst butting up against the café culture of the twenty-first century.

The gulls cawed overhead as he got out of the car and Janssen caught his colleague eyeing the small cafeteria on the promenade overlooking the slipway. DS Cassandra Knight realised he was watching her, snapping her attention back to him and apparently stifling a yawn.

"Sorry, sir. Where do we go from here?"

He pointed past the café in the direction of the promenade, stretching east along the extensive sea defences. A mammoth wall of concrete that protected the town and the cliffs from the ravages of the North Sea. This was most likely Cassie's first visit to the town. He wondered what she would make of it. It was no doubt very different to her native north east. There would be similarities in the small coastal communities but every town in Norfolk would be a stark contrast to what she experienced back in Newcastle.

Leading the way, he set off. The sun was already above the horizon and the sky was clear. Despite the strong breeze carried in from the east, the day promised to be pleasant, suggesting the arrival of spring might not be too far away. Even so, he drew his coat about him and turned his collar to the wind. Glancing across as he walked, he noted Cassie seemed less than bothered, hands thrust into her pockets but her coat remained open, flapping in the breeze as she took in her surroundings.

Once clear of the café and other public facilities they came to the colourful beach huts. These were chained to the concrete retaining wall, securing them against the possibility of being swept into the sea if the conditions arose. There were notable spaces where others had been removed and Janssen considered how things had changed. Where once the promenade was lined with concrete shacks, shuttered and in a state of disrepair, vandalised with graffiti and abandoned, an effort had been made to rejuvenate the area. What couldn't be repaired or utilised had been replaced, cleaned or made good. The last surviving concrete shack was now a coffee hut. Cassie had her eye trained on it already. His too, if he was honest.

From here, the sea defences became less substantial as they moved beyond the edge of the town. The retaining wall ceased and became a crumbling cliff face made up of sand and earth. The sea wall was still maintained here but to a lesser degree and it was where the modern, solid defences gave way to the ageing wooden barriers that they could see the police cordon and the activity beyond.

The path came to an end at the same point as the sea wall, dropping down to the patchy, broken surface of sand and stone. They were dwarfed here by the old sea defences, a wooden palisade running as far as the eye could see. Periodically, there were breaches where the sea had broken through. At some point in the past, the cut-off point was drawn as to where the town would be defended and where nature would be allowed to take its course. The coastal erosion was evident, the cliff face slipping to the shoreline around them all along the east beach.

DC Eric Collet saw them arrive as they ducked under the cordon, assisted by a uniformed constable tasked with keeping the onlookers at bay. He came to meet them, acknowledging Janssen first and smiling towards Cassie by way of greeting.

"What do we have?" Janssen asked, looking beyond Eric to where he could see the CSI team in their coveralls setting up their equipment.

"An unidentified male," Eric said, glancing back over his shoulder too before turning to lead to the scene.

Janssen fell into step alongside him and the three made their way over to the scene. Eric read from his handwritten notes as they walked.

"He was found a little over an hour and a half ago by a local couple walking their dogs. It was around first light and from a distance they thought it was a seal carcass."

They approached the scene and were met by the medical examiner, Dr Williams. Janssen bid her good morning.

"Morning, Tom," she said. "Not quite what you might have expected this one to be, I should imagine."

He found his curiosity piqued. It wasn't unheard of for people to die along this stretch of the coast. A prolonged spell of heavy rain could leave the cliff face prone to collapse and people walking close by at the foot of the cliffs were at risk. Sadly, accidents of this nature did occur. As did situations where people might choose to take their own lives or indeed accidentally fall from the path running the cliff edge above. The discovery of a body wasn't a surprise. The medical examiner's expression, however, was.

Coming to stand alongside her, he dropped to his haunches to assess the body, gesturing for Cassie to do similar. She came closer, appearing not to baulk at the prospect of being so close to death. She shouldn't be of course. It was often a matter of routine in this job and being a detective sergeant, Cassie would have seen her fair share already.

The victim was a black male, he judged to be around fifty years of age, perhaps a touch older but it was difficult to tell. He was clean shaven and must have been over six feet tall, although his body was twisted at an uncomfortable angle at the waist. He could immediately see what Dr Williams was referring to. He was dressed in a grey suit, white shirt and smart shoes, polished to a high sheen. This wasn't the attire many would choose for walking the seafront or cliff path above. His clothing bore patches of mud and sand, streaks of which ran the length of the arms and much of his legs. Janssen looked up. The cliff face towered above them, roughly a hundred feet high. There were outcrops yet to collapse but it was obvious that the land slipped towards the sea on a regular basis.

"My thinking is he fell from above, too," Williams said, reading his mind.

Janssen turned his gaze back to the man. The fall itself would most certainly have been enough to kill him. If not, the iron bar protruding from his chest would have secured his demise. Examining it closely, it was an L-shaped length of rusty iron. He imagined it was part of an old sea defence or groyne, left over from years ago and revealed by the sea wearing away the sand around it. There were many of these to be found along the coast.

"Well, if the fall didn't kill him, then that would have," he said, indicating the metal. "Do you think he would have survived the fall?"

Williams' brow furrowed as she thought about it.

"Possibly. The autopsy should be able to tell you for certain. Although it's more likely to tell you he was dead prior to the fall. The bleeding around the wound is indicative of that. If the heart was still beating during the fall, there would be far more blood."

"What do you make of this?" Janssen asked, gesturing to a wound on the forehead. He turned his gaze back to the cliff face searching for a rocky outcrop or something similar. The doctor lowered herself, leaning over, her eyes narrowing.

"Curious. At first glance, I thought it must have been caused by something he struck on the way down."

"Unlikely," Janssen concluded, assessing the composition of the injury as well as the cliff face the victim would have tumbled down. Although he was reticent to tell a medical examiner her job.

"Agreed," Williams said, looking closely at the impact point.

Janssen could trace what appeared to be a straight edge to the depression above and to the left of the eye socket.

"What do you think could make that outline? It's an irregular-shaped wound from either a blow or a fall," he said.

"I've never seen anything like it," she said, tilting her head as she spoke. "Something blunt and uncompromising, almost certainly. We'll have to get him under an X-ray and take it from there."

"Any ID?" he asked, looking between her and Eric.

It was the latter who stepped forward with a transparent evidence bag folded over in his hand. Eric offered it to him and he took it, turning it over in his palm. Inside was a set of keys attached to the key fob of a Range Rover.

"No wallet. No identification," Eric said.

"Any sign of the car?"

"Uniform says there's a Range Rover parked near to the cliff-top path but I haven't been able to check it out yet."

"We can do that," Cassie said from her kneeling position where she was still examining the body. Catching Janssen's eye, she quickly added, "If that's okay?"

He nodded, inclining his head back towards the promenade.

"Why don't you grab us a coffee at the shack, then we can head up. The nearest path up is near there anyway and I can see you're salivating at the prospect."

Cassie laughed.

"How do you take it?"

"Black. No sugar."

"Please," she said, frowning.

"Please and thank you," he replied with a grin.

Turning to Eric, he spied the onlookers nearby. Word would no doubt be around the town already. It was a tight community and news surrounding events like this travelled fast.

"I want you to increase the cordon, push people back," he said to Eric. "There's no need for anyone to come by here today. The dog walkers and the ramblers will need to take a detour."

"Right you are," Eric said, looking around. The only detour available would be through the sea.

"It's low tide now, so forensics will have until early afternoon to get the scene squared away before their feet get wet. Do you recognise him?" Janssen asked, always keen to pick the young detective constable's knowledge of the locals. He'd been quite adept at knowing what was going on in the community in the past, information that could only come from being born and bred in the area. Janssen's personal knowledge had lapsed for the better part of a decade when he departed for a spell in the

Met, only returning when his marriage failed and he sought comfort in familiarity.

"No," Eric said, scanning the deceased as if he expected to jog his memory by increasing the intensity of his stare. "I can't see him being local... at least not for any length of time. I can't say why I think that but... his clothes, appearance... stands out you know. I'd remember him if I'd seen him before."

Janssen nodded.

"While you're here coordinating things, have a casual word with those milling around," he said, flicking an eye towards the onlookers. "Someone always has an eye out around here and let's face it, newcomers who hang around stand out."

"Will do," Eric said. "I'll have some uniform go door-to-door along Cliff Road and the neighbouring streets as well while I'm at it."

"Good man," Janssen said, turning and heading off to catch up with Cassie. "Keep me posted if anything turns up," he said over his shoulder.

CHAPTER TWO

MEETING CASSIE AT THE SHACK, just as the coffees were being handed over, he took out his wallet and passed the assistant a ten-pound note before the DS was able to protest. He accepted his change and scooped up his cup, gesturing towards the nearby steps behind them. They led up to the car park above, servicing the flats overlooking the town. From there they would cross a couple of streets and pick up the path running the length of the cliffs. It was a popular walking route with locals and tourists alike, giving access to stunning views along the coast towards Cromer.

They started the steep climb up the steps and if Cassie thought they should have taken the car and driven round, then she didn't mention it. Janssen's towering frame made the ascent relatively steady for him, taking the steps with ease, whereas Cassie was barely five foot six tall and approaching the halfway point her breathing became more laboured but she didn't complain or let up.

Janssen reached the summit first, stopping to look back across his hometown. The skyline must have changed little in years with many of the buildings in the centre dating back centuries. The whites of the distant breakers reflected the early morning sunshine and the ever-present gulls searched for food. Behind him to his right was an art-deco building housing flats overlooking the sea. It had seen better days and was in need of a lick of paint, but the sea air routinely battered everything in the area. Necessary maintenance was a constant.

"Take your time," he said with a grin as Cassie joined him at the top, stopping to draw breath.

"I thought Norfolk was supposed to be flat," she said.

"It is. Apart from the high parts. Come on."

Janssen took the lead and Cassie fell into step alongside him.

"What did you make of our victim?" he asked her, glancing sideways, sipping at his coffee. It was strong, slightly bitter and as good as he'd come to expect.

Cassie thought about her response before she responded. He liked that. It demonstrated an analytical character, thereby making her less likely to be impulsive. This was his own favoured approach although he had been known to deviate from it on occasion much to the chagrin of the DCI, Tamara Greave.

"No wallet or mobile," Cassie said. "Back in Newcastle, I'd have suggested a robbery but not here. Not him."

"Why not?" Janssen said. He agreed but chose to play devil's advocate. "People get mugged here as well, you know. It's not as idyllic as outsiders seem to think."

"I don't doubt it but not that guy. Did you see the size of him? I'd bet he would give you a run for your money if you went up against one another," she said, referencing Janssen's height and build; far larger than the average man standing at well over six feet tall and powerful in stature. "Albeit before he died…" she added swiftly, "Less so now, clearly."

Janssen smiled. "He's a big guy, certainly."

"Yeah, tall and muscular with it," Cassie said, sipping at her own drink before meeting his eye as they walked. "And I reckon he knew how to handle himself. Did you see the tats on his neck and forearm?"

Janssen had to admit, he hadn't noticed the arms and didn't see the body art as significant.

"What of it?"

"I've seen similar. If I had to say, I'd wager they're fashionable on the street. Something of a marker to make you stand out from the crowd."

He wasn't so sure. The victim was in his fifties, not a twenty-something seeking street credibility with his local gang.

"The ink didn't look new," he said.

Cassie shook her head.

"No. He's carried that for a while. Doesn't fly with the suit, though either. That's not off-the-rack kit, you know. A bloke that size would struggle to get a suit to fit. His was tailored. Same with the shirt. He didn't pick that up in one of the high-street chains. That sets him a cut above the average bloke. But his palms are rough which speaks of manual work of some kind. That doesn't fit with his clothing either. And did you see any facial injuries...... other than the head wound, obviously?"

Janssen shook his head.

"Exactly. There were some scratches on the backs of his hands and a graze to the right side of his face but I'd argue that was down to the fall rather than the result of a physical confrontation with someone else. There was no swelling to the face or hands, no cuts to his knuckles, and the suit was in good shape aside from what you might get from taking a swan dive from a hundred feet. No, he wasn't involved in any sort of scrap."

"Then what do you think he was doing up there? If he wasn't forced over the edge then we must consider this as a suicide," Janssen said.

"Doesn't fit with any jumper I've ever investigated," she said with a shrug. "How many suicides have you been to where they're as smartly turned out as he was? If they have the impulse in the privacy of their own home, maybe, but those I've seen where someone has taken themselves out of their way to do it...

no, they are usually a mess which is only magnified upon impact."

Janssen exhaled loudly, accompanying the action with a dry laugh and a shake of the head.

"You have a way with words, Cassie. Don't ever let anyone tell you different."

She grinned at the comment.

"It has been said before." She cast a sideways glance in his direction, almost apologetic. "If his wallet and mobile are in the car, then I might lean back towards a suicide but if not then I think we'll need to dig deeper. I've never attended a suicide where they've ditched their ID before doing themselves in so as to go out anonymously."

"It takes all sorts," Janssen said, tilting his head to one side and observing her. She noticed, suddenly becoming self-conscious.

"What?"

She was nervous, worried she'd said too much or perhaps not enough?

"Nothing," he said, not wanting to heap too much praise on her assessment.

Her take was not too dissimilar to his own despite his efforts at debate. Tamara had been right; there was something about Cassie Knight that elevated her from the rest of the crowd, making her the stand-out candidate for the position. It was just as clear to him what Tamara saw in her. He could imagine the two of them sitting alongside one another, the same assertive character, the same intellect at work. Only a week into her new role, a promotion no less, and settling into an unfamiliar region and she didn't seem out of place at all.

"Seriously. What is it?"

He shook his head and smiled, turning his gaze to the sea beneath them. A red fishing trawler lay at anchor a little way off the coast. Cassie didn't press him further as they walked. Conversation dropped as they reached the top of the shallow incline, giving them a sweeping view of the vista along the coast towards Cromer.

"Damn," Cassie said.

"What is it?"

"It's beautiful," she said, stopping to admire the view. "My mam said it was lovely down here but she didn't do it justice."

"Your mum has visited?"

She shook her head.

"No, she's from here... originally, like, you know. Well, not here exactly, but Norfolk in general. She always said she wanted to move back one day but the old man would never wear it. *Too far south*, he always said."

"What does he do. Your father?" he asked.

"Ah... well, he's on the sick," Cassie said, her tone lowering and Janssen figured they were into uncomfortable territory for her. He didn't seek anything more on the subject but was surprised when she offered. "Has been for a long, long time."

"I'm sorry to hear that," he said, resuming their walk. "What's wrong with him?"

She shrugged.

"Sticky mattress syndrome, if you ask me," she replied, pointing ahead. "Is that the car?"

Up ahead of them they could see a black Range Rover. The liveried police car parked alongside it arguably gave the game away and Janssen figured she was taking the opportunity to change the subject. He didn't mind.

"So what is it that brings you to Norfolk?" he asked casually. The county was a wonderful place in his opinion but recruitment was an issue with many of those seeking adventure being drawn to the capital, much as he had been years previously. "I mean, it's quite a shift for you, isn't it?"

"I saw it as an opportunity," she said without breaking step. "Besides, I worked with DCI Greave on a national investigation a few years back and when she called... well, you know."

He nodded. This was news to him that the DCI already knew

Cassie. He was surprised how she hadn't chosen to mention it to him. Maybe she feared he would question the appointment more and make assumptions about Tamara's motivation. If so, that would disappoint him. He thought their working relationship was closer than that. Then again, it didn't change his initial view of his new detective sergeant.

The uniformed constable tasked with keeping an eye on the Range Rover got out of his car as they approached, nodding a greeting to Janssen and another to Cassie. His smile seemed warmer towards Cassie, his eye lingering on her longer than Janssen would have liked. Janssen knew the constable, at least, his reputation preceded him.

"Has anyone touched the car, PC Tomlinson?" he asked, drawing the constable's attention towards him.

He shook his head. "No, sir. Not since I've been here."

"Good. You can get back in your car now but don't go anywhere, there's a good lad."

The constable seemed momentarily confused before Janssen's stern look made him acknowledge the instruction and he departed, appearing somewhat embarrassed. Cassie was mildly amused. Apparently, this wasn't the first time she had made an impression on a young man.

"Was it something he said?" she asked, once the constable's door closed and he was out of earshot. Back in his vehicle, he removed his cap. His face was a picture of thunder.

"I'd give that one a wide berth, if I were you," he said, not wishing to detail Tomlinson's well-documented exploits and attitude towards women.

"I don't know," she said, glancing in the constable's direction. "I'll bet he wouldn't know what he was up against!"

Janssen laughed. He could see he was going to have his work cut out when both Tamara and Cassie were in full flight. Eric was likely to struggle.

"Let's take a look at this car then."

CHAPTER THREE

THE RANGE ROVER was parked at an irregular angle, appearing to have been left where it stopped. Cassie pulled on a set of latex gloves and tried the handle to the driver's door. The vehicle wasn't locked. She flicked an eyebrow in his direction and pulled the door open. The interior of the cabin was clean and well presented. She scanned the door linings as well as the fabric of the roof for any indications of a scuffle having taken place within the vehicle; blood stains, scuffs or scrapes to the linings. There were none that she could see at first glance.

The leather upholstery was a dark tan colour, useful for inadvertently concealing any telltale signs of blood but she was confident the victim hadn't been involved in an altercation, not a stand-up fight at least, so there wasn't likely to be any. The passenger door opened and Janssen dropped to his haunches, examining the interior much as she was. He was an interesting man, thoughtful and articulate, exuding a reserved confidence that appeared to put everyone in his company at ease. She liked him which was a massive improvement to what she was used to recently.

Janssen took the evidence bag Eric had given him from his coat pocket, placing it down on the passenger seat and gestured towards the ignition button. She pressed it and the dashboard lit up, thereby confirming the fob belonged to this particular vehicle. She looked at the digital dash and read the mileage. From the plate, she knew this was a recently registered vehicle and judging by the recorded miles it can't have been on the road for more than a month or two. It was also a high-specification model. She wasn't an expert on cars, they weren't really her thing, but she knew enough to mark this as a model costing upwards of eighty-thousand pounds. Perhaps more.

Turning her attention to the DI, Janssen's eyes moved around the cabin before settling on the glove box. He opened it. From her vantage point, Cassie could see a leather-bound case which she presumed contained the service record and handbook. Janssen paid it a cursory inspection before putting it down beside the evidence bag on the passenger seat.

"There's nothing in here to suggest it's a hire car. The DVLA should be able to tell us the owner," Janssen said.

He then reached back into the glove box and drew out a leaflet, taking a brief moment to read it before passing it across to her with an accompanying flick of the eyebrow.

Cassie accepted it from him, giving it the once over. It wasn't glossy and mass produced as one might find with a promotional leaflet for an attraction or a takeaway, this was a low-quality paper, most likely printed on a domestic printer. The colours were streaky in places suggesting the cartridge was running low on ink. The subject matter detailed a local food bank highlighting why it was necessary in the local area, actions people could take in order to get involved along with the contact details of the organisers. On the back were directions to where people could make donations, both financial as well as physical drop-offs. He must have picked it up, or been given it recently, because paper of this quality would easily degrade in a short period of time once thrust into pockets or stuffed into a glove box, rapidly taking on a weathered and dogeared appearance.

Glancing towards the rear seats, Janssen nodded his approval and the two of them retreated from the front of the cabin to examine the passenger seats. They opened the rear doors to find the interior to be in a similar condition to the front, although Cassie paused as her eye caught sight of mud on the edge of the seat behind the driver's. It was a small patch, not much more than a smear a couple of inches long but it was at odds with the condition of the rest of the car. Inspecting the door, she found a scuff to the trim along with more mud at the foot of the inside panel of the door lining but curiously none on the floor mats. It was dry but fresh enough to still have the appearance of a recent deposit.

Moving to the back of the car, Cassie opened the boot. The linings here were immaculate. Whatever the owner used the car for, he didn't spend much time loading or unloading items from it, reinforcing the view that this vehicle was new on the road. Janssen came to join her and, from his expression, she thought he was disappointed.

Lowering the boot lid, it closed with a smooth and reassuring click. She took out the radio she was carrying in her pocket, meeting Janssen's eye.

"I'll find out who the registered keeper is."

Janssen nodded and left her to make the call. He made his way past her and around to the driver's side. Making contact with the control room, she read out the licence plate and confirmed the index as it was read back to her. Then she waited. At the foot of the cliffs the breeze coming in off the sea was strong but comfortable. Standing on the high point as she was now, exposed and out in the open, it was a different experience as she leaned into the wind to keep herself stable. Casting a glance back towards the extensive sea wall protecting the town, and knowing how fierce the North Sea could be when roused, she wondered how different this little coastal haven might look. Their victim echoed this contrast, an event of pure ugliness depicted in such beautiful surroundings. The more she thought about it, the more she doubted this was either an accident or a suicide. It was an instinctive conclusion but the evidence would follow. She was confident of that.

The radio in her hand crackled into life, snapping her from her thoughts. Turning to put her back to the wind, sheltering the handset, she acknowledged the controller.

"Go ahead."

"Vehicle is a black Range Rover, first registered at the beginning of October last year…" Cassie did a quick mental calculation, that meant the vehicle did less than a thousand miles per month; precious little in this era. The information continued to flow. "The registered keeper is a company by the name of AMK Logistics Solutions, a limited company based in London."

The controller read out the address recorded on the database along with a landline telephone number he had found lodged against the company on the Police National Computer. Cassie placed her radio on the roof of the car as she made a note, awkwardly writing in her notebook whilst trying to listen. No more details about the company were forthcoming and Cassie tucked the radio back into her coat pocket, taking out her mobile. She had a strong reception which she found both pleasing and surprising in equal measure. Opening up a browser window she did a google search for the company by name. The list of returns came back negative with the search engine offering alternatives and querying her spelling. It was unusual for a business to have no online presence these days, reputable and legitimate ones anyway.

Janssen came back to join her, raising an inquisitive eyebrow at her thoughtful expression.

"Just checking something," she said in response to his unasked question, tapping numbers into her mobile before hitting the green button on the screen. Raising the handset to her ear, she waited for the call to connect. Almost immediately, she heard a mechanical voice repeating a recorded message.

The number you are calling has not been recognised. Please check the number and try again.

Double checking the number she dialled against the one provided by the control room, she shook her head, returning the mobile to her pocket.

"What can you tell me?" Janssen asked.

"The car's registered to a logistics company based in London, AMK Logistics Solutions. Somewhere in Lewisham. Sorry, I'm not familiar with where that is."

"South east London," he said.

She tilted her head thoughtfully to one side, considering the potential relevance of the location but nothing came to mind.

"I've done a quick search but the business has no online presence at all. If its trade is in logistics then that's moving stuff around; people, commodities or related services. The telephone number is either bogus or disconnected."

"Gone bust?" he said.

"Perhaps."

"Focus on putting a name to our victim first and the rest will follow."

"Yes, sir," she said.

Janssen frowned. She realised her error. The basic level of familiarity within the team was going to take a bit of getting used to.

"Sorry… Tom."

"Better," he replied with a warm smile. "You'll get there."

"I will," she said, inwardly knowing that she would definitely make the same mistake again.

Janssen produced the evidence bag containing the keys from his pocket.

"This one is interesting," he said, holding the bag up and pointing to one of the keys in particular. The blade of the key was brass, or was at least coloured to appear so, with the bow being made up of a plastic mix of black and orange. The bow bore an imprinted name of the manufacturer, one she had never heard of, and alongside the name was a serial number. The cuts were also unlike anything she'd seen before being inlaid concentric circles, rather than notches.

"Good luck getting Timpson's to cut you a spare for that," she said.

Janssen nodded.

"The blade is magnetic as well. Strikes me as high-end, technology-based security."

"Who uses that around here, do you think?"

Janssen shrugged.

"I don't know. Since the town has undergone its regeneration in recent years and seen the property money flowing in... it could be anywhere. It might be nothing."

"I'll call the manufacturers. Something that bespoke will need to be registered with them for spares and so on. Maybe they can help us out."

"Good thinking," Janssen said. "In the meantime, all we have locally to follow is that leaflet."

"The food bank?"

Janssen nodded.

"He might have just picked up the leaflet from a passer-by."

"Quite possibly," Janssen said. "But you never know. It's run by one of the local church groups. We can pay them a visit on the way back to the station. Maybe they can put a name to the face."

"Do you know them, the organisers?"

He shook his head. "No, can't say I do. My parents were never too fussed about religion and it's been a long time since I've set foot in a church."

"You and me both. I wouldn't be surprised if I burst into flames as soon as I cross the threshold."

Janssen grinned. "In that case, I'll keep a respectable distance."

CHAPTER FOUR

THE ENTRANCE to the property from the main road was narrow and Janssen felt he had to ease his way onto the drive. The brick wall encompassing the flint-fronted house was extensive and most likely original to when the building was first constructed. The pillars set to either side were not designed with modern cars in mind. The gravel-lined drive wound its way to the front of the house, sweeping past and back to the highway via a separate access gate.

"Nice place," Cassie said, eyeing the exterior of the rectory as the wheels crunched the gravel.

"It's unusual for the church to hold onto these old houses," he said, following her gaze as he brought the car to a stop outside the front door.

The building was large and set within extensive grounds. Often, these characterful properties were sold and replaced with a more modest, modern home that required much less in the way of upkeep. The sound of their approach must have carried because Janssen saw a curtain move in one of the downstairs rooms. It could have been caused by a draught but it was a significant movement. No sooner were they out of the car than the front door opened and the vicar appeared.

"Good morning," he said, accompanied with a warm smile that spread the width of his face.

"Reverend Ebling?" Janssen asked.

The vicar nodded. "The very same. What gave it away?"

The initial impression of the ageing vicar was that of a convivial man. He appeared to be in his mid-seventies, tall and slim. If Janssen hadn't already looked him up, he would most certainly have thought he was much younger than his years. But then again, he often found those who were strong in their chosen faith appeared to be more settled in themselves with a positive outlook. The thought was a sweeping generalisation but it was his experience.

"Detective Inspector Janssen and DS Knight from Norfolk Police," he said, not feeling the need to offer his warrant card unless asked.

"Good morning, detectives," Reverend Ebling repeated. "Please, do come in."

"Thank you," Janssen replied as the vicar stepped to one side and gestured for them to enter.

"What can I do for you on this fine day?" Ebling said, closing the front door behind them.

"We just have a few questions regarding the food bank that you run, if you don't mind?" Janssen said.

"Not at all," Ebling replied. His expression demonstrated mild confusion as to why they might be asking but also a measure of curiosity.

They were in the entrance hall, a wall-mounted clock ticked in the background. Whether it was the highly polished parquet flooring or the lack of furnishings to deaden the sound was unclear. Ebling directed them through a nearby door and into a sitting room. This was much as one might expect. The walls were painted a shade of dark green, but dominated by paintings of sailing ships at sea. An open fire crackled away in the hearth. Despite the sunshine and largely blue skies, the day was not warm and here, in a house built long before any thought was given to insulation or air-tightness. The house felt cold.

Ebling offered them a seat on either of the two floral-print sofas facing one another adjacent to the fireplace.

"Now, what is it I can do for Norfolk's finest?" Ebling said, addressing Janssen.

"Unfortunately, we have some sad news. This morning, a body was found at the foot of Sheringham cliffs and we were hoping that you might be able to help us identify him."

"Oh, that's dreadful news, Inspector. Truly dreadful," Ebling said, the attentive, warm smile dispersing to be replaced with a look of genuine concern. "Do you suspect this to be one of my parishioners?"

"We don't know as yet, is the honest answer," Janssen said. "However, we found this in what we believe to be the victim's car."

Janssen produced an evidence bag containing the food bank's leaflet, offering it to Ebling who reached for a pair of half-rimmed spectacles on an occasional table beside him. Leaning forward, glasses perched on the end of his nose, he held the leaflet at arm's length and his brow furrowed as he inspected it.

"Yes, this is certainly one of ours. We print them here in the rectory."

He handed the bag back and Janssen thanked him.

"As yet, we have been unable to identify the victim. He could be local, or not. He had this leaflet in his possession, so we thought he might be connected to your charity work or at the very least passed your way at some point. We were hopeful you might be able to put a name to him."

"If I can, Inspector. Can you describe him to me?"

In some circumstances, Janssen would take a photograph of the victim's face to help in these cases but with the head wound, on this occasion he figured it unsuitable. They were going to have to rely on a verbal description until they could bring in a sketch artist later, if it proved necessary.

"A well-dressed black man, most likely in his early to mid-fifties. Clean shaven with close-cropped hair," Janssen said.

Reverend Ebling thought hard, looking down and to his left in the direction of the dancing flames of the fireplace as if searching for inspiration.

"He has extensive and distinctive tattoos, as well," Cassie said, "covering his arms and protruding up from the collar of his neckline."

"I must admit that doesn't *sound* like any of my flock, Inspector," Ebling said. "But, my wife is really the driving force behind the food bank. Bear with me one moment, if you please."

Janssen nodded his approval and Ebling crossed the room to stand at the threshold to the room and poked his head out into the hall.

"Louise!" he called. "Would you come through to the sitting room for a moment?"

A voice acknowledged the request and Ebling returned to his seat. They didn't have long to wait before they were joined by Louise Ebling. She was busily drying her hands on a tea towel as she entered, her eyes flitting between her husband and the visitors.

"They are from the police, Louise," Ebling said. His wife was momentarily taken aback but quickly recovered from her surprise with great agility.

"How curious. What is it we can do for you?"

Janssen quickly repeated the information, aided by her husband who managed largely to repeat exactly what Janssen had just said.

"Is this someone familiar to you?" Janssen asked, once he'd recounted all of the relevant information.

Louise's brow furrowed and she exchanged a look with Ebling, who splayed his hands wide, turning the corners of his mouth down to indicate he was at a loss.

"You don't think that might be Devon, do you?" she asked her husband after a reflective period.

"Who's Devon?" Janssen asked, his eyes dancing between the two of them. Ebling's brow furrowed as he looked to the ceiling. "Devon? Is he that man who came to last Sunday's service?" "Hmm… yes. I think that description would fit him," Louise said, turning her gaze to Janssen and then smiling at Cassie, who made a note of the name.

"Do you have a surname?" Cassie asked.

Louise shook her head. "No, I am sorry. He only came the one time… with Helen, I believe."

Ebling shot her a brief look, one that was instantly lost as he nodded his agreement to his wife's suggestion that Devon could well be their man. Janssen picked up on it nonetheless.

"And who is Helen?" he asked.

"Oh… Helen Kemp," Louise said, smiling in his direction. "She is a regular at our food bank. She's ever so helpful. I don't know what I would do without her really. She needed our help once or twice herself and chose to repay us by volunteering from time to time."

"Is she one of your parishioners as well?"

Ebling rocked his head from side to side, scrunching up his face as he did so.

"Not so as you would notice but Louise is right, she did attend Sunday Service with a black man who could be your… unidentified man. Is that how you would put it?"

Janssen bobbed his head. "And you're sure that Helen Kemp attended service with him?"

"Yes, absolutely," Louise said.

"Is that unusual for her?" Cassie asked.

"She's certainly not a regular, no. Far from it," Ebling said.

"She is at the food bank, mind you," Louise said. Her husband nodded sagely.

"I can't say I remember her attending service prior to that occasion but, sadly, my memory isn't quite what it once was. Do you think it is significant?"

Janssen shrugged. "We're merely looking to build up a

picture at this time. Identifying the man is our first concern. Mrs Ebling—"

"Louise, please."

"Louise, was this Devon a friend of Helen's? Did he ever assist with your work at the food bank?"

Louise shook her head. "No. I mean, he didn't help at the charity but I would say he was close to Helen. Far closer than he should be, if you ask me."

Janssen found the overt accusation quite telling and he seized upon it.

"Could you elaborate?"

Ebling appeared none too impressed by his wife's intimation either, slowly shaking his head with disapproval. Louise exhaled in mock disgust at her husband's reaction.

"Honestly, Charles. You know what I am talking about. You've said as much yourself!"

"Yes, I have but… *in private*, my dear."

"Why would their relationship be… frowned upon?" Janssen asked.

"Well, she's married for one thing," Louise said.

This revelation sparked a strong interest in both detectives who exchanged a glance. Janssen wondered if Devon's fate could revolve around a scorned husband taking revenge. Clearly, Cassie was thinking similarly.

"And you believe they are more than just friends, this Devon and Helen Kemp?" Janssen asked.

"Idle gossip—" Ebling said.

"It is neither, Charles, as you well know." She dismissed her husband and turned to face Janssen. "Helen is a lovely young woman but… troubled. It's hard for her with her husband always away as he is. She started helping at the food bank partly to occupy some of her time. No children. No work of her own to speak of because her other half won't allow it. She was able to get permission for charity work. Is it any wonder why she might look elsewhere?"

"That's enough, Louise," Ebling said, placing a gentle hand on her forearm to restrain her from saying more. He addressed Janssen. "Despite my wife being far closer to Helen than I am, I must say this is speculation on my wife's part." Louise bristled but didn't offer a counter argument. "Now, it may turn out to be accurate but, at this time, it is purely conjecture and I beg you not to take Louise's opinion as gospel."

"Don't worry unduly, we never do," Janssen said. "Tell me, what do you know of Helen's husband? What is it that keeps him away?"

"He's a fisherman," Louise said.

"Based in Sheringham?"

"Yes," Louise nodded affirmatively. "Obviously, Shaun is out at sea a lot of the time."

"Shaun Kemp?" Janssen asked.

"Yes, that's him."

Janssen held his breath for a moment, noting Cassie watching him through the corner of his eye.

"Do you have any idea where Devon was living?" he asked.

"Charles is right. He wasn't local but I believe he had a place in the town. I guess he was renting somewhere. Helen will know."

"Thank you. We'll ask her."

Without anything further to ask, the two detectives thanked them for their time and rose to leave. Charles Ebling escorted them to the front door and it was closed before they reached their car.

Janssen shut his door and found himself drumming the steering wheel with his fingers, absently staring ahead at nothing in particular as Cassie got in and drew her seatbelt across her.

"Penny for them?" she asked, snapping him out of his reverie.

"Oh, nothing. Just the mention of Shaun Kemp threw me a little, that's all."

"You know him?" Cassie asked. He looked across to her. "It's written all over your face, then and now. Did you nick him once or something?"

"No, it's nothing like that."

"But you do know him?"

"Yes. I went to school with Shaun… and his brother, Jamie, come to mention it."

"Friends, like?"

Janssen drew breath, looking away from her and exhaling loudly. "No. No, I wouldn't say that at all."

CHAPTER FIVE

CHARLES EBLING CLOSED the door as the officers walked towards their car. As the latch clicked into place, he left the palm of his hand resting against the frame of the door and lowered his head. With his eyes closed, he took a deep breath and slowly released it in a controlled manner before returning to join his wife in the sitting room.

He found Louise knelt in front of the fire, adding another log to the grate.

"Did you see them out okay?" she asked over her shoulder without turning to look at him.

"Hmm…"

"Well… did you?" she asked pointedly, turning to face him.

"Sorry. What did you say?"

He found himself distracted, preoccupied with the conversation they'd just had, the details turning over in his mind. His gaze drifted towards the window overlooking the drive. The detectives' car was waiting at the gates, indicating left. Moments later, the car moved off again, soon disappearing from view behind the conifers lining the boundary wall of the rectory.

"Did they say anything else as they left?"

"What about?"

"Oh, Charles! You really should pay more attention—"

Louise was exasperated with him. That was a common occurrence.

"Perhaps you are right," he said, smiling weakly in her direction as she stood. The action was slow. Her left leg was clearly still causing her discomfort. "Do you think it was wise to say what you did?"

She looked at him with a puzzled expression.

"I didn't say anything that isn't widely known in the community."

She was defensive; a trait that he'd never admired in her for the fifty years of their married life.

"Widely *suspected* is not the same as known, Louise," he said, tilting his head to one side as he spoke. "And we both know what Shaun can be like."

"Helen has made her bed and she must lie in it."

"That is… a little harsh. I fear the police arriving at her door will only cause more problems than it solves. I do hope you thought that through before raising it."

Louise didn't respond to the question directly. Her expression was set as she headed for the hallway. If he had to label her look, then it would be one of defiance. Louise saw every given situation as a matter of black or white with no leeway in between the two for any shade of grey. No space for nuance. Over their many years together, he often saw this as advantageous in life; a stance that served her well. In hindsight, it was this strong belief system that he thought underpinned her unquestioning faith. At other times, however, he found the narrowness of her approach restrictive.

"Did you consider it?"

"I'll make a pot of tea," she said lightly, reaching the doorway.

"Not for me, love. I think I'll pop out for a bit."

He glanced in her direction as she turned to face him, her eyes narrowing.

"Where on earth do you need to go this morning?"

"I thought I would go for a walk. Maybe along the seafront."

She looked beyond him and out of the window. Grey clouds were rolling in from the direction of the coast, shrouding the early promise of the day in darkness.

"It looks like the weather might be about to change," she said. "You don't want to be caught outside if it does."

He held her gaze for a moment. There was something unsaid behind her comment, evident in her eyes. He was sure it was unrelated to him heading out. Fear, perhaps. Uncertainty. He forced a smile but it didn't seem to allay her anxiety.

"I won't be long," he said.

"I could come with you… if you like?" The question was asked tentatively. Hopefully.

"No. I would rather go alone if that's okay?"

She nodded and left the room without another word.

CHAPTER SIX

PARKING SPACE WAS at a premium on Cliff Road, a residential street leading away from Sheringham town centre in the direction of the caravan park, set back from the cliffs on the edge of the town's boundary. The street was a mix of semi-detached homes, some modern but most constructed at various points over the last century or prior. Building trends of the day were clear to see in the house designs. Tom Janssen pulled the car into the kerb and switched the engine off.

"I think it's the white one," he said, indicating a house three doors along.

Cassie followed his gaze. The house was a three-storey Victorian semi, painted white but the paint was lifting off in various places such was the exposure to the salt of the sea air. It was set back from the road with enough off-street space to squeeze in two cars. The bay windows on the ground and first floors were lined with heavy net curtains, restricting the view of the interior. The house faced towards the coast and there was every chance a sea view was visible if looking between the buildings opposite. The front door was made of plastic, at odds with the period of the house, but was also white and discoloured with age.

"Do you know the wife, Helen?" Cassie asked.

Janssen shook his head. "Not as far as I know. I went to school with a Helen but I doubt she would have been up for marrying one of the Kemps."

Cassie was first to the door and she pressed the bell. A tune played inside the house. Janssen peered through the bay window but nothing could be seen through the nets. The interior appeared to be in relative darkness.

"Maybe nobody's home," Cassie said.

At that moment, a shape appeared on the other side of the door and it cracked open. A set of pale blue eyes, dark-rimmed, eyed them warily.

"Yes?" she said, looking Cassie up and down.

"Detectives Knight and Janssen," Cassie said, holding up her warrant card for her to see. "We're looking for Helen Kemp."

"That's me," Helen said, opening the door wider. The wary expression remained. "What can I do for you?"

Janssen took her measure. She was in her mid-thirties, he guessed. Her hair was tied back but when loose would hang to her shoulders, blonde and almost certainly highlighted. Her general appearance was dishevelled, by circumstance and not design in his reckoning. She wore a loose-fitting shirt over a white vest and leggings.

"We would like to speak with you about a friend of yours, Devon," Cassie said.

There was a flicker of recognition in Helen Kemp's expression, her lips parting ever so slightly at mention of the name.

"Devon? What about him?" she asked, looking past them to the street. Janssen glanced over his shoulder but there was no one around.

"Could we speak inside?" Cassie asked.

"If you like," Helen said with a shrug, stepping back and pushing the door open to its fullest.

She turned away and headed into the house, not checking to

see if they were following. Janssen and Cassie exchanged glances. Cassie took the lead, hurrying to catch up with her, whereas Janssen ensured the door was closed. He cast an eye around the property as he slowly followed. The interior was similar to the impression of the house from the outside; in need of some care and attention.

Helen guided them to the back of the house and a large galley kitchen opening onto a small yard. It was a dogleg tacked onto the rear of the house. It looked as if they'd knocked through into the old outbuildings that would once have housed the coal shed and outside convenience, making a larger space for modern living. Aside from that, the kitchen was in a poor state of repair. Everywhere they looked, clutter was piled up. If it wasn't newspaper or junk mail, it was dirty crockery and foodstuffs. Helen noticed Janssen's attention and addressed him directly.

"Sorry about the mess."

From the tone in her voice she wasn't sorry at all, sounding irritated, possibly by her perception of his judgement. She was wrong. People lived how they chose to. It was none of his concern.

"You said this was about Devon?" Helen asked.

"Yes," Cassie said. "When did you last see him?"

Helen shrugged. "A few days ago… last week, maybe. Not sure. Why?"

"Can you describe him to us?"

If Helen was fazed by the nature of the question, she didn't show it. Rolling her eyes to the ceiling as she thought through her response, inhaling loudly.

"Black. Fifty-something, I guess. Works out. Tattoos." She folded her arms across her chest, appearing disinterested, watching Cassie intently who was listening to the description and nodding along with every detail. "What's this about?"

Cassie looked to Janssen and he nodded his approval. Sheringham was a small town and the likelihood of two men matching such a distinctive description was unlikely. Helen's description fitted their victim to a tee.

"I'm afraid we have some bad news. The body of a man was found this morning."

Helen sank back against the kitchen worktop, her mouth falling open.

"And… you think it's Devon?"

Cassie inclined her head. "It would appear so but we are yet to identify him officially."

"Is that… what's been going on up there, this morning?" Helen asked, turning her head in the direction of the cliffs barely a hundred feet away from them, almost as if she could see through the brick wall to the crime scene. The proximity of the Kemp residence to where the body was discovered had not gone unnoticed by Janssen.

Cassie nodded. "Yes. I'm afraid so. How well do you know him?"

Helen remained staring at the wall for a moment longer. Janssen wondered if she had even registered the question. Cassie looked about to repeat it when Helen turned back to them. He thought he could see her welling up but the tone of her reply offered no hint of emotion and he questioned his assessment.

"Not well. We speak from time to time."

"Where did you meet?" Janssen asked. Helen met his eye and he held her gaze. He sensed hesitation, as if she was considering which answer would be best to give. "It's not a trick question."

Her eyes narrowed and then she broke their contact.

"Around… you know how it is."

"Is he friends with your husband?" Cassie asked.

Helen shot her a dark look but it melted away as quickly as it had come to her.

"What's Shaun got to do with this?"

"You tell us," Cassie said.

Helen looked away, tightening her arms across her midriff.

"Nothing," she said, stepping forward and appearing flustered. "Can you excuse me for a minute?"

She didn't wait for permission and brushed past them, heading into the hall, walking with purpose. Janssen watched her go but said nothing. Cassie raised her eyebrows in his direction, which he took as an unspoken indication that Helen Kemp was holding something back.

They waited in silence. It was another couple of minutes before Helen reappeared from the cloakroom, located in a converted cupboard underneath the stairs, to the sound of a flushing toilet in the background. She walked back into the kitchen but didn't make eye contact with either of them. Janssen thought her skin was flushed with a sheen of sweat on her brow. The dark rings beneath her eyes also appeared more pronounced.

"Are you okay?" he asked.

"I'm fine," she said, glancing at him and then away. "Why are you here asking me about Devon anyway? I barely knew him."

Janssen took up the questioning, Helen's stance indicated she was about to adopt an aggressive attitude towards them.

"We understood you and he to have a closer relationship than that."

"Is that right?"

"Is it not the case?"

"Like I said. We hang out sometimes."

"Do you know why anyone might wish to do him harm?" Janssen asked, watching closely for a reaction. Helen's expression remained unchanged, fixed in a scowl.

"No. Why would anyone want to hurt him? He's a good bloke is Devon. Has someone done him in?"

"Too early to say," Janssen said. "How would you describe him?"

"What do you mean? I just did, didn't I?"

"Confident... arrogant... depressed, maybe?"

Helen snorted back a laugh, putting the back of her hand

against her mouth. "Depressed, Devon? You're kidding, right. No, not at all, not Devon."

If Helen was right, her emphatic denial could probably rule out suicide as the cause for him falling to his death.

"We don't have a local address for him. Do you have any idea where he was staying?"

She nodded. "Yeah. He had one of those apartments they've just converted on the other side of town. On the esplanade."

"The Beaconsfield?" Janssen asked.

Helen nodded. "Yeah. Nice place. It's not his. I mean, he rents it."

"But you hardly know him?" Cassie asked.

Helen met her eye with a dark look.

"Yeah. That's what I said. Do you have a hearing problem?"

Cassie ignored the sarcasm, her expression remaining neutral.

"If he's not local, where does he come from?" Janssen asked.

Helen shrugged. "Down London way, I think."

"London's a big place," he replied.

"Yes, I know," Helen said, raising her eyebrows and taking a deep breath while looking directly at him. He sensed they were reaching the limit of what they were going to get out of her. For now, anyway.

"What was his surname?" he asked. Helen shrugged, a gesture he found irritating. There was being unhelpful to the police and then there was bloody-minded obstinance. She must have read his expression, rolling her eyes away from him and answering quietly.

"Bailey. Devon Bailey."

"Thank you," he said flatly.

The door to the rear yard opened and a man walked in. He was startled by their presence, bringing himself upright as it dawned on him they weren't there for a social call. Janssen recognised the newcomer. It may have been the better part of twenty years since they'd seen one other, and they'd both aged, but Janssen knew the weasel-like features well enough despite some added girth and receding hair. By the expression on his face, he remembered Janssen just as clearly.

"I heard you were back," the newcomer said.

Janssen flicked him a welcoming nod. It was slight and made out of courtesy rather than being heartfelt.

"For a while now," he said. "How have you been, Jamie?"

"Alright, *PC Tommy*," Jamie Kemp replied.

Janssen didn't rise to the dig. He'd heard it before and chose to smile, one that was mirrored by Jamie.

"Is your brother around?" Janssen asked.

"Shaun?" Jamie said before answering the question. "Nah. He's still out. I spoke to him yesterday. He had a problem with the boat and had to put in along the coast. He was due back today, but… you can't help old boats, can you. What do you want him for anyway?"

"Any number of things, I should imagine. But for now, we're looking into the death of a man staying here in town."

"The jumper?" Jamie said.

"Jumper?"

"Yeah. The guy who threw himself off the cliff last night. That's what everyone's saying."

Janssen didn't wish to confirm or deny anything.

"What do you know about him?"

Jamie shrugged.

"They think it's Devon," Helen said. Jamie looked over to her, raising his eyebrows in response.

"Really?" Jamie said, looking between his sister-in-law and Janssen. The latter nodded. "Oh well. Can't say I'll miss him. I guess I'm one car length up in traffic this morning."

Janssen caught sight of Cassie's reaction to the comment in the corner of his eye. The callous nature of Jamie's attitude clearly surprised her. Not him. Janssen remembered Jamie Kemp only too well.

"Sounds like you don't care much for him," he said.

Jamie fixed him with a stare, casually chewing his lower lip, but said nothing.

"Of course, we don't know how he came to fall from the cliff top. Any suggestions?" Janssen asked.

"Always looking for the angle, aren't you, Tommy?" Jamie said. "Never mind reality... just look to make trouble for people."

"But you didn't like him, did you?"

"No. Can't say I did," Jamie said, looking at Helen who averted her eyes from his gaze. "His sort don't belong around here."

"What do you mean by that?" Cassie asked.

Jamie looked to her. "What do I mean by what?"

"*His sort.*"

"You know... dodgy and that."

"How is he dodgy?" Janssen asked.

Jamie shot him a withering look.

"You're the policeman, not me. Unless you want to pay me to do your homework?"

"No. Just like back in school, I'd need the right answers."

Jamie's face split a broad grin but it didn't meet the eyes, they remained trained on Janssen, who held the gaze. Neither spoke and yet something still passed between them.

"If we're unable to locate a next of kin," he said, turning to Helen. "Would you be willing to help us identify the deceased?"

Helen Kemp met his eye, nodding without speaking a word.

"Thank you. We'll see ourselves out," he said, gesturing for Cassie to lead. He lingered where he stood for a moment. Jamie remained unmoved. Cassie headed back into the hall and Janssen broke the mutual stare, turning to follow. He saw Helen and Jamie exchange a brief look at one another as he passed before she turned her eyes back to the floor.

CHAPTER SEVEN

THE SOUND of the latch clicking into place carried through to the kitchen and Helen Kemp glanced towards the front door, making sure the detectives had indeed left. She glared at Jamie. He didn't seem bothered by her attention, shrugging it off and moving to the fridge. He opened the door and casually eyed the contents before clicking his tongue against the roof of his mouth in disgust and pushing it to.

"Don't you ever do any bloody shopping?"

"If you don't like it, you can sod off back to your own flat," she said, drawing a sneer from her brother-in-law. "What are you doing here anyway?"

"Shaun asked me to stop by."

"Why?"

Jamie raised his eyebrows, fixing her with a knowing look.

"Oh, get stuffed, Jamie!" she said, turning her back on him. She would have stormed out if she had anywhere worth going to.

"Well, you can't blame him can you? Not with the way you've been going at it these past few months."

"And what would you know about it anyway?" she said.

"I know you well enough," Jamie said, his eyes on the hunt

around the kitchen. He dropped to his haunches and opened a cupboard in front of him, rooting through the contents. He paused his search and looked up at her. "And it's a good job I did really. Seeing as you're having chats with the police behind his back."

"Am I hell. They knocked on the door. What am I supposed to do? Ignore them?"

"Yeah. That's exactly what you're supposed to do, Hel," he said, with a frown. "Or, at the very least, don't knock around with people who'll bring them to your door. You know what Shaun's got going on at the moment—"

"That's just it, I don't, do I?"

Jamie sighed, abandoning his search and rising, pushing the cupboard door closed with his knee as he stood up.

"Tommy Janssen knocking around at the moment is the last thing we need. I would've thought that much was obvious."

"That's not my fault."

Helen felt under attack, she adopted a defiant stance, folding her arms across her chest.

"Maybe you should have kept some distance between yourself and Devon," he said, eyeing her up and down. "Any distance would have been good."

"What's that supposed to mean?"

"You know damn well what that means, girl! I'm not stupid… and neither is my brother."

"I think you should leave."

Jamie moved towards her with a swagger she'd come to despise. His posturing exaggerated no doubt by her dismissal of him. He came to stand before her, so close that she could feel the warmth of his breath on her face and the smell of the stale cigarette smoke clinging to his clothes. He reached up with his right hand and ran his fingertips through the loose strands of hair on her left side. She averted her eyes and flinched, moving her head away from his touch. He reacted instantly, gripping her hair and snapping her head towards him. Leaning in, their foreheads touched. She yelped but didn't cry out, nor did she seek to free herself.

"I know what you are," he said, barely above a whisper. "Remember when we were together? I got to know you very well, better than anyone else... even Shaun. And you should know something. We need this, me and Shaun. I don't care what my brother says, if you screw it up for us..." He tightened his grip and she tensed, letting out an involuntary whimper, grimacing with discomfort. "I'll make sure that you don't walk away... no one will be finding *you* at the bottom of a cliff. They won't find you at all."

He released her by thrusting his arm out and shoving her away. Helen staggered back and stumbled, half-falling against a cupboard where she allowed herself to sink to the floor. Her eyes were screwed tightly shut and her lower lip quivered as she crossed her arms in front of her, drawing her knees to her chest in an effort to provide both self-defence as well as a small measure of comfort.

Jamie moved to the rear door. He grasped the handle and opened it but stopped at the threshold to look down on her. She dared not meet his eye. He stepped into the yard without saying another word, allowing the door to swing closed without his assistance. Helen remained where she was. The silence seemed to weigh heavily upon her. Only now did she allow herself to cry. The tears rapidly developed into sobs. Yesterday, she thought there was a way out of this but now, and not for the first time, it seemed less likely than ever.

CHAPTER EIGHT

THE DOOR CLOSED behind them and Janssen was first to reach the pavement, turning left in the direction of the town centre. After a moment, he realised Cassie wasn't alongside him. Looking over his shoulder, he saw her hesitating to follow.

"The car's over there," she said, indicating behind her with a casual flick of the thumb, replying to his unasked question.

"I figured we would check out Devon's apartment at the old Beaconsfield. Come on, it's only a short walk across town."

He turned and set off, not waiting to see if she would follow. She did, hurrying to catch up with him as his stride lengthened. Coming alongside, he caught her glancing at him as they walked. Cassie Knight had only been with them for a week or so and although a lack of confidence was something she would never be accused of, he sensed she was still trying to work out the boundaries within the team. Cliff Road became Wyndham Street and he led them back towards the seafront. Once they were at the beach, Devon's resting place at the foot of the cliffs would be off to their right but they would turn left and head in the other direction along the promenade past the lifeboat museum towards the esplanade. It wasn't the most direct route but any chance to walk alongside the sea was his preferred option. Janssen turned his thoughts to Devon's likely movements the previous night. Sheringham was a small town by most measures, although large by coastal Norfolk standards, with everything easily accessible by foot for most people. The notion that a fit, healthy man would feel the need to drive from his apartment to where the car was found at the top of the cliffs seemed incongruous to him. Perhaps he had been elsewhere earlier in the day. Maybe he'd been to see Helen Kemp, parking the car nearby but not close enough to be too brazen. Cassie caught his eye once more.

"Something on your mind, Detective Sergeant?"

She didn't need any further encouragement.

"I was just wondering…"

"Wondering what?" he said, glancing at her as they walked.

"It's obvious you and Jamie Kemp go way back."

"Yeah. Not seen him in years, though. To be fair, if I hadn't seen him for another couple of decades, I wouldn't have minded too much."

The last was said with a wry grin, bringing a smile to Cassie's face.

"Is it fair to say the two of you didn't get on?"

He shrugged. "I didn't care for him, that's true. Jamie was obsessed with being top man, if you know what I mean?" he said, tilting his head to one side. "I'm not sure anything has changed."

"I know the type. Hard to imagine him going up against you, though."

Janssen laughed.

"Well, I was something of a late developer."

"What about Helen's husband, Shaun, wasn't it? Did you get on any better with him?"

"Nah," he said, shaking his head, directing them to the left along the promenade. They passed a couple of locals, making way for them on the pavement. "Jamie and I had the better relationship when it comes to the two of them."

Cassie raised her eyebrows, turning the corners of her mouth down in an exaggerated knowing look and bobbed her head up and down.

"Please can I be there when you speak to him?" she asked with a playful smile.

Janssen ignored the question. Helen Kemp came to mind and he replayed their conversation, prior to Jamie's arrival, in his mind. She'd been defensive. That alone wasn't unusual, many people were when the police came calling. This was different. Despite her apparent ambivalence towards the news of Devon's death, if that was what she was trying to convey, he had seen a notable reaction. Louise Ebling was certain Helen and Devon were carnally, if not romantically, involved. Knowing Shaun as well as he did, at least the Shaun Kemp of twenty years ago, he could understand why. He wasn't the type of man who would take kindly to his wife having an affair but then again, who would? One thing was certain, they would need to check up on Shaun's whereabouts. There was no way he'd take it on trust that Jamie was right and his brother was out at sea the previous night. If he had indeed put in for emergency repairs along the coast as Jamie claimed, then it was quite possible Shaun Kemp was on land when Devon had taken the fatal fall.

"What did you make of Helen?" he asked.

Cassie had been looking out to sea as they climbed the steps alongside the entrance to the museum. She turned back to him as they reached the top, another blast of wind striking them as they did so.

"Nervous," she said. "More so than just because two detectives turned up asking questions. Scared, I reckon."

"Scared of what?"

Cassie thought about it as they made their way up the steady incline. There was an old hotel on the corner, overlooking the sea. It had seen better days, the paintwork peeling and the render cracking. Janssen noted the planning application stuck to one of the doors facing the street.

"The easy answer is the affair... worrying that it would become common knowledge but I think it's more than that."

"How so?"

Cassie screwed up her face in mock anguish. "I'm from a large family, sir... Tom," she said, correcting herself. "The youngest of four sisters and a brother."

"Wow," he said, finding the thought of growing up in that environment challenging.

"You're not wrong," Cassie said, grinning. "One bathroom. Four girls. You can work it out."

He nodded at the sentiment.

"Your point?"

"I'm not only the youngest sibling but I'm the only one without children and also the coolest aunt you could wish for. With the amount of detective shows and serial-killer films knocking around these days, my nephews and nieces think I have the most exciting job going... little do they know having a drunk regularly throw up on you is usually about as exciting as it gets."

"Living the dream," Janssen said.

"Right. But I'll tell you one thing, all of my sisters have kids and I've been around enough pregnant women to know one when I see one."

Janssen stopped dead in his tracks, turning to face her. She was clearly amused by his expression of surprise.

"Are you sure?"

"The sudden rush to the toilet... the rosy cheeks and sheen of perspiration on her face when she came back," Cassie said with a knowing look, bobbing her head in confirmation. "Oh, yes. Undoubtedly morning sickness. I'd put my house on it. If I had one anyway."

"She wasn't showing, so... how far along would she be?"

"You've not got kids then?" Cassie asked.

An image of Saffy popped into his head but he declined the

opportunity to explain his circumstances. Instead, he shook his head.

"She'll be first trimester. A couple of months... around then, at any rate."

Janssen found various scenarios permeating his thoughts with one major question coming to the fore.

"I wonder who the father is?"

Cassie nodded solemnly. "I wonder if anyone else has been having the same thoughts?"

They continued on along the promenade for another hundred yards before they came to another flight of steps running up past a shack that would soon be selling coffee and ice creams once the tourists flooded the town when the season kicked into gear. For now, the shutters were down. Cassie stopped, eyeing the incline before them. These steps were cut into the side of a steep bank, making the ones they took earlier in the day seem like a breeze in comparison.

"Are you kidding?" she said, her eyes flitting between him and the steps. He laughed.

"I would have thought cool aunts would be used to charging around and be in better shape."

"I'm in good shape. Better than you," she said over her shoulder, setting off in the lead.

Janssen moved to catch up with her, which was a challenge as she set a swift pace. The steps led up to a small green overlooking the seafront. At one end was an enclosed children's play area and to the other was open grass. Beyond this stretch was the esplanade itself, made up of a mixture of residential properties ranging from houses to apartments. At one end stood the old Beaconsfield Hotel. When Janssen was growing up the hotel was still in use and had been up until very recently. It was the last of three traditional hotels dating back to Sheringham's heyday with their period decor, wrought-iron elevators and were all well known for their splendour. However, the Beaconsfield had seen better days and, although the last to close its doors, had been sold to developers recently. The new owners transformed the building into luxury apartments with the addition of a contemporary block added to where a car park once stood. The decision to allow the development was a contentious one amongst many local people who felt something of the town's history was being lost.

They rounded the playground and crossed the narrow road to the building's entrance. Once inside, they could see some of what would have greeted visitors of the past. The lobby, situated in the hotel's original reception, had been modernised but still tipped its hat back to the golden age. The reception desk of the former hotel was still manned by a concierge who looked up and welcomed them with a practised smile. Even his uniform was reminiscent of a bygone era. Janssen brandished his warrant card as he approached, his shoes squeaking on the marble floor.

"What can I do for you, Inspector," the concierge said, rising from his seat and inspecting Janssen's credentials. If he was disturbed by the police presence then he didn't show it, unsurprising when considering his job role. He would need to maintain a neutral, implacable stance whatever came his way. By the look of the interior, these apartments, in particular those with balconies overlooking the sea, would surely be priced upwards of half a million, perhaps more.

"We believe one of your residents was found dead this morning."

The concierge's mask slipped for a moment displaying surprise. Whatever he'd expected their visit to be about, that wasn't it.

"How awful. Who?"

"Devon Bailey."

"Mr Bailey. How awful," the concierge repeated, looking past Janssen to the outside.

"How well did you know him?"

The concierge considered his response. "Not very. He's not a permanent resident here, you see. I understand he was here on a temporary basis."

"How temporary?" Cassie asked.

"For the past few weeks or so. Perhaps a month but no longer."

"And when was he due to leave, any idea?" Janssen asked.

Again, there followed a period of reflection.

"That's a curious thing, I must say. You see, I was advised by the owner that Mr Bailey would be leaving at the end of the month but only yesterday that was changed. I received an email to say he would be staying on."

"How long for?"

The concierge shook his head. "I'm afraid I don't know the answer to that."

"The landlord, could they tell us?"

"Almost certainly. I can provide you with the contact details. He lives in Dubai, though, and I should warn you he is something of a devil to get hold of."

"We need access to Mr Bailey's apartment. Do you have keys?"

"I do indeed," the concierge replied, gesturing for them to accompany him to the lifts. Janssen was disappointed to see the original lift had been replaced with a modern system. The concierge glanced to Janssen as he summoned the lift to the ground floor. "What happened to Mr Bailey? Was it some kind of an accident?"

"That remains to be proven," Janssen said as the ping sounded and the doors parted before them.

CHAPTER NINE

DEVON BAILEY'S apartment was located on the third floor of the contemporary addition to the original building. They stepped out of the lift and the concierge directed them to the left. Allowing him to pass by, he led them along a well-lit internal corridor. Upon reaching the entrance to the apartment, he produced a swipe card and tapped it against a small silver pad fixed to the wall. A green light lit up and he gestured to Janssen with an open palm to suggest he entered.

Both Janssen and Cassie donned a set of latex gloves and Janssen tried the handle. It moved effortlessly and he pushed the door open. He told their escort to wait outside which he dutifully agreed to. Once inside they split up and moved through the interior. The apartment was large and predominantly open plan. Janssen figured the interior of his boat would fit inside this three-fold.

The interior was flooded with natural light, a result of the wall of glass lining the balcony which ran almost the full width of the apartment. The curtains were open giving them an uninterrupted view of the vista beyond the building. The apartment overlooked the sea and Janssen moved to the doors out to the balcony. They were high-end, much as this entire building was, powder-coated aluminium bi-folds that he knew would move to one side, fully opening the interior to the outside.

Producing the evidence bag containing the key found on Devon's body, he took it out of the bag and slid it into the lock of the primary door. The key turned easily and he was able to open it and step out. The wind buffeted him as Cassie came alongside. From this vantage point, they could see across the town centre and to the coastline beyond. Despite the bracing weather, the sky was clear at this point and the Sheringham Shoal wind farm was visible on the horizon. When the weather closed in, the turbines were often shrouded in mist and cloud.

Returning inside, he cast an eye around the room. It didn't look like any bachelor pad he had ever frequented before. The place was immaculate. The furnishings were high quality and the apartment as a whole was decorated in neutral, pastel tones. He pointed to the corner sofa. It was cream leather. Cassie smiled.

"In the north east, cream leather sofas are favoured by drug dealers. Does that follow down here?" she asked with a flick of an eyebrow.

Janssen laughed. "Maybe we should put a call into *House and Home* magazine to answer that question."

"Clean though, isn't it?" she said, her tone turning professional as she entered the kitchen area. "It doesn't look like he spent a lot of time in here."

As if to emphasise the point, she opened the oven which was mounted at chest height for Janssen, almost head height for Cassie. The interior looked brand new and unused.

"When did you say these apartments were done?"

"Over the last few months," he said. "Maybe Devon liked to eat out a lot."

Cassie nodded, moving towards a closed door. She opened it and Janssen saw the bedroom beyond. Even from where he stood, he could see the bed was made and there were no clothes scattered around. The worktops in the kitchen had nothing of note upon them and an inspection of the kitchen cupboards revealed very little. It wasn't clear if Devon spent much time here at all. He made a mental note to check on how the apartments were cleaned. He doubted that the occupants would do so and the block was probably serviced via the concierge facility.

Moving into a small corridor joining the living area to the rest of the apartment, he found a spacious bathroom and a second, smaller bedroom overlooking the rear where parking was allocated. Not many cars could be seen and the thought occurred to him that many of the residents could be at work but there was every possibility that the apartments may not be currently occupied. If the latter was the case, they might struggle to put together a decent timeline of comings and goings. The bathroom was spartan, a few toiletries were present but they looked like complimentary provisions, much as one would find in a hotel. No doubt there was an ensuite bathroom off the main bedroom and that would be the most-used facility.

The second bedroom, similarly with the bathroom, appeared to be unused, although even here the bed linen was clean and dust free suggesting it had been recently changed. Cassie called to him and he made his way back through to join her in the master bedroom.

The wardrobe doors were open and he scanned the contents. Several suits were on hangers, neatly pressed and he judged them to be of good quality, alongside a number of shirts. Other clothing was neatly folded on shelves below but this wasn't what Cassie was drawing his attention to. She was standing next to the bed and moved aside as he came alongside her, indicating the bedside cabinet. The drawer was open and he peered into it. She pursed her lips as his eyes widened, looking across to meet her gaze.

"I wasn't expecting that," Cassie said.

Janssen exhaled deeply, turning his attention back to the only item visible in the drawer: a semi-automatic pistol. Taking out his mobile he snapped several pictures of it in situ. He could see the safety catch was on. Putting the mobile back into his pocket, he took out a pen and slipped it through the pistol's trigger guard, lifting it clear of the drawer.

Holding it aloft, he examined it. The weapon was not large with a short barrel, easily concealable which was arguably where its strength lay. It was certainly not one he deemed would be used for show or street credibility as he had occasionally found among young dealers in the East-end of London. There were a number of scuffs and scratches to both the handle and the barrel, suggesting the weapon was well travelled. Despite this, it appeared to be a modern design and well maintained. He brought it close to his face and sniffed the area around the hammer. All he could smell was the oil used to clean it and even this was faint. Any weapon recently fired carried a distinctive smell, a pungent aroma caused by a mixture of nitroglycerin-soaked sawdust coated in graphite. It was a smell not easily forgotten but it wasn't present here.

"Any chance we can trace it?" Cassie asked.

"The serial number has been filed off," Janssen said with a shake of the head, looking at the slide where the number had clearly been removed by force.

The manufacturers name and model identification number were however still visible. It was a Steyr C9-A1; a brand he was unaware of. It was most likely German or Austrian made, judging by the name although it could just as easily be an East-European marque for all he knew. His knowledge of weaponry was limited to what he'd come across in the job. London was awash with cheap firearms and gun crime was a growing problem in the capital along with many major UK cities. Arguments that were once settled with fists or knives were now being dealt with differently and even low-level drug pushers were regularly known to carry. It was inevitable that such an escalation would eventually make its way out to regions, even to Norfolk, unbeknownst to many.

"It sounds like there's much more to Devon Bailey than we imagined," Cassie said.

Janssen met her eye.

"Wherever he was heading last night, he felt safe. Safe enough not to need this," his eyes indicated the weapon, "at any rate."

"Unless he was taken out of here under duress?" Cassie said.

Janssen looked around the room. It was as tidy and well presented as the rest of the apartment. There was always the possibility it had been cleaned but any blood stains would be apparent due to the colour of the carpets and soft furnishings. If Devon received his head wound here, then there must be evidence of it. Cassie followed his lead and her eyes tracked around the room. She stepped back into the living room and began checking for those telltale signs that could easily be missed by someone seeking to cover up an attack; the carpet at the edge of the sofa where table legs met the floor, the places easily missed in a hurry. Her expression conveyed her disappointment. There was no indication of an altercation.

"We should still have CSI turn this place over, just in case," he said. Cassie nodded. She produced an evidence bag and Janssen released the magazine into the palm of his hand. It was fully loaded and there was also one round chambered. The weapon was prepared. Devon Bailey had dangerous enemies or, perhaps, dangerous friends.

He placed the magazine alongside the gun in the bag and Cassie sealed it. Indicating towards the front door, Janssen crossed to the balcony and closed the door, locking it and putting the key back in its evidence bag. He then joined Cassie in leaving the apartment. The entrance door was ajar and as Janssen pulled on the handle he heard a shuffling of feet in the hall. Pulling it wide, the concierge was still there looking somewhat flustered. If he had to guess, Janssen figured he'd been at the door eavesdropping. It was probably the most exciting thing he'd experienced in his role to date.

"Are you finished?" the man asked Janssen.

"Not quite," he said. "We'll be sending a team over to examine things more closely."

The concierge seemed both interested and disappointed in equal measure at that announcement.

"Tell me, who cleans the building?"

"We have contractors for the communal areas as well as for the exterior."

"Windows and corridors?" Janssen asked. The man nodded. "What about the apartments themselves?"

"We provide a service for those who require it. Some owners choose to have their own staff but most use what we provide."

"Mr Bailey?" Janssen asked.

"They use ours, yes."

"When was it last cleaned?" Cassie asked.

The concierge thought on it. "I would have to check our records. The standard is for alternate days but that can be increased if requested."

"We will also need the names of all those who have access," Janssen said. "And no one is to go into that apartment until we give permission. Do you understand?"

"Absolutely."

"Were you working last night?"

"No. My shift ends along with our service at 7PM. I was here until then."

"What about Mr Bailey. Was he here when you left?"

The concierge frowned as he sought to remember. Eventually, he shook his head. "I'm sorry. I couldn't say. I didn't see him leave but it is possible he slipped out while I was otherwise engaged."

"Okay, thank you. Do you have a number we can contact you on?" Janssen asked. "We'll let you know when our technicians are coming."

The concierge produced a business card from an internal pocket and passed it over. Janssen scanned it briefly. The name of the management company was emblazoned within a stylish crest and the man's title was listed as 'Facilities Manager'.

"Thank you, Mr Dixon," Janssen said, reading from the card.

"Please, call me Ewan," he said with a ready smile.

Janssen bobbed his head in acknowledgement. "Thank you, Ewan. We'll be in touch later." He jabbed his thumb in the air over his shoulder, indicating Bailey's apartment behind them. "No one goes in there, right?"

"Clear," Ewan said, bobbing his head affirmatively. Cassie pulled the door closed behind them and they headed for the lifts.

Once they reached the ground floor, they said goodbye and headed straight outside. Janssen turned and looked up at Devon Bailey's apartment. Cassie thrust her hands into her pockets, evidently feeling the cold breeze.

"What are you thinking?" she said, following his gaze up.

He met her eye. "What's a guy like that, flash, money… shady… doing spending so much time in Sheringham?"

"Doesn't seem like his type of place, does it?" she said, looking around. "Hiding from something or someone."

"That's a thought," he said, bracing against the breeze coming in off the sea. "He was going and then changed his plans at the last minute. What could have caused that?"

"You'd love it if the Kemp brothers had a hand in this wouldn't you?" Cassie said.

By her tone, he knew she was only half serious. It brought a smile to his face. He turned to leave, a black SUV catching his eye parked further along the street. It looked out of place somehow. It was a BMW, nearly new with privacy glass all round. The daytime running lights were on but he couldn't see anyone in the interior. Almost as if his attention had been noted the vehicle pulled out and drove away from them. Something had piqued his curiosity but he couldn't explain why.

"Tom?"

He turned. Cassie was looking at him expectantly.

"Sorry, what did you say?" he asked, realising he'd completely missed what she was talking about.

"I said, shall we go and get something to eat now?"

"Yeah, sure," he said, his gaze drifting back along the street as he struggled to shake the sense of unease. The BMW was nowhere to be seen.

CHAPTER TEN

"I'M PRETTY certain this is our guy," Cassie said, drawing Janssen's attention. He rose from his seat in the ops room and crossed over to where she sat, chewing on a mouthful of the sandwich he'd bought on their way back to the station. Cassie angled the screen of her laptop so that he could see properly. The head shot was clearly recognisable as Devon Bailey. He was younger, clean shaven and somewhat thinner in the face and upper body but that was to be expected. "This was taken when he was arrested twenty years ago."

"What for?" Janssen said, swallowing the last of his mouthful and touching the back of his hand to his mouth.

"It was an arrest for assault. He was involved in an altercation outside a central London nightclub. The victim was admitted to hospital with multiple injuries and Bailey was arrested a couple of days later along with a number of others."

Cassie sat back in her seat, reaching for the coffee cup next to her laptop. It was still warm and she cupped both hands around it.

"An arrest for assault doesn't exactly make him gangster number one," Janssen said, his eyes scanning the detail on the screen in search of more.

To Cassie, he sounded disappointed. She sipped at her drink while he turned and perched himself on the edge of her desk, folding his arms across his chest.

"It doesn't, you're right. However, reading through the investigating officer's notes, there was a suggestion that the attack was motivated by gang affiliation."

Janssen met her eye, the disappointment dissipating as she spoke. He encouraged her to go on and she sat forward, opening another tab on the screen.

"From what I've been able to find out about him, Devon Bailey was something of a tearaway from his early teens. He was excluded from the high school he graduated from on several occasions and expelled from two others prior to that. He was on our radar from the age of thirteen. He has multiple arrests throughout his teenage years and into his twenties, ranging from his first arrest for theft, then receiving and burglary. Throw in a peppering of offences for violence and you see a developing picture."

Janssen's brow furrowed as he thought hard. "Sounds like a pattern of escalation to me."

Cassie agreed. "He was moving up the ranks, starting small and building a reputation for himself."

"You said they figured the assault was gang related?"

She nodded. "Aye. The victim was a known runner for a local dealer and the suspicion was that he crossed the boundary and the attack was the result."

"He was encroaching," Janssen said, thinking aloud.

"That was the theory but it didn't go anywhere."

"Let me guess," Janssen said, retrieving his own coffee from his desk and returning, "they couldn't find any witnesses?"

She smiled. He was spot on. It was often the reality when these cases reached court, if they ever got that far.

"The attack was caught on the security cameras mounted outside the entrance to the club," she said. "Bailey and his mates messed up. They were traced by the licence plate of the car in shot."

"Probably wouldn't make that mistake these days. CCTV wasn't as widespread as it is now, even in London."

"It was Bailey's car and they found him with three others who were all detained. The footage was enough to identify three of them, including Bailey, and to ensure the CPS pressed the case but no witnesses could be brought at trial."

"No witnesses, on a Saturday night in a central London nightspot?" Janssen said, not bothering to mask his incredulity.

"Oh, they had witnesses. Many of them," she said, bobbing her head, "but none of them appeared in court. Neither did the victim. In the end, all they had was the CCTV. Devon Bailey got three months. Served half that in the end."

"Gang connections?"

"Nothing specific on file," she said, putting her coffee down. "I'll dig a little deeper and see what I can find."

The sound of someone entering ops made them both turn to see Eric hustling his way, laden with two plastic carrier bags; his arms full. He was seemingly preoccupied and didn't notice their presence at first. Upon seeing them looking at him, he paused, the bags appearing to get heavier with each passing moment. The young DC seemed compelled to explain.

"Mum asked me to pick up a few things… you know, for later."

Cassie found herself struggling to refrain from laughing as Eric's visible discomfort increased.

"I did it in my lunch break… after the crime scene was processed."

Janssen shook his head slowly. "I didn't say a word, Eric." He nodded towards the bags which Eric placed on his desk, the constable moving quickly to brace the side of one as the contents threatened to spill out. "Did you get everything she needed?"

"Oh… erm…" Eric said, looking between his boss and the

bags. "She wanted an aubergine... a large one, but the shop didn't have any."

It was too much for her and despite a further attempt to withhold it, Cassie snorted a laugh, looking to the floor. She missed seeing Eric's puzzled expression.

"You'll have to stop off at the supermarket on the way home," Janssen said.

His tone was so dead pan, she couldn't tell if he was serious or not.

"Yes. I'll do that," Eric said. Cassie looked up and met his eye. Eric looked between her and the DI, frowning. "What?"

"Nothing, Eric," Janssen said, smiling warmly. "Nothing at all. Did CSI get the crime scene squared away?"

Eric nodded enthusiastically. "There was a concern that the incoming tide would put them under pressure but, as it turns out, the wind dropped and they processed everything well ahead of time."

"And the car?"

"Impounded. The techs will process the interior today and we should get prelims by tomorrow."

Eric's eyes drifted to Cassie's lunch, the open packet containing the second half of her tortilla wrap. She noticed his attention and for a moment could have sworn she heard his stomach murmur. Janssen looked up at the white boards. So far they were looking pretty spartan in content.

"Eric, can you get the boards updated with everything that we know from the crime scene so far. Cassie will fill you in on what we've turned up on Devon."

"Devon?" Eric asked. He had spent the day on the sea front overseeing the recovery of the body and was as yet unaware of what they'd already uncovered.

"The victim," Janssen said without elaborating. Eric nodded and took out his pocketbook, approaching the information boards in search of a marker pen. Janssen turned back to Cassie. "Is that the last we've heard of him, Devon, I mean?"

"Yes, the next time we hear from him is at the foot of Sheringham cliffs."

"That's odd, don't you think?"

"I'll say. It's not inconceivable that you can drift into a life of crime when you're barely out of short trousers and inexplicably fall out of it again in your twenties but, in my experience, it's unlikely," she said, glancing back at the image of a young Devon Bailey on her screen. Her thoughts turned to his association with Helen Kemp and their presence at the food bank. "Maybe he cleaned up his act... found God or something?"

Janssen followed her gaze to the screen, his eyes narrowing. "How many of His flock feel the need to carry an unlicensed firearm?"

She had to agree, the gun left them with some searching questions. It was a serious piece of weaponry as well. Illegal guns were readily available in the UK if you knew where to go and who to speak to, despite the belief of many to the contrary. More often than not, these were either older weapons brought in from Eastern Europe or converted weapons that used to fire blanks. The gun found in Devon's apartment was another level entirely. It was modern, would be expensive on the black market in the UK and the fact the serial number had been filed off suggested the possibility it wasn't a clean weapon. That is to say, one that had already been used in a criminal offence. Such weapons were cheaper to buy, coming with the inherent risk of attaching the owner to a serious crime. Ballistics checks would need to be performed and the results entered into HOLMES, the police database, to see if a match could be found. She glanced back at her screen.

"We have his last known address in London. Granted it's from a long time ago but in the absence of anything else to go on..."

Janssen appeared to think on it. "Yeah, let's see if we can find out what he's been up to around here first. If we draw a blank then we'll have no choice but to go backwards in time. You and

Eric can go door-to-door at the Beaconsfield, see if anyone there knew Devon or saw him knocking about with anyone local. Sheringham's a small town. The kind of place where everyone knows someone who knows someone. Secrets aren't usually kept quiet for long."

"Right," she said, glancing at the clock and then at Eric's shopping, teetering on the edge of his desk and threatening to topple over at any given moment.

"First thing tomorrow will be fine," Janssen said, reading her mind. "See what you can find out about the company who owns the Range Rover as well. I want to know what they do along with Devon Bailey's connection to it."

"Leave it with me," she said.

"I'll advise Tamara where we are," Janssen said, referencing the DCI. "Somehow I don't see this as a suicide."

"I'm with you on that," she said.

Janssen left, heading for his office, scooping up the empty packet that had contained his sandwich along with his coffee cup. Cassie saw Eric look longingly at the packaging as Janssen dropped them into the bin next to the door before disappearing into his office.

"What's up, Eric? Didn't you pick up something for yourself while you were shopping for your mum?"

The comment was only semi-serious in its mocking nature. In any event, Eric appeared not to notice. He glanced towards her, marker pen wavering in his hand having half-written a word on the board in front of him.

"No. I didn't think."

His tone was forlorn. A newcomer could have been mistaken for thinking something gravely serious had befallen him. She stood up and crossed the short distance between them, thrusting the packet containing the second half of her tortilla wrap into his hand. Eric's expression lit up, taking on the look of a six-year-old on the morning of his birthday. Returning to her desk, Cassie opened a new tab on her screen and directed it to the Companies House portal. Entering the company name the Range Rover was registered to, AMK Logistics, into the search box, she tapped return and waited. The results came back immediately.

AMK Logistics was an active company with private limited status. It was initially set up and incorporated three years previously and a quick check of the filing history revealed submitted accounts on time with the next confirmation statement due in a couple of months. The company was listed as a business offering support for transportation activities, which she found to be wonderfully vague. Changing the page to review the people listed against the company, she found several directors and a company secretary. None of those listed was Devon Bailey. The managing director was a man by the name of Gavin Reynolds. Switching to another screen, she did a search on the name but it returned no information at all which she found odd. Returning to the government portal, she took a screenshot of the company details before noting the company's registered address. It was the same as that she'd been given earlier by the control room operator, an address in Lewisham, south east London. She copied the address and googled it, bringing up a map and enlarging it on the screen but it offered her little by way of useful information. This was partly because she was so unfamiliar with London's geography and she shut it down again. *What was it that would bring a man like this to Sheringham?*

The sound of tins clattering against the desk before tumbling to the floor, accompanied by Eric cursing loudly, snapped her from her reverie. Eric scampered over, half-eaten wrap in one hand, and began recovering the items, some of which had rolled under the desk and tantalisingly out of his reach. Cassie moved to help, patting Eric on the shoulder reassuringly as she knelt down beside him. He offered her a grateful smile.

"My mum will go mad if any of these are dented," he said, examining the tins as he picked them up.

"Your mam is lucky to have you, Eric," she said. He met her eye, seemingly unsure of whether she was making fun of him. She smiled. "You can do my shopping for me anytime."

CHAPTER ELEVEN

"COME ON, Eric. Get a move on. The sooner we're done, the sooner you can be off," Cassie said in response to Eric's gaze, lingering on the shopping bags on the back seat of his car. She was keen to find out what Devon Bailey might have been up to as well as who he was associating with recently. If Helen Kemp wasn't willing, or was unable, to offer up any information and with Jamie unlikely to be forthcoming, the only opportunity they had to shine a light on Devon's life was at the Beaconsfield. There was always the chance that forensics might lift something useful from the car or the apartment, a fingerprint or similar, but until the techs had time to properly process them, it was a waiting game. Cassie wasn't good at waiting. Besides, the best time to catch people at home would be in the evening. If they left it until the following day, there was every chance they'd find no answer at most of the doors they knocked on.

Janssen was right when he'd told her this was a small town, and small towns were the same the world over; everyone knew everyone else, where they worked and who they mixed with. Much of the information would be rumour, idle gossip or pure fabrication as people loved to talk about others. If they didn't know genuine facts, they might choose to see an inference where one didn't exist or fill in the gaps with their own details.

This was what made eyewitness testimony such a minefield when it came to prosecutions. Five people could all see the same events but what they recalled could be vastly different and usually was. However, wading through the random recollections of people's memories wasn't entirely a waste of time. Sometimes, more regularly than one might realise, the most innocuous of comments could offer a shard of light that cut through the murk to reveal a breakthrough. Those moments were special but the reality was they only came from knocking on doors and speaking to people face to face.

"I know," Eric said, grumbling. "It's just…"

"There's nothing refrigerated in there, is there?" she asked, eyeing the shopping bags.

"No… but Mum likes to eat at half past six, on the dot," he said, looking at his watch.

"We'd better be quick then," Cassie said, pushing her door closed. The thud of the door sounded the death knell for Eric's hopes of getting home on time. By the expression of disappointment on his face, Cassie figured his mother must be a formidable woman. Eric struck her as a lovely guy, a bit wet behind the ears for her tastes, though. They entered the lobby of the Beaconsfield apartments. Ewan Dixon, the concierge, was behind his desk as he had been earlier in the day. He was into the final hour of his shift but he looked as fresh as if he'd just started. Part of the job, she figured.

"Back again so soon?" he asked, glancing up as they approached. The question was asked without any hint of genuine surprise, spoken as more of a greeting. "Do you need access to Mr Bailey's apartment again?"

Cassie shook her head. "No, we're here to canvass the neighbours."

"I see," Ewan said, acknowledging their goal with a bob of the head. "Well, you know your way around," he said, gesturing towards the lifts. "But... I would appreciate it if you could be discreet." The latter was said with a lowered voice and he glanced around the lobby as he spoke, seemingly concerned their conversation would be overheard. It was a daft concern in Cassie's mind. She had no intention of leaving the building until she'd knocked on every door. If the residents were unaware of Devon Bailey's demise, and that he was one of their own, they certainly would be by the time she left.

"Tell me, has anyone spoken to you regarding Mr Bailey today?" she asked, ignoring his request.

"No. Not with me, at any rate."

"Any tradesperson entering the apartments, or visitors coming to see residents, are required to sign in with you before going in. Is that right?"

Ewan nodded agreeably. "That's correct. Unless they're accompanied by a resident. In that case I'm not involved."

"What about after you clock off? Seven, isn't it?"

"The main doors are locked and visitors need to buzz the resident via the intercom in order to gain entry."

Cassie looked around, searching for cameras. She couldn't see any which surprised her.

"What about Mr Bailey, has he drawn attention to himself recently?"

"Attention? In what way?"

"Strange visitors... out of the ordinary incidents, strange comments... anything like that come to mind?"

Ewan Dixon's brow furrowed while he considered the question. "I can't say anything springs to mind."

"Any visitors recently. The last few days in particular? How about the other residents? Was he familiar with anyone in particular, as far as you know, either in a professional capacity or socially?"

Again, Dixon thought hard about it before replying. "Mr Bailey pretty much kept himself to himself. Almost the perfect resident." Cassie nodded slowly, taking in the information. Dixon met her eye. "You will be discreet, won't you?"

"We'll do our best," she said. Ewan held his gaze on her, watching intently. She guessed he was assessing her sincerity. Not that it bothered her. She turned and headed for the lifts. Eric hurried to join her, arriving as she pressed the call button.

"He's a bit officious," Eric said under his breath, looking back towards the desk and the man apparently busying himself behind it. "Doesn't seem to know very much about what's going on around here either."

Cassie sighed, shooting a quick glance towards the reception desk. Dixon was already head down and getting on with whatever he was doing, shuffling paper by the look of it.

"I always thought a concierge was supposed to have their finger on the pulse of the building; there to anticipate the wants and needs of the people they serve."

"Like some kind of a politician," Eric said, glancing at his watch again. "How many apartments do you think are in this block?"

Eric looked up at the counter displaying what floor the lift was currently at. Cassie assumed he was already working out what time he would be able to make it home to limit his mother's wrath. Eric's comment struck her as poignant, though. Whether he knew that himself, she wasn't sure. A concierge did indeed walk the line of a politician, trying their best not to put anyone offside and please as many people as possible. It was the job role. They heard the lift approaching the ground floor; a ping sounded as the doors parted and they entered. Cassie hit the button to take them up to the floor Bailey's apartment was on before turning around and facing out. Her eyes focussed on Ewan, standing behind his desk as the doors closed. Perhaps, it was a case of *see no evil, hear no evil* when it came to what they got up to at the former Beaconsfield Hotel.

Stepping out of the lift, Cassie glanced towards Bailey's apartment. The door was closed with blue and white crime scene tape criss-crossing it. Forensics hadn't been able to get to it yet and this was the best they could do for the time being, aside from asking Ewan to ensure no one sought to enter. Looking along the corridor, there were three other apartments to this floor. One other overlooked the sea, directly next door to Bailey's, while the others faced towards the rear. They would have views across the rooftops of the town and, if they were lucky, might be able to see the water in the distance but would be far less prestigious.

"Why are we starting halfway up?" Eric asked, following Cassie's lead as she strode along the corridor.

"Makes sense. I should imagine a place as well kitted out as this will have a decent sound barrier in place between floors, so it's probably best to start with those who might see comings and goings, bumping into people waiting for the lifts. That type of thing."

"This one first?" Eric said, coming before the door to the front-facing apartment. Cassie nodded and Eric rapped his knuckles on the door. They didn't have long to wait before it opened and they were greeted by a man in his late seventies. He looked the two of them up and down with a wary eye. Cassie brandished her warrant card and identified herself, then introduced Eric. The DC smiled warmly but the pleasantries were lost on the resident.

"I saw the tape across next door. What on earth is going on?" the man asked, without introducing himself.

"I'm afraid your neighbour was found dead this morning."

"Really? Here?"

"No. His body was discovered on the shoreline at the foot of the cliffs, just beyond the sea wall," she explained.

"That is a shame," he said, looking past them to the far side of the corridor. Cassie followed his gaze but there was nothing there of note.

"Did you know him well, Mr…?" Cassie raised her eyebrows, encouraging him to be forthcoming with detail.

"I'm terribly sorry. Scott, Geoff Scott," he said, snapping out of his reverie and introducing himself, directing his attention to her. "No. I didn't know him at all. I think we may have exchanged words once or twice... on my way to get the morning paper but that's about it."

"Forgive me if this sounds a little off, Mr Scott," Cassie began, choosing her words carefully, "but do you spend a lot of time here. I mean, are you retired?"

The man laughed.

"Very much so, young lady. I've paid my dues and now it's time for me to put my feet up."

"Have you noticed any comings and goings from next door? Anything that you found a little curious, perhaps?"

Scott looked along the corridor, first in the direction of Bailey's apartment and then across the hall to the next apartment. His reticence was obvious.

"Anything at all might prove useful," she said warmly, accompanied by a wide smile.

"Well... I'm not one to pry," Scott said quietly. Cassie had the distinct impression that he was prone to exactly what he denied but she said nothing, allowing him the space to elaborate. "But there was something of an altercation the day before last."

"What type of altercation?"

"Oh, an argument... it got rather heated, I must say. My hearing isn't very good these days but even so, I felt uncomfortable listening to it."

"Was Mr Bailey, your neighbour, involved?"

"I dare say! It was inside his apartment."

"Who was he arguing with, do you know?" Cassie found her curiosity piqued.

"Couldn't say," Scott said, accompanied by a shake of the head and another nervous glance beyond the officers.

The door to the apartment opposite opened and a woman stepped out. She cast them an inquisitive look as she passed them in the corridor, Scott averting his eyes as she glanced in his direction. Cassie gestured with her head for Eric to have a word and he quickly caught the woman up before she reached the lifts, already taking out his ID as she turned to face him. Cassie returned to the conversation at hand.

"What were they arguing about?"

Scott shook his head, glancing at the woman chatting with Eric. She looked in their direction once again and Scott retreated a step into his apartment, out of sight.

"I couldn't really say and I wouldn't like to cause trouble."

"Please, Mr Scott," Cassie asked, reaching out and placing a reassuring hand on his forearm. It did the trick and he smiled at her, easing the tension in his face.

"It was all muffled… but there were definitely raised voices."

"How many voices… male or female?"

Scott thought on it. "Three, I would say. All men. At least, I wasn't aware of a female voice but as I said, my hearing isn't quite what it used to be."

"And this was two nights ago?"

"Two days ago, yes but it was mid-afternoon, not in the evening."

"Are you sure?" Cassie asked, recollecting the earlier conversation with the concierge.

"Absolutely. I'd just finished a late lunch. My hearing might be off but my faculties are intact," he said with a grin that revealed pristine white teeth. She figured they must be implants.

"I don't suppose you happened to get a look at these visitors?"

Scott shook his head emphatically. "No, stayed well out of it. Discretion being the better part of valour and all that. You could always ask Sandra."

Cassie raised her eyebrows in query. "Sandra? Is she your wife?"

Scott laughed again. "No, nothing like that. Sandra Leaford. Do you not know her?" Cassie shook her head. "She's a local estate agent. I've seen her coming and going regularly. She's frequently been in and out of next door."

"Are you sure it was her?" Cassie asked, making a note of the name.

"Yes, of course. Her office handled all the sales of these apartments. I know her well."

Cassie tilted her head to one side. "I wasn't aware Mr Bailey was involved in property."

Scott snorted with derision. "That's a gentle euphemism if ever I heard one." It was clear to him that his statement wasn't going to be allowed to pass without more detail and after a moment of silence, he relented. "I'm not sure it takes all night to discuss property acquisitions. Looked like she'd had a bit of a rough night, if you know what I mean?"

"Are you saying she spent the night?"

"More than once," he confirmed, tapping the side of his nose with the tip of his forefinger. "Definitely more than once."

"And when was she last here, do you know?"

Scott's brow furrowed as he thought about it. "The night before last, I would say."

"You're certain?"

"Oh yes," he said. "I was a military man in my youth. Royal Air Force." He raised himself upright. "Attention to detail was important. Mistakes weren't tolerated."

Eric returned, slipping his pocketbook back into his coat pocket. He offered a slight shake of the head to an unasked question, implying his conversation hadn't borne fruit. Cassie handed Scott one of her contact cards. He scanned the detail as she thanked him for his time.

"If anything else comes to mind, do give me a call," she said.

"Be sure that I will, young lady," he said, beaming and tapping the card against the side of his head before withdrawing back into his apartment and closing the door as the detectives turned to walk away. Cassie made to go towards the last remaining apartment on that floor only for Eric to stop her.

"That one's empty. It's a holiday home and the owner lives in London."

"Okay, I think we have enough to go with at the moment anyway," she said, turning and heading for the lifts. She recounted Scott's account of recent events while they waited for the lift to come up. "Do you know her, Sandra Leaford?"

"I know of her business. It's the longest running independent estate agent in town," he said, checking his watch for the umpteenth time. "Sandra runs it with a couple of staff. It's not one of the biggest in town. Not that you'd know it based on how much business they seem to be involved in. Her husband is a financier, I believe. He must push a lot of clients her way."

"Husband? That's interesting," Cassie said with a knowing wink. "I wonder what he would make of Sandra's overnight stays here?"

Eric didn't answer immediately, merely blowing out his cheeks as the doors parted before them.

"I doubt he'd be very pleased."

"I doubt he would, Eric. I doubt he would."

CHAPTER TWELVE

Cassie Knight saw Tom Janssen hunched over the desk in his office as she entered the ops room. She was up early, keen to get in and get ahead of the game. It looked like she wasn't the only one. He hadn't noticed her arrival and she watched him from the corner of her eye as she hung up her coat and went to turn on her computer. She'd spoken with Tamara Greave about her potential boss prior to agreeing to apply for the role. Despite Tamara's assurances, she still hadn't been sure upon their first meeting. It wasn't so much his physical presence, although that alone was intimidating enough, but more his reserved nature.

The DI was a very hard man to read which unsettled her. She wanted to know where she stood. She needed to.

He looked up, catching her watching him. She cursed internally and offered a slight wave in his direction. To pretend he hadn't caught her eye would be futile. Janssen beckoned her into his office. Crossing to the office, she leaned on the door frame with the palm of her right hand but remained at the threshold.

"Morning, sir," she said, grimacing at the use of the title.

Janssen smiled but didn't mention it. "Good morning,

Detective Sergeant. I'm just going over some of the initial findings from the pathologist."

"How on earth did you manage that so soon?"

Janssen laughed. "I asked nicely." She frowned, indicating a lack of enthusiasm for his response. "I asked for a quick assessment regarding the head wound. It's only based on an early X-ray and examination, so it's most certainly subject to change."

"Even so," Cassie said with a raised eyebrow. "They'd have told us to whistle for it back home."

"Yeah, well," Janssen said, sitting back in his chair, "we do things a little differently in Norfolk."

"So I gather. What can we learn from it?"

Janssen turned his laptop one hundred and eighty degrees and pushed it towards her. Cassie felt an instinctive pull to remain where she was but fought it, entering and crossing the short distance to Janssen's desk. The image of the X-ray was displayed on the screen and she could easily make out the shape of the wound along with the damage to both the surrounding tissue and bone.

"That looks nastier than I first thought," she said.

Janssen nodded.

"Could it be a result of the fall?"

He shook his head. "It doesn't appear so. Had he fallen from the cliff closer to the town, landing on the promenade and sea defences, then possibly."

"But he didn't."

"That's right. CSI picked over the route of his descent, as best they could, and there was nothing they could find that would have resulted in such an injury," Janssen said, sitting forward and resting his elbows on the desk and interlocking his fingers before placing them under his chin.

"Any suggestion as to what we may be looking for?" she asked, looking closely at the scan of Devon Bailey's skull. The depression was extensive, punching through the cranium and sending shards of bone inwardly in each direction from the impact point. With the naked eye, it appeared to be roughly two inches wide and yet shallow. In her experience that ruled out makeshift weapons that may have been close at hand, such as a hammer or garage tool. The object was more likely to be wide and flat.

Janssen pursed his lips, appearing thoughtful. "No. She's a little stumped; never seen the likes of it before. It's a hefty object, blunt with smooth, regular edges. That rules out an incidental knock against an outcropping or the remnants of shale concrete we found at the foot of the cliffs. She thinks it's more reminiscent of an assault."

"That would also suggest a lack of premeditation if that's the case," she said. Janssen looked up from his thoughtful pose, his eyes narrowing. "The gun we found in his apartment suggests Devon is something more than what we've seen so far, or has reason to see himself as under threat. The people he sought to protect himself from, the likes of whom would require an armed response, would surely have weapons of their own. We'd be looking at gunshots or stab wounds, surely?"

Janssen sat back again. "I see your point."

"It follows that if this was a planned attack, we'd see an obvious weapon… right?"

"Agreed."

"Any feedback on where such an attack may have taken place?"

Janssen sighed. "I don't think we've identified the crime scene yet. The pathologist reckons there's no way Devon would have been able to walk himself off the cliff. The head wound would have seen him unconscious, so unless he has a superhuman capability to somehow sleepwalk his way off a cliff while neurologically impaired, then we are looking at a murder. We'll have to wait for the full report to see if he was alive when he went over the edge and it was the fall that killed him but that remains open to debate right now."

"It'd be good to get CSI around to Devon's apartment today, if only to rule it out as the crime scene."

"They'll get there as soon as they can," he said, looking to his left and picking up a sheet of paper. His eyes drifted over it before he handed it across to her. "That's their preliminaries from the car. It's been wiped clean. Steering wheel, door handles, buttons... all devoid of prints."

"That's efficient," she said without looking up, reading through the documented bullet points.

"Very. I've asked them to pick it over... see if they can find anything that might help us figure out who drove the car up there. The local criminal fraternity isn't overly large and if they can pull together a print of any kind then we'll have a good shout at picking someone up."

Cassie found her thoughts drifting to the Kemps and wondering whether Janssen was silently hopeful his childhood adversaries would loom large in the investigation but she didn't mention their names.

"Eric and I pulled a good lead last night when we went door knocking at Devon's apartment block."

"Go on."

Cassie outlined the conversation she'd had with Geoff Scott the previous night, as well as Ewan Dixon's failure to mention Devon's visitors several days before his death. Janssen listened intently, only speaking when he wanted clarification on specific points in the narrative. When she was done, he sat in silence, chewing on his lower lip.

"There's every possibility Ewan was unaware of the visitors to Devon's place but, you're right, it is a substantial deviation from the man Ewan Dixon described to us. Devon seems unlikely to be the man who keeps himself to himself."

"Similarly, Ewan would know Sandra Leaford too," Cassie said. Again, Janssen nodded. "How should we play it with her?"

They both noticed Eric Collet entering the ops room and Janssen tipped his head in the young man's direction. "Go and have a word with Sandra. Take Eric with you but play things close to your chest and see what develops."

"Leave out the malicious gossip, you mean?"

"Yes," Janssen said, absently rubbing at the back of his neck. "We've no reason to doubt the validity of the neighbour's accusation but if you mention it, then it could spook her into throwing up barriers. It might be better to hang back and see how she reacts to the news of Devon's death."

"And what she does afterwards," she added.

Janssen nodded slowly.

"In the meantime, I'll go and have a word with Shaun Kemp. Jamie said he'd be putting back in today."

Cassie nodded, standing up and heading for the door. She had genuinely wanted to be there when Janssen spoke with Shaun, not only to witness the apparent needle between him and the Kemps but also because she wanted to get a bead on Shaun. Helen bore all the hallmarks one would expect to find in a household where domestic violence was an ever-present. She'd seen enough of them to know. Devon Bailey's death could easily be the result of a confrontation with a jealous husband. The question on her mind at the moment was *which* husband was most likely. Devon Bailey was looking more and more like something of a player when it came to other men's wives.

Eric was taking his seat in front of his computer as she strode towards him. He clicked his tongue against the roof of his mouth and hissed quietly under his breath, placing a plastic vending machine cup down on the desk. Evidently, he'd spilt some of the contents and burned his fingers in the process. He was shaking the excess liquid from them as Cassie clapped him on the shoulder.

"Come on Eric, get your coat."

He looked up to his right as she passed by him, swivelling to his left to answer her as she scooped up her coat.

"Where are we going?"

"To see Sandra Leaford, remember?"

Eric nodded, looking forlornly at the steaming cup on the desk in front of him, a small pool of coffee spreading out from the base. "But... I was just hoping—"

Cassie came back to him, coat looped across her forearm, and looked over his shoulder. The grey film floating on the surface of the drink made for an unappealing sight. She never used vending machines. They were almost always awful.

"Come on," she said, playfully elbowing him in the arm, "I'll buy you a proper one while we're out."

Eric smiled, rising from his chair and following her to the door. He retrieved his own coat from the hooks by the entrance and slipped one arm through as he hurried to join her. Coming alongside her, she caught a familiar whiff of something. Leaning in towards him, he recoiled from her, a confused expression on his face.

"What is it?" he asked.

"You missed yer dinner last night then?"

He glanced sideways at her. "Erm... yes," he said, sounding puzzled. "How did you know?"

"Your fish and chips was nice though, was it?"

Eric shook his head in defeat. "I told you... Mum doesn't like to eat late."

Cassie couldn't help but smile. Even so, she resisted the urge to mock him any further.

CHAPTER THIRTEEN

"YOU'VE LIVED around here all your life?" Cassie asked. Eric nodded briefly before reversing the car into a parking space between a hatchback and an SUV. They were in Sheringham, at the car park situated alongside the train station. They got out of the car. An engine with three carriages was waiting at the platform and Cassie was surprised to see smoke billowing out of it. "What's with the old school trains?"

Eric first looked to where she was pointing before frowning at her. It was an expression of his that she was becoming familiar with. Like many people who are born and raised in one particular location, never leaving, when newcomers exhibit surprise at something they consider routine they often find it confusing.

"It's the Poppy Line," he said as if it was the most obvious answer possible.

"Say again?"

"The North Norfolk Railway. It's a heritage line running from Sheringham through to Holt," Eric indicated the best route to the high street and Sandra Leaford's estate agency. "Don't you have steam lines up your way then?"

"Yes, of course. I just wasn't expecting to find it… you know, here."

"In the back of beyond, you mean?" Eric said, his tone sounded accusatory.

"No. That's not what I meant at all," she said, wondering whether Eric was actually offended. He didn't seem particularly thin-skinned but she chose to drop it. "What do you know about Sandra Leaford?"

Eric guided them to the left and they headed into the town centre. This was one of the main routes in and out and cars buzzed past them as they negotiated the narrow pavements and pedestrian traffic.

"I've never met her personally but she's well known in the area," Eric said. "Both Sandra and her husband."

"They have something of a reputation?"

"I've heard nothing negative," Eric said, raising his voice to be heard above the passing cars. "They moved out here from London a few years back. I remember the office opening. That was the summer before I joined up, so I remember it well."

Cassie was surprised. She'd been in the job for six years before she had a shot at CID. Eric couldn't be more than in his early twenties. How long could he have been on the force? She figured she could ask Janssen later or perhaps Tamara when she was next in.

"Do they both work in property?"

Eric shook his head. "No, the estate agent is her thing, as far as I know. He's some kind of big shot in the city I think or, at least, he was. I'm not sure now."

They walked for a couple of minutes until they hit the area of the town where all the estate agents seemed to be located. None of them were particularly large by city comparisons. Leaford's was on the other side of the street and they waited for a break in the traffic before trotting across. The business was located in a small traditional building set back from the road behind a collection of public benches, all arranged in a semi-circle for shoppers to take a break and watch the world go by. As with many of the older buildings that still remained in the town, they had small windows and appeared claustrophobic by modern standards; designed to provide functional respite from the harshness of the coastal weather rather than maximising the retail experience.

Cassie entered first. What little natural light penetrated the interior was further restricted by the advertising boards hanging in the window. Despite the sunshine outside, they found themselves bathed in artificial light from recessed spots. A young woman sat at a desk facing the door speaking on the telephone. She acknowledged their presence, silently mouthing a hello, and holding up a forefinger, before continuing on with her conversation. There were two other desks. One was unoccupied, very tidy and didn't appear to be in use today. The remaining desk was set back to the rear of the office and had more in the way of files in comparison to the other two. Beyond this was a narrow hallway and Cassie could see a staircase leading off it and another closed door. She figured the closed door offered access to the facilities.

Cassie cast an eye across the properties for sale locally, their details hanging on the walls all around the office. There were several she might consider herself. Only flats, mind you, as any house was well out of her reach financially right now. The conversation finished and she heard the sound of the receiver being put down.

"Good morning," the young woman said, Cassie turning towards her. Her face split a broad grin, the type that was forced and easily seen as fake by anyone who spent their working day dealing with professional liars and con artists. Even so, Cassie returned it with a warm smile. "I'm Stephanie. How can I help you today?"

Cassie inclined her head towards the properties on offer. "Pricey around here, isn't it?"

Stephanie applied a suitably apologetic expression to her

features. "This is a high-demand location, I'm afraid. There is limited stock and the market sets the price. What are the two of you looking for?"

Cassie met Eric's worried glance in her direction. Clearly, Stephanie thought they were a couple and Eric's reaction didn't do much for her self-confidence. *He should be so lucky.* Shaking her head, she reached for her identification.

"We're from Norfolk CID," she said, offering her warrant card. "We're here to see Sandra Leaford. Is she available?"

Stephanie followed Cassie's gaze towards the rear.

"Sandra should be in shortly."

"Is she usually in later?" Cassie asked, wondering if the owner's absence could be deemed unusual.

Stephanie shook her head. "I opened up this morning. We tend not to get much footfall first thing, so one of us can manage. It's largely chasing people up, progressing chains and the like. Why, what's going on?"

"Oh, we just need to have a word about a couple of things," Cassie said.

At that moment, the door from the outside opened and another woman entered. Cassie took her measure. She was in her forties, tall for a woman, far taller than herself, and immaculately presented. Her blonde hair, professionally dyed without visible grey to the roots, was loose and hung to her shoulders. Her make-up was equally well crafted, subtle and classy, rather than baked on with excessive use of powder as tended to be commonplace these days. She was adorned with minimalist jewellery and sported a stylish business suit, and Cassie knew enough to recognise it as a designer label. If there was a description of a 'high-end' estate agent, then this woman would fit the bill.

"Sandra Leaford?" Cassie asked with an accompanying smile.

"They're from the police, Sandra," Stephanie said, her tone was tinged with excitement for some reason. Maybe this was a turn of events that titillated her.

"Police?" Sandra asked as Cassie produced her identification once again. "What can I do for you? Is everything okay?"

"We just have a few questions for you. Is there somewhere we can talk?"

Sandra eyed Cassie and then Eric, glancing to the rear of the office.

"Not really. The kitchen would be a bit of a squeeze. We tend to see clients out at properties rather than here. How can I help you?"

"We wanted to discuss your relationship with Devon Bailey," Cassie said, watching closely for a reaction. There was one and it wasn't subtle.

"Devon?" Sandra said, following a brief pause where any warmth radiating from her towards them seemed to dissipate. Her expression became fixed, pensive. "I haven't spoken with him in quite some time."

Cassie glanced at Stephanie who was making a show of getting on with her work but she wasn't much of an actor.

"Can you define what *quite some time* looks like?" Cassie said.

Sandra stumbled over her words. "Weeks… if not longer. Why do you want to know?"

"Mr Bailey was found deceased yesterday morning," she said. The veil momentarily slipped and Sandra's mouth fell open. "I'm very sorry to have to tell you. He was found at the foot of Sheringham cliffs."

"That… was Devon?" Sandra asked, Cassie confirmed it with a slight nod.

Cassie noticed that Stephanie was no longer typing, her hands frozen in mid-air above her keyboard. Sandra noticed too.

"Steph, why don't you pop out and get us some milk… and then I can make us all a cup of tea," Sandra said, with an entirely unconvincing smile.

Stephanie shrugged, gesturing over her shoulder and pointing her forefinger in the direction of the kitchen. "There's no need. We have milk in the fridge."

"Get some fresh," Sandra said, producing a purse from her handbag and taking out a ten-pound note.

"No. It's fine. I just made—"

"Just do it!" Sandra snapped. The adopted tone must have been unfamiliar because Stephanie seemed visibly shocked. Sandra caught a hold of herself, drawing breath before gently pushing the money into Stephanie's hand and forcing a casual smile. "Please. Maybe get some cakes or something while you're there."

Stephanie was visibly taken aback, her lips parting momentarily before returning the smile as she stood up. The others made room for her to pass and she stepped out into the street, the sounds of the town centre carrying to them on the blast of cold air from the outside. Once Stephanie was out of sight, Sandra turned, folded her arms in front of her and perched herself on the edge of the unused desk. She took a deep breath, apparently steadying herself. Her body language only confirmed Geoff Scott's assessment of her relationship with Devon. Whether Sandra Leaford would admit it, however, was quite another matter entirely.

"What is it you want to know?" Sandra asked, avoiding eye contact.

"What was the nature of your relationship with Mr Bailey?"

Now Sandra looked up, meeting Cassie's gaze with a stare. "Professional."

"I see. So, Mr Bailey was what… a client of yours?"

Sandra looked to the ceiling, drawing breath as she considered her response. "Of sorts, yes. Devon was looking to make investments in the local area."

"What sort of investments?" Cassie asked, looking to Eric to make sure he was documenting the conversation. He was.

"High-end residential, in the main," Sandra said, sniffing and touching the back of her hand to her nose. "He knew our office handled the sale of the Beaconsfield apartments. That's what drew him to me… us."

"I see. And when did you say you saw him last?"

Sandra locked eyes with her again. "Like I said. A couple of weeks ago, maybe. I'm not sure."

"To your knowledge, was Devon involved with any other local businesses?"

Sandra appeared puzzled by the question, her eyes narrowing as she thought about it.

"Your competition perhaps?" Cassie said.

Sandra shook her head. "Not that I know of. Why?"

"It seems odd, that's all. We understand Devon was due to be moving on but at the last moment changed his plans and arranged to stay on here. Why would that be, do you think?"

Sandra pursed her lips, gently rocking her head from side to side. "I'm sorry. I wouldn't know."

"It's curious though, isn't it?" Cassie said, glancing at Eric and then back to Sandra. "He extends his stay for some reason and then winds up dead the following day."

"You say that as if… "

"As if what, Mrs Leaford?"

Sandra shook her head once more, only this time more emphatically. "Like… it is somehow untoward."

"Well, it doesn't look like he died from natural causes."

Cassie paid close attention to her, sensing that mentioning the suspicion of murder could catch her off guard and prise open her thoughts a little. However, Sandra had already recovered from the shock and had her poker face back in position.

"It's coincidental, is it not?"

"Are you saying Devon was killed?"

The question was asked in a dead-pan tone, too neutral to infer anything from it.

"It is a distinct possibility, yes," Cassie said, replying in kind.

Sandra held the eye contact for a few seconds before looking beyond them to the street outside.

"Do you know anyone who may have taken issue with Devon?"

"Enough to kill him?" Sandra asked, immediately dismissing the suggestion with a flick of her head. "I'm sorry, I have no idea. How would I know?"

Cassie maintained her watchful gaze in the silence that followed, waiting to see if anything else would be forthcoming. Sandra offered nothing further and she decided, for now, to leave it there.

"Okay, thank you for your time, Mrs Leaford. If you can think of anything else you think might be useful, please do get in touch." Cassie offered her a contact card. Sandra took it, giving it a cursory glance before slipping it into her pocket.

"I will, Detective Sergeant."

Cassie followed Eric to the door, turning back as he opened it to the sound of traffic. Cassie frowned as she thought about how to phrase the question, keeping it casual. "How much business were you doing with Mr Bailey?"

"How do you mean?"

"Well, you said he was into property. High-end residential, didn't you say?"

Sandra nodded.

"How close was he to completing some purchases?"

"It was all in the preliminary stages."

Cassie bit her lower lip, bobbing her head. "I see… but he planned to leave." Sandra was unfazed by the comment and remained tight-lipped. "And what of your husband?"

She appeared to tense at the mention of her husband, only by a fraction, but Cassie was watching for it.

"What about him?"

"Would he have been involved in business dealings with Devon as well?"

"No. My husband works in finance."

"Right, okay," Cassie said, smiling. "Thanks again."

Eric led the way out into the sunshine. After time spent in the gloomy interior, Cassie found herself shielding her eyes from the brightness whilst they adjusted. They began the walk back to the car.

"She's an accomplished liar," Eric said as they walked, careful not to say so within earshot of passers-by.

"She's an estate agent," Cassie said. "That comes with her job."

"Emotional attachment makes it harder though."

She nodded. "Yeah, she was unconvincing when it came to the relationship between her and Devon. Professional, my arse."

"Nice way to drop the husband into things. That threw her a bit. You didn't fancy telling her we know she was at Devon's apartment the night before he died, though?"

Cassie smiled, casting a sideways glance in his direction. "All in good time, Eric. All in good time."

CHAPTER FOURTEEN

THE DOOR CLOSED and Sandra Leaford watched as the two detectives walked away to their left and out of sight. Only then did she feel the tightness in her chest. She'd been holding her breath. A sensation coursed through her body, leaving a feeling of disembodiment, and she laid a palm onto the nearest desk to steady herself. What should she do? Barely a minute passed before the door to the street opened once more. Stephanie hustled through clutching a plastic box of pastries in her free hand with a small bottle of milk nestled between forearm and midriff. Pushing the door closed behind her with a foot, she turned and was surprised to see only Sandra present.

"Oh, have they gone?"

Sandra nodded. She made to speak but the telephone rang on the desk beside her and she shot it a dark look. Stephanie put down the items she was carrying and tried to accept the call from her own desk but struggled to transfer it in time. The call rang off. She looked to her boss with an apologetic expression.

"Sorry. Do you want a cup of tea?"

"Yes, please," Sandra said but her response was, at best, lukewarm. The question didn't really register and it was only when Stephanie scooped up her purchases and slipped past her towards the rear did she respond properly. "Actually, Steph..." she said, not finishing the comment.

Stephanie turned to her, raising an eyebrow in query and lingering at the far end of the office.

"I'll pass on the tea," Sandra said, forcing a smile. Stephanie pursed her lips and nodded, turning away and taking another step. She didn't make it far. "What have you got on today?"

Stephanie paused, turning back and looking to the ceiling as she thought through her appointment schedule. "I've got that viewing out at Beeston at eleven. Then nothing until after lunch. Why?"

Sandra met her eye, holding her attention. "It's a pretty quiet day, not much lined up."

Stephanie shrugged. "I've got chains to chase."

"Yes, yes... of course, but you can do that from home."

"From home?"

"I was thinking we'd shut up early today, transfer the calls to the mobile and run things light."

"Why?"

Stephanie's expression was one of confusion. She wasn't the brightest. Pleasant, friendly when she needed to be and quite a shark when it came to pushing for a sale, but not altogether particularly intelligent. That was a blessing in many respects.

"Because I said so," Sandra replied, in a tone far harsher than intended. She forced herself to soften her approach. "There's no need to keep the office open. Footfall is well down and will likely stay that way until spring kicks in."

"I guess," Stephanie replied, looking at the milk in her hand.

"Take whatever you need with you for the next day or two and we'll open up again before the weekend."

Stephanie met her eye. She seemed unconvinced. Nevertheless, she smiled and glanced at the bottle in her hand. "Okay. I'll put this in the fridge," she said. "What shall I do with these?"

Sandra looked across at the small box of mini pastries in her other hand. "Take them with you... whatever. Are you okay locking up?"

"I can do, yes."

"Good."

Sandra picked up her handbag from the desk alongside her, rummaging through the interior to ensure her keys and mobile were present as she made her way to the door. It was an afterthought to look back over her shoulder before passing out onto the street. Stephanie was still standing at the other end of the office.

"Give me a call if you need to," she said and left.

She was already on the street with the door closing behind her and therefore didn't hear her sales negotiator mutter *what would be the point*, under her breath.

The wind caught her hair as she walked and it blew across her face. She brushed it aside with her manicured nails and reached into her bag for her mobile phone. Dialling as she walked, Sandra glanced around her as she pressed the handset to her ear. A few people were milling around, going about their daily business but no one seemed to be paying her any particular attention. Crossing the street and rounding the next corner, she glanced over her shoulder finding herself assessing anyone who she passed or who came into her line of sight and taking their measure, judging why they might be there. Her anxiety was building. She could feel it. The call cut to voicemail and she cursed inwardly as she came in sight of her car.

"Typical," she said, lowering her hand and glaring at the handset. As if someone heard her, the screen flashed into life with an incoming call. She stopped to answer it, noticing a dark SUV parked opposite her car. It stood out. Only business owners and residents ever parked in this side street and she was familiar with most vehicles that would usually be left there. This wasn't one. Brushing her hair aside once again, she tapped the green tab on her screen. "Hi. Yeah, it is important. Thanks for calling me back."

"What's up?"

Sandra reached her car, turning her back and leaning against it. "We might have a problem."

"Really, how so?"

She took a deep breath. "It's Devon."

The voice sighed. "Devon? What's he done?"

"He's dead." Silence followed. A pause was to be expected but this carried. So much so that Sandra checked her screen to ensure the call was still connected. "Did you hear me? Devon is—"

"Yes, yes, I heard you. That is… unexpected."

"Unexpected? He fell from the cliffs… it's a bit bloody more than that—"

"Yes, it is. I know. I didn't mean to sound flippant." There was another pause. He was thinking. She waited. "It doesn't necessarily need to change things. Arrangements are already in place. I'll make some calls but, in the meantime, we will just have to muddle through."

"I guess so," she said, drawing breath and rubbing absently at the back of her neck. "Although…"

"Although what?"

Sandra bit her lower lip.

"The police called round."

She could hear his breathing down the line. Oh, how she wished she could read him but she'd never been able to, no matter what they were talking about.

"To see you?"

"I think so," Sandra said with a shake of the head, irritated by her lack of certainty. "I'm not sure."

"Perhaps someone placed the two of you together. When did you last see him?"

"Erm… a week or two ago… maybe. I'm not sure," she lied.

"Why are they asking questions?"

"They think… someone may have killed him. That he was somehow pushed rather than falling accidentally."

"But they don't know."

"I… I… don't know. They didn't really say. They were asking me about his business interests."

"And what did you tell them?"

His tone had changed. His question was open ended, searching, as if he was already calculating their next move. This was his strength.

"I didn't tell them anything, not really. Just that he was interested in property." He didn't reply. "Does that change things?"

"Not necessarily. Leave it with me, for now. I'll see what I can find out. In the meantime, don't do anything different to your normal routine. Try not to draw attention to yourself. I know that will be somewhat difficult for you."

She ignored the barbed comment, her thoughts turning to the business. "I've shut the office, told Stephanie to take a couple of days working from home."

"Well, that's exactly what you shouldn't have done."

She felt like a schoolgirl, caught red-handed by the teacher somewhere she wasn't supposed to be. She felt her cheeks flush.

"Do I… open up again?"

"No," he said, sounding displeased with her. She hated it when he adopted that particular manner. "What's done is done. You'll only attract more attention if you do that."

She looked around, thinking hard. "Then what should I do?"

He thought about it for a moment before adopting a more conciliatory tone. "Go home. Like I said, I'll look into it and see what I can find out. Then, we can take it from there."

"Okay, I'll wait for you to call. When do you think—" She didn't get to finish the question. He had already hung up on her. Her fingers curled tightly around the handset as she lowered it from her ear and closed her eyes, drawing a deep breath. *Why did she have to lie?* The answer was obvious. Because she had no choice.

CHAPTER FIFTEEN

Tom Janssen turned left onto Beach Road, the direct route leading from the centre of Wells-next-the-Sea out towards the sea mouth, lifeboat station and holiday park. The water of East Fleet lay to his right, the traditional access to the town for all water traffic prior to the construction of the outer harbour. Protected by salt marshes and a sand bar, the town had been prolific as a trading port for centuries prior to industrialisation. Even then, commercial trading continued well into the 90s with grain shipments arriving from the continent before the business eventually wound down.

These days, the harbour was still used by local fishermen and visiting commercial vessels, with the greatest increase in traffic coming recently since the construction of the wind farm located off the coast.

Janssen observed the Lifeboat Horse on the far shoreline, looking resplendent in the sunshine. A metal statue, crafted from steel bars and beer barrels, standing proudly overlooking the access to the old quay. Funds were raised by locals in order to buy the sculpture; a tribute to the animals who used to tow the lifeboats out to the sea over a century earlier.

Only two boats were situated in the new harbour, one was a

trawler while the other looked like a survey ship and probably tied to the wind farm. Janssen pulled up, switching off the engine and casting an eye across the trawler. One figure was on deck, dressed in bright yellow waders with loops over his shoulder.

Janssen got out of the car, immediately facing the onslaught of the wind coming in off the sea. The skies were presently clear and the sunshine belied the harshness of the wind chill. Drawing his coat about him, Janssen made for the trawler. The figure onboard didn't see him coming, he had his back to the quay and was busy hosing down the deck with a pressure washer. Janssen crossed the bridge and came to stand alongside the boat, looking it up and down. He was surprised at how much he remembered. The boat was considered old back in the day but now, more than twenty years on, it was faring badly. Janssen knew he'd forgotten more than he remembered about how the boat worked but wear and tear alongside repeated repairs were obvious to the eye.

"It's been a while."

Janssen hadn't realised the noise from the pressure washer had ceased, so engrossed was he in reminiscing. Shaun Kemp hadn't changed much. Like his brother, Jamie, his hair line was on the retreat whilst the advent of his forties had seen him gain weight in all the wrong places. He sported several days' growth of stubble, not unusual for a man who'd spent time at sea.

"Yes, it has," he said, glancing up and shielding his eyes from the sun currently silhouetting the skipper. "How have you been, Shaun?" He looked away as he asked the question. Shaun followed his gaze along the quay.

"Been better," was the curt reply. "You here to see me?"

Janssen nodded.

"Somehow I don't see it as a social call."

"It isn't. Permission to come aboard?"

"If you like," Shaun replied, turning and stepping away. "Watch your footing. The deck's wet."

Janssen walked towards the stern of the boat and climbed

aboard onto the aft working deck. He found Shaun struggling with the hydraulic boom. The mechanism looked worse for wear.

"Need a hand?" he asked.

Shaun continued on for a moment longer. Janssen thought he'd chosen to ignore the offer rather than not registering it. He didn't comment, merely waited. Shaun exhaled heavily, stopping what he was doing and looking off the starboard side and into the salt marsh beyond.

"I see you've still got your dad's boat running," Janssen said, casting an eye around the deck. "She's holding up well. How's business?"

Shaun turned back to face him, casually keeping one hand on the boom to steady himself and fixing him with a stare.

"Well... what you see here is one of the last full-time commercial trawlers operating out of Wells, so you figure it out."

Janssen heard the frustration in his tone, touching on despair. He glanced across the harbour. Although today appeared quiet, the quay looked well used. Shaun followed his gaze.

"I thought Wells had seen something of a mini-boom in recent years."

"Yeah, a lot of foreign boats coming and going... not many of us locals left, though."

"Must be difficult."

"What are you doing here, Tom?"

Shaun was cutting to the chase. Although his welcome wasn't as cold as that of his brother, Janssen was well aware that the animosity of their past was still relevant even after all these years.

"Devon Bailey. You know him?"

Shaun rolled his tongue along the inside of his bottom lip, warily eyeing Janssen.

"Yeah. A bit."

"How well?"

"We play cards once in a while, that type of thing. Why?"

"Because he's dead," Janssen said, watching closely for a reaction. Shaun chewed on his lower lip momentarily before flicking his eyebrows up and drawing breath.

"That's bad. What happened?"

"He fell from Sheringham cliffs."

The corners of Shaun's mouth dipped downwards and he flicked up his eyebrows in an exaggerated expression. "That's *really* bad. What's it got to do with me?"

"We're looking into his connections, trying to build a timeline for his last few days."

"So, you reckon he was pushed rather than jumped," Shaun said by way of a statement and not a question, making a show of examining the equipment before him.

"What makes you say so?"

"Devon doesn't strike me as a jumper, if you know what I mean."

"You knew him well, then?"

Shaun shook his head. "Nah. Not really. And if you're looking for those who were with him recently, you can count me out. I've been at sea for the past four days."

"Jamie told me you'd put in along the coast. Is that right?"

Shaun's eyes narrowed and he didn't respond immediately. Janssen figured he was weighing up what his brother might have said.

"The truth shouldn't be difficult to remember, Shaun. It's only the lies that get tricky."

"Yeah. I put in for a day, that's all."

"What for?" Janssen said, glancing towards the wheelhouse as if he might see an explanation.

"Engine trouble."

"What kind of engine trouble?"

"The broken kind," Shaun said flatly. "Look, Tom, if you're after someone who had a problem with Devon, it wasn't me okay. I barely knew the bloke."

"We heard he was familiar with others in your circle. Your

wife, in particular. Apparently, he worked with her at the local food bank. The one run by the church."

Shaun's expression remained fixed. "Is that so?"

Janssen nodded, ensuring his own expression was also unchanged.

"Helen is the friendly sort," Shaun said.

"Jamie didn't seem to care for him much."

Shaun snorted, an expression of derision. "Sounds like Jamie."

"He hasn't changed much, your brother."

Shaun laughed bitterly, looking away. "No. Did you honestly expect him to?"

Janssen shook his head. It was a fair comment. Both of the Kemp brothers were quick to temper but Jamie was far more volatile than his elder sibling. Whenever the two of them got up to mischief in their youth, invariably it was Jamie who was the instigator but Shaun never needed much encouragement to join in.

"You on your own?" Janssen asked, flicking his hand in a gesture to indicate the trawler. It necessitated a three-man crew but only Shaun was present.

"Things have been better," Shaun said, sounding despondent. "If I could afford to hire then believe me, I would."

"How can you handle a boat like this alone?" It wasn't the largest of trawlers, far from the likes of the big commercial operators that trawled the waters these days but even so, it was a big ask for one pair of hands.

"You fancy some part-time shifts on the quiet, Tommy?" Shaun said with a sideways grin. "Just like back in the old days."

Janssen shook his head, an image of Shaun's father giving him the lowdown of what went where.

"Couldn't Jamie lend a hand?"

Shaun laughed then. It was a genuine sound but one tinged with sarcasm. "Jamie... on Dad's boat? You must be joking. He'd be spinning in his grave."

"Yeah, I guess you're right," Janssen said, remembering the man's acrimonious relationship with his youngest child.

"The old man always hoped you'd take to the sea, Tom."

Janssen pursed his lips before taking a deep breath but he chose not to comment.

"In some respects, I figure he would have preferred you to take the wheel rather than me."

The suggestion irritated Janssen. It was typical of Shaun. He hadn't changed either, still looking for something to beat those he cared about over the head with. Even the man who cared for him the most, forgiving and excusing his mounting misdemeanours when any sane man, father or not, would have walked away. And yet, here he was, still trying to score cheap points against a memory. The man deserved so much better.

"Your father was a decent man, Shaun. He wanted nothing more than to have two sons he could be proud of."

"Hah!" Shaun retorted. "And what did he leave me? A business built on debt and this rusty piece of shit," he said, kicking the hull with the edge of his boot. "Thanks a bloody lot!"

"He did the best he could," Janssen countered.

"You haven't changed, Tom. You still look for the best in people, see things in black or white."

"And what's wrong with that?"

"The world is grey, Tom."

"For some, maybe," Janssen muttered. "But you're wrong. It's not black or white, it's right and wrong, and that's very different."

"Still a boy scout, aren't you," Shaun said, raising three fingers in a mock salute. "Any more questions or can I get on with cleaning up? I wouldn't mind getting home for some kip."

"Sure. I expect you'll have missed your wife as well."

Shaun shrugged, returning to his inspection of the boom. Janssen turned and made to disembark. Once back on the quay, he looked towards Shaun who appeared to be paying him no further heed at all. His thoughts turned to Frank, the Kemp brothers' father. He was a special man, a man who showed a young Tom Janssen a genuine level of care and kindliness when he lost his own father. It was a memory that he would always treasure. Was that at the root of the antagonism between himself and the two brothers or would their relationship with their father always have turned out this way? He didn't know. What he did know was that Frank Kemp had earned greater respect than that which he garnered from those two. Somehow, he still thought that there would have been a sense of pride in seeing his son carry on the family business. Although, by the looks of it, how long Shaun could keep it going was anyone's guess.

CHAPTER SIXTEEN

SHAUN KEMP KEPT a watchful eye on Tom Janssen as he walked back to his car and got in. He was careful to keep himself occupied in such a way as to give the impression he wasn't interested in the visit. Of all the people, it would have to be him. There had been talk a while ago that Tom was back in the area. There was no reason for their paths to cross, not unless one of them went out of their way to make it happen. Now, here he was. Back again. Still the air of arrogance, looking down on both him and Jamie. Just as before, judging him on their family dynamic. What the hell did he know? He only ever saw the best of their father. The man who had so much love to offer strangers but precious little left for his own children.

The sound of an engine made him look towards the quayside as Janssen's car drove away. Once it disappeared from view, he headed into the wheelhouse. Retrieving a screwdriver and a mini LED torch from a toolbox housed in a cupboard beneath the control panel, he returned outside and made his way to the hold. Lifting the hatch, he cast a sideways glance to the shore before descending the ladder into the empty hold, dropping lightly into the water that pooled at his feet. Making his way to the forward section, he approached the hull and clicked the button on the base of the torch.

A shaft of light punctured the darkness, illuminating the interior with its rust patches and flaking paint. Gripping the torch between his teeth, he dropped to his haunches and angled the light towards a panel in front of him and fished out the screwdriver from his pocket. The tips of his fingers were numb, a result of the cold water he'd used to wash down the deck, and he struggled to find the screw heads. With some difficulty, he managed to undo the screws and then felt around the edges, eventually managing to lift the false panel clear. It was fashioned from steel, and although it was thin, it still required a great deal of effort to move it aside.

Shaun ignored the packages, tightly wrapped in blue plastic, and instead withdrew a mobile phone that was tucked inside the hidden compartment. He took the torch in one hand, the mobile phone in the other, touching the latter to his chin as he considered what he should do next. Switching the mobile on, he waited for it to start up. Taking a deep breath, he opened the contacts list. There were only two numbers listed and neither had a name against their entry. He selected the first number and dialled it. The call was answered immediately.

"I figured you'd be calling."

Shaun was annoyed. Obviously, he wasn't the only one who had been paid a visit by Tom Janssen.

"Have the police been to see you already too?" he asked.

"Yes... of sorts."

His irritation grew. "You might have let me know."

"Why?"

"Maybe... so I could have been prepared. That might have been bloody useful, don't you think?"

"No. The more natural you were, the better, I reckon."

Shaun didn't reply. The logic was sound but he was still angry.

"How are we fixed?"

"Good to go, my end," he said, looking around as his voice echoed around the hold. "When is it arranged for?"

"I'm working on it."

"Working on it!" Shaun hissed. "You need to get this bloody sorted now. It should have been done already."

"Like I said, I'm working on it. You need to calm down—"

"Calm down?" Shaun felt his anger rising but he kept his tone in check. Now wasn't the time to be a hothead. "That's easy for you to say. I've got—"

"I'm well aware what's at stake... for all of us. I said I'm dealing with it and I am. Okay?"

"Okay," Shaun said. "Look, if the police are sniffing around, you're going to need to sort this sooner rather than later. Things are starting to come to a head, what if they—"

"I know. If you needed to, how soon could you put out to sea?"

Shaun thought about it, looking over his shoulder in the direction of the engine bay as if he could see through the bulkhead. The idea didn't appeal.

"I could limp around the coast if I had to but... I wouldn't fancy it."

"It'll not be long now. Just stay cool for another couple of days."

"Will do," Shaun said, hanging up. He touched the handset to his lips, assessing whether he felt truly reassured or not. He was no longer in control of events and he didn't like it. At sea, he was the skipper and in many ways he knew where he stood in the relationship between himself and the water. On land was always where he found himself out of his depth. Only time would tell if this was the case.

He switched off the phone and hurriedly stashed it back inside the compartment alongside the packages. Replacing the cover panel, he tightened the screws back in place and retreated to the ladder. Clambering back towards the block of daylight the open hatch provided, he squinted in the brightness as he came back atop deck. The quay was still devoid of people and he slid the hatch cover back into place. Slipping a padlock into place, he snapped it shut and stood up, sniffing loudly and wiping his nose with the back of his hand. His thoughts drifted back to Tom Janssen.

"Always the bloody boy scout," he muttered under his breath.

CHAPTER SEVENTEEN

TOM JANSSEN GLANCED in the rear-view mirror as he pulled away from the quayside. The figure he could see was Shaun Kemp, still standing where he was when Janssen left him. The discussion hadn't gone quite as he'd expected. Perhaps the earlier meeting with Jamie had left him a little jaded.

The conversation with Shaun seemed to fare far better under the circumstances. Clearly, there was still a great deal of enmity present in Shaun that was aimed squarely in his direction. Could he have expected much else? The last time they'd met was nearly two decades previously, at Frank Kemp's funeral, and it had almost ended in a physical confrontation.

He sighed. That was a long time ago and for his part, he'd moved on. Whatever Shaun was, he could never be considered a great actor. His appearance on the trawler seemed to come as a complete surprise to Shaun. He'd expected Jamie to have tipped his brother off, allowing the latter to be prepared. That didn't seem to have happened. It was Jamie who dominated his thoughts. The offhand, callous nature with which he'd greeted the news of Devon Bailey's death shocked him. A feeling that he'd since struggled to shake.

Reaching the town, he pulled in to the side of the road and

picked up his mobile. Calling through to the control room, he requested a check on Jamie's address held on the Police National Computer. Armed with the address, a street he knew well in Sheringham, he set off.

The Kemp brothers were tight, they always had been, but in the past it had often been an uneasy relationship. At times they seemed to be almost symbiotic but there was always the potential for a flare up. Shaun didn't appear to hold his brother in high regard at present, shunning the possibility of following their father into the family business. Help that it appeared Shaun was in desperate need of. And yet, Jamie was very comfortable making himself at home when they called in on Shaun's wife, Helen, the previous day. The decision to drop in unannounced was instinctive, he had no real cause to, other than to shake the tree and see what, if anything, fell from the branches.

He was also well aware of his own prejudice towards the Kemps and the concern came to mind that he might be allowing his judgement to be shaped by their strained relationship.

No conclusion had been forthcoming by the time he pulled up on Beeston Road on the outskirts of Sheringham town centre. He struggled to find somewhere to park. The street ran away from the centre and was a mixture of 1930s-built semi-detached houses and terraces of traditional fishermen's cottages. Parking was at a premium, as it was in much of the town.

Getting out of the car, he glanced at the house numbers and made off in the direction of Jamie Kemp's property. It was one of the terraced cottages and stood out from the others nearby and not in a positive sense. Adjoining properties were well presented whereas Jamie's had seen better days. The wooden window frames were rotting in places and they were still single glazed. He approached and, in the absence of a bell or a knocker, he thumped the flat of his fist against the door. Stepping back, he tried to see through the one ground-floor window but it was shrouded in a thick net curtain, unsurprising as the front door opened straight onto the street. Any passer-by may as well be walking through the interior of the house for all the privacy available.

Moments later, a key turned in the lock and the door squeaked open. It was wooden and ill-fitting, probably the result of repeated swelling and contractions over the course of many years. A woman stood before him. She was in her forties with shoulder-length brown hair, dressed in jeans and a casual blouse. She met him with a warm smile. He offered her his warrant card.

"I'm Detective Inspector Tom—"

"Janssen," she finished for him. He was taken aback. "I know who you are. It's me, Tom, Kerry-Ann."

For a brief moment, Janssen found himself mentally scrabbling to put a face to the name. Then it came to him in a flash. They'd also been at school together. He remembered her as a redhead though. That was pretty much the only detail he could recollect.

"Yes, of course," he said as convincingly as he could. "I'm sorry. You've thrown me. I understood this was Jamie Kemp's home."

"It is," she said, her smile fading. "Or, at least, it was. Come on in."

She stepped back, opening the door wider and gesturing for him to enter. The smile was back and he returned it, following her into the interior. The house was a two-up-two-down with a small galley kitchen attached at the rear. The front door opened into the living room and with just the two of them present, it already felt cramped.

"Kerry-Ann Wittey," Janssen said, trying not to sound triumphant. If she noticed the delay in his recollection of her name then she didn't show it.

"It's Kemp now, though," she said.

He smiled. "Of course. I'm sorry."

"Not half as sorry as I am, believe me!" she said, grinning. He couldn't help but match it.

"Is Jamie here?" he asked, looking around. The interior was in stark contrast to the impression offered by the outside. The house was incredibly well kept. Furniture was limited, due to the lack of space, but everything was fresh, clean and tidy.

"Jamie doesn't live here anymore," Kerry-Ann said flatly, looking pensive. "Not for a while now."

He sensed deep sadness contained within the statement, recognising it in her expression as well.

"I'm sorry."

The words seemed inadequate, and he wasn't sure about the sincerity he conveyed. If he was honest, he imagined life without Jamie Kemp would be infinitely preferable.

"That's okay," she said, indicating for him to join her in the kitchen.

She led the way and he followed, ducking under the beam separating the living and dining room. The ceilings tended to be low in these houses as it is and knocking out a wall seemed to reduce the head height even further.

"Do you know where I can find him these days?" he asked as Kerry-Ann sat down at one of the two chairs beside an occasional table at the far end of the kitchen. He took the other seat opposite her. There was a set of French doors next to them that opened out into a small enclosed courtyard where wild flowers grew.

She shook her head. "No, sorry. I can't help you there. He calls by occasionally."

"The two of you are still talking then?"

Again, she dismissed the suggestion with a shake of the head. "Not really. It's usually when he's had a few drinks or is feeling sorry for himself." She cut a wry smile. "Come to think of it, those two are by no means mutually exclusive."

Janssen grinned. "What happened? If you don't mind my asking," he added. "I know it isn't any of my business."

"That's okay, Tom," she said, reaching over and patting the back of his hand affectionately. "You remember Jamie?"

"Only too well."

"Then you'll not be surprised to find out he went the way most of us thought he would after we left school."

"And yet you married him?" he said, careful to not sound as if he was mocking her. He needn't have worried.

"Yes," she said with a laugh. "Yes, I did. The quality of my taste in men never bore well under any form of scrutiny, Tom. But I'll say one thing for Jamie, and that's his entertainment value. There was never a dull moment."

"So what did happen?"

She sighed, looking through the window at some nondescript point in the courtyard outside. "Don't get me wrong, Jamie could be a great guy... funny, charming... he was handsome once as well." She rocked her head from side to side as if remembering happier times. "But... he also has his demons." She met his eye and he chose not to speak, giving her the space to talk. "It wasn't long before we were having financial problems. At first I thought he was the unluckiest guy alive. He was always the last one in the door and therefore the first one out when things turned bad."

"You mean, he kept being laid off?"

She nodded. "Yeah. At least that's what I thought. It took a while for me to realise that *just having one with the lads after work* was actually the cover for having one after work, having one at work and having one *before* work."

Janssen put a hand across his mouth and chin, casually stroking his chin as she talked.

"But it wasn't just alcohol he had a problem with. When the bailiffs came calling, I realised things were far worse than I could ever have imagined. Jamie's keen on the horses, the dogs... pretty much anything he can place a bet on, regardless of whether he actually has a clue what's going on. I just wish the bastard hadn't put my name as co-signatory on the loans and cards he racked up. I should have realised but I was too bloody stupid."

"He always was pretty full on, as I recall," Janssen said, sitting back in his chair. He could see the pain etched into her expression. She was putting a brave face on it all but the damage was evident. "So, where are you now?"

She smiled but it was one without genuine warmth. "Hanging on," she said, drumming her fingers on the table in front of her. "I work two jobs and that just about keeps them from putting the door in and turfing me out into the street."

"That's rough," he said.

"Yes, it is," she said, blowing out her cheeks. "What do you want him for anyway? What's he done?"

Janssen attempted to sound casual, shaking his head as he spoke. "He's not necessarily done anything. His is a name that's come up in an inquiry, that's all."

She rolled her eyes heavenward. "Well, that's all I bloody need. Jamie bringing the old bill to my door on top of everything else."

"It's okay, Kerry-Ann, really, it is. There's no need for you to worry."

"Who's worried? Next time he comes round I'll give him a good hiding, that's all."

Janssen raised his eyebrows, trying not to smile. Kerry-Ann couldn't help herself. She burst out laughing and Janssen followed suit.

"So, how's Alice? The two of you getting on okay?"

He was taken aback at the depth of her knowledge. She grinned at him.

"It's still a small town, Tom. Word travels, you know."

"I didn't realise my love life was such a hot topic," he said, mocking her interest.

"Not much happens around here, Tom. That's why people leave. Including you and Alice as I recall."

"True," he said, bobbing his head.

"Besides, I bumped into Alice a while back and she told me the two of you were seeing one another."

"Did she now?"

He felt his cheeks flush.

"I think she's quite proud of it too," she said, leaning forward and touching his forearm. "Why didn't I ever make a play for you back in the day?"

He smiled then. "Because I'm quite dull, remember?"

She sat back as a smile swept across her face. "You were never dull, Tom. And to be honest, dull seems quite appealing right about now. You're looking great, by the way. It's really good to see you again."

He didn't get the impression she was flirting with him. She seemed to be contemplating how differently her life could have gone if only she'd made better choices.

"Any idea where I can find Jamie at the moment?" he asked, changing the subject. She met his eye, inclining her head to one side.

"Are the bookies still open?"

CHAPTER EIGHTEEN

TOM JANSSEN WALKED into the ops room, finding it to be a hive of activity with more people present than he expected. Eric was hunkered over his computer screen and didn't notice his presence. He caught sight of Cassie in his office with her back to the door. Someone else was with her but several bodies passed in front of him obscuring his view. He didn't recognise these people.

"Eric!" he said, raising his voice to be heard above the hubbub. The detective constable looked up, saw no one before him and then looked around. Upon seeing him, Eric got up and made his way through the throng to speak to him.

"Hi Tom. Busy in here, isn't it? I can hardly hear myself think."

"Eric," Janssen said, gesturing with a circular hand movement, "who are these people?"

Eric looked around, eventually returning his attention to him. "They're here for the press conference, I think."

"What press conference?" Janssen said, frowning. Eric became nervous, glancing towards his office. Janssen followed his gaze. "Never mind," he said, moving in that direction.

He entered his office. Cassie looked round and smiled a

greeting. She was sitting in front of his desk, one leg crossed over the other with a notebook in her lap, pen poised to make an entry. Behind his desk, DCI Tamara Greave was sitting in his seat, elbows on the surface, her clasped hands supporting her chin. She smiled warmly. She was dressed in a business suit, charcoal pinstripe and a cream blouse. It was far removed from her usual presentation, that of casual jeans and a large jumper. Even her hair was tied up and styled.

"Tom. I'm pleased you're back."

"What's this about a press conference?" he asked. He only realised his tone was perhaps too brusque when he saw her reaction to his question.

"It's good to see you too, Tom."

He shook his head, glancing at Cassie who in turn looked to the DCI. Tamara flicked her head in the direction of the door and Cassie rose from her seat, swiftly departing. She offered Janssen a brief nod and smile as she passed him, closing the door behind her.

"What's this about a press conference?" he repeated.

"We need to give the public an update."

"An update on what exactly?" he said, irritated. "Right now we only have a suspicion of murder."

"I agree," she said. "I've read through the preliminary findings of the pathology report, along with the CSI reports from the fall site and the car, and it does strongly indicate foul play."

"Why haven't I seen those reports?"

She seemed taken aback, almost insulted. "No one's going behind your back, Tom," she protested. "The seniors are taking an interest in this one and pressed for me to get involved."

"Why?" His question was curt.

"*Because* it's my job," she said.

"No, it isn't. It's my job," he countered. "And as for carrying out a presser at the moment, I really don't think that's a good idea."

She sat back in her seat, his seat, and put the tips of her fingers together, forming a tent.

"How so?"

"We've barely scratched the surface of this guy's life, let alone figured out what he was doing here in Sheringham. One of the few advantages we have is the limited knowledge in the public domain."

Tamara considered what he'd said. She wasn't rash, far from it. He found her arrival, unannounced as it was, and the calling of a press conference without discussing it with the lead detective to be out of character.

"You think if we announce we're treating this as a murder inquiry it will drive the perpetrator underground?"

"As well as any potential witnesses," Janssen said. He sat down in the chair Cassie had vacated. He wasn't bothered about the DCI sitting behind his desk, he usually spent his time with the others anyway. "The connections we've already been able to establish are curious. If we start identifying them we could lose the advantage."

Tamara took a deep breath, adopting a pensive expression. "Speaking of which, are you going to be able to maintain distance in this investigation?"

Janssen narrowed his eyes. "What kind of a question is that?"

"I know you're connected to the town," she said, avoiding eye contact. He got the impression she was working up to something. "Do you think you'll be able to stay… objective?"

"*Objective*," he repeated, not bothering to keep the derision from his tone. He glanced into the ops room. Perhaps it was her sixth sense, the feeling of his eyes upon her, because Cassie looked up, catching his eye. She looked away again as he turned back to Tamara. "It'll be fine."

"Don't be too hard on her, Tom. It was merely a passing comment."

He brushed it off. "I grew up in the town. Stands to reason I'll come into contact with people I'm familiar with."

"And don't for a second believe that I haven't got absolute faith in you," Tamara said. "But I had to ask. That *is* my job."

He exhaled deeply, regretting the harshness of his earlier tone. "So is overseeing a murder investigation."

Tamara smiled in response to the sideways acknowledgement of his overreaction.

"I see your point but we still have the issue of the press conference. It's been called and we can't cancel it."

"Why not? Release a statement instead. You know, ongoing investigation... more to add when appropriate in the coming days. That type of thing."

She grinned. "Yes. I've been there too. Not this time, Tom. Other factors are in play."

He was perplexed by the mysterious comment. His expression must have conveyed that to her.

"Spring is almost upon us, Tom. You're a Sheringham boy. You know what that means for the town."

He did. Only too well. The previous summer hadn't been quite what the local businesses had been hoping for. A lean winter meant many were banking on a strong start to the tourist season to recoup where they fell short the previous season.

"I know a murder isn't a good advertisement for tourism but—"

"But nothing, Tom. A murder can happen anywhere and in a small place like this, with an economy dependent on tourism, we need to be as transparent as possible with our investigation. I don't want the rumour mill getting underway."

Janssen shook his head. "The current word is that it's a suicide."

"Which won't last five minutes once we release the deceased's name. Journalists are just as adept at digging up a background as anyone in your team. With Devon Bailey's record in the public domain, gossip is going to spread like wild fire."

He had to admit, she made a good point. Combining Devon's history with his current lifestyle, it was only a matter of time until speculation surrounding his death got out of hand. He rubbed at his face with the palms of both hands.

"What do you want to do?" he asked.

"Ideally, bring the investigation to a conclusion as quickly as possible before things run away from us. Regarding the press conference, media interest is already building up a head of steam, so I think we need to confront it head on." He was about to make his point about the need to keep things close again but she raised a hand to cut him off. "But we can make sure not to reveal too much. We'll offer up the victim's name, that's unavoidable at this point, and go with the *ongoing enquiries* line."

"Thank you."

"That will buy you a little time but not much, Tom. I'll hold them off for a day or two but you'll need to have made some headway."

He nodded his understanding.

"What about those upstairs," he said, raising his eyes to the ceiling as if the top brass were in a room above them.

"I was talking about them," Tamara said with a shake of the head. He laughed. "The press will be easy in comparison. Let's talk about next steps. What have you got planned?"

He cleared his throat. If truth be told, they were still in the foothills in the search for a motive. Devon's criminal record suggested he was rising through the junior ranks of criminality from an early age but the fallow period in recent years implied he'd moved significantly up the chain. The discovery of an illegal firearm concealed in his apartment was a pretty good indicator that he was still involved in crime, the nature of which remained something of a mystery. Similarly, his movement within a social and professional circle that spanned a local businesswoman and the likes of the Kemp brothers seemed odd. How, or even if, any of them fitted into all of this presently escaped him. Could it be as simple as Devon Bailey was something of a player and enjoyed clandestine relationships with married women? His earlier conversation with Jamie's estranged wife, Kerry-Ann, only confirmed that he would never understand a woman's choice of partner. She knew what he was like and still married him.

"We need to get to know Devon better. His recent past is a mystery but we do have a company that he is somehow attached to, if only by way of the car he was driving, and he is obviously well financed judging by his accommodation. So far, we've been unable to contact the company registered to the car. Sounds like someone needs to go on a road trip."

"Right," Tamara said, looking towards ops and getting Cassie's attention, signalling for her to come in, and to bring Eric with her. The two junior detectives filed in. Once they were present, she addressed Cassie. "We need you to follow up on this connection Devon Bailey has to this logistics firm in London. The two of you can travel down to London tomorrow."

"Both of us?" Eric asked.

Tamara nodded. "Yes. Is that a problem?"

Eric shook his head. "No, not at all."

The words may have said there was no issue but his body language suggested otherwise. No one chose to press it.

"We need to know what Devon was doing here in Sheringham. He doesn't strike me as the type to settle here on the coast. Whatever he was up to, it probably got him killed. I imagine that was an occupational hazard he roundly accepted. That's why I'm sending both of you. This is a murder investigation and where he was from is well off our patch. I'm not having anyone walking around blindly. Not alone at any rate."

"Is it worth tapping into local resources while we're down there?" Cassie asked, looking to Janssen.

In most circumstances, he would almost always say yes but he hesitated. Tamara picked up on it.

"What is it, Tom?"

"It might prove beneficial to drop in under the radar," he said, thinking aloud. "Triggering local resources might tip our hand just as much as giving away too much in a press conference. I'd say we keep it to ourselves for the time being but should we need to tap them up, then do so."

"Agreed," Tamara said. "In the meantime, Tom and I have a date with the gathering sharks."

"And why do I feel like the Mayor in Jaws?" Janssen said, drawing a smile from two of the three people with him in the room. Eric looked over with a confused expression. Janssen stood up, clapping the younger detective on the shoulder. "Don't worry, Eric. You'll just have to wait for the remake."

It was a comment that did nothing to enlighten Eric, who remained puzzled as everyone around him smiled.

CHAPTER NINETEEN

"I THINK THAT WENT WELL, all things considered," Tamara said, pushing through the double doors and leading them into the corridor out of reach of the throng. Several of the gathered journalists were still calling out questions as she and Tom Janssen left the room, an indication of their unhappiness with the information offered.

"I reckon they were hoping for more," Janssen said, glancing sideways towards her.

"Well, they can blame you for that," she said, with a wry smile. "Besides, once they put Devon's name into the system, they'll have enough to run any number of front page headlines. They're not being stonewalled anywhere near as much as they might think. Any chance of a lift to my hotel?"

Janssen's brow furrowed. "Did you not drive here?"

"I was in London for a conference before I got the call to head up here. I didn't even get the chance to go home, so my car is still parked at a rural train station. In about an hour, it will probably have a parking ticket which will be reclaimed on expenses."

"A conference. That explains it," Janssen said, bobbing his head slightly.

"Explains what exactly?" she asked, stepping in front and turning to face him, stopping them both in the corridor.

Janssen looked her up and down before tilting his head to one side. "Nothing, really. It's just... you've made something of an effort."

"I'm going to ignore that, Thomas," she said, spinning on her heel and setting off.

Janssen grinned and easily pulled alongside her again within a few strides, such was his height and step advantage over hers.

"I meant no offence," he said lightly.

"None taken. As it happens, you're right. I did make an effort. I was in the capital, surrounded by the great and the good, not mixing with the likes of you," she winked in his direction. "And that means I have to make an effort but, if you mention it again, I'll have you directing traffic for the foreseeable. Understood?"

"Crystal clear, Ma'am," he said, smiling.

THE WESTCLIFF HOTEL was located in a prominent position overlooking the town, offering unparalleled views across the rooftops of Sheringham town and along the coast. The sun was already setting as Janssen approached the front entrance of the hotel, bringing the car to a stop on the gravelled driveway.

Tamara stifled a yawn as he engaged the handbrake. It had been a long day. She was scheduled to be in the capital for three days and hadn't expected to be hauled away on day two. Tom had been put out by her sudden appearance. He'd hidden it well, up to a point. It was understandable. He was more than capable of leading this investigation without her direct involvement but everyone had their superiors and she answered to hers as much as he did to her.

Thinking about it, she could have called ahead and given him forewarning. Maybe next time.

"Join me for a drink?" she asked.

He glanced at the display on the dashboard, screwing up his face as he considered it.

"No, sorry. I can't. I promised I would tuck Saffy in tonight and I'm cutting it fine as it is."

The mention of Saffy, the daughter of Tom's girlfriend, Alice, put an image in her mind. If memory served, Saffy would be six or seven years old now. As far as she knew, Tom and Alice weren't living together but maybe things had changed. He was quite cagey about his private life. Either that or she didn't show enough interest in her friends' lives.

That was certainly true around children. They had never been foremost in her mind. Not that she didn't appreciate what the little darlings could bring to one's life, her nephews and nieces were wonderful, it was just that she had never seen herself in that role. The realisation of which put an end to her prospective marriage to Richard. It was devastating news for him, and even surprised her, but it had been for the best. The decision not to have children, the right one for her, which is what she kept repeating to herself anyway, left her in limbo as to what she was supposed to be doing with her life.

"Tamara?"

She glanced across at Tom. He was looking directly at her, waiting for a reply to a question she'd not heard him ask.

"I'm sorry. What did you say?"

"I said, do you want me to pick you up in the morning?"

"Yes. That'd be great," she said, smiling and reaching for the door handle.

She got out and he followed, walking to the rear and opening the boot. He lifted out her bag. She realised that she was travelling impossibly light for an extended stay and would need to go shopping in the next day or so. Looking across the town, lit up as dusk passed into night, she could hear the sound of the waves breaking on the shoreline. Tom made to walk into the hotel but she took the bag from him instead. It was delightfully charming of him to do so, but entirely unnecessary.

"I'll see you in the morning, Tom," she said.

"Good night."

She waited for him to get into the car, waving him off as he turned it around and headed off. She turned and walked towards the entrance. The gravel was difficult to negotiate in heels and she couldn't wait to get out of them. The reception desk was staffed and she was warmly greeted.

The Westcliff was a traditional hotel, well established and presented in a contemporary and stylish decor, very grand, and a cut above what she would normally expect when working a case. However, she didn't make the booking so there was no guilt. The receptionist checked her in and called another member of staff to take her bag to her room, offering her a drink in the lounge. Suddenly, the length of the day, coupled with the travel, caught up with her and the offer of a drink was too good to refuse.

Leaving her bag at reception, she walked through to the lounge. A bar was at one end, running the width of the room. An extensive casual seating area separated the bar from the dining room at the far end. There were a few guests chatting in small groups, adding to the warm ambience. Several deep bay windows overlooked the front of the hotel, offering wonderful views of the town and the coast which was now rapidly disappearing as it was enveloped by the approaching night.

Walking up to the bar, the barman smiled and left the customer he was talking to and came over to meet her. She ordered a glass of white wine and leaned against the bar while she waited. The drink was complimentary and she thanked the barman as she raised it to her mouth. The alcohol passing her lips reminded her that her stomach was empty. She hadn't eaten since breakfast. The snack food available on the train journey, along with multiple cups of terrible coffee, didn't count.

Glancing beyond the lounge and into the dining room, she saw the tables were set. A few people were already eating. She wondered whether she needed to book a table or not. Turning to ask, the barman was now nowhere to be seen. She hadn't noticed him leaving. Lifting her glass again, she took another sip, savouring the taste.

"Have you been stood up as well?"

She heard the question but was unsure if it was meant for her. The man sitting at the other end of the bar was looking directly at her.

"I'm sorry?" she asked.

"I was due to have a meeting here over dinner tonight, but it's been cancelled," he said, raising a glass containing either sparkling water or gin and tonic, she couldn't tell which.

"Short notice," she replied.

He smiled. The expression was warm and appeared to come naturally to him. He was in his late forties, she guessed, dark haired and with angular features. He stood up and crossed the distance between them. He was tall, perhaps as tall as Tom Janssen although more athletic in build than the powerhouse frame of her colleague, and cut a dashing figure in a well-tailored three-piece. He walked with confidence, a swagger that only a private education or a supreme personal belief could deliver. *Did he work in sales?* Coming alongside, he gestured to the stool next to hers.

"May I?"

She nodded and he sat down, placing his drink on the bar in front of him. The glass was nearly empty.

"I'm Max," he said, offering his hand. She took it.

"Tamara," she replied with a smile.

"I've never met a Tamara before."

She angled her head towards her shoulder. "And I've never come across a Max, either."

"Well, please don't shorten it in front of my mother. To her I will always be Maxwell."

"Even rarer," she said, grinning.

"It is true. There are fewer of us around these days. I am the latest in a long line. It's… a *family thing*," he said, picking up his glass and finishing the contents. The barman returned and Max summoned him. "Could I have another, please, and..." He looked to her, indicating her glass. She nodded, picking it up and raising it to her mouth.

"Pinot Grigio," she said before sipping at the contents.

He smiled. "And a dry white wine, if you please."

The barman nodded and collected a fresh tumbler, depositing ice cubes into it before dispensing a measure of gin and reaching for a small bottle of tonic water. Inwardly, Tamara smiled. Max spoke with such charm and authority. Her tiredness was forgotten and she found her gaze drifting to the ring finger of his left hand. It was clear with no hint of a visible tan line. She'd fallen foul of that misjudgement once before.

"So, who were you supposed to be meeting?" she asked, finishing her drink just in time as the replacement was set down on a fresh paper mat in front of her. She was surprised how quickly the first had gone down.

"A frightful number of *frightfully dull,* and rather tiresome people," he said, grinning and lifting his glass, angling it towards hers. She lifted her own glass and touched it against his. "The cancellation has saved me from what was promising to be an awful evening. Here's to much more interesting company," he said.

"Much more interesting company," she repeated as their glasses rang out.

"What brings you here, Tamara?" he asked.

She wasn't keen to discuss work. More often than not a warrant card sent people running for the nearest exit.

"I have business, here in the town."

"What is it that you do?"

She thought about her response, opting to keep it suitably vague seeing as deception didn't come easy to her. "I work with people."

"Ah… human resources?"

She took on a thoughtful expression. "After a fashion." It

wasn't strictly accurate but she chose to run with it. "How about you?"

"Investments," he said, adopting a glum expression. "I'm good with numbers. They are, however, very dull and I even bore myself talking about it. Would it be okay if we avoided professional conversation for the remainder of this evening?"

"How very presumptuous of you," she said, smiling. Max seemed momentarily taken aback before the default position of his charm and confidence reasserted itself.

"I see no point in either of us dining alone. What a terrible waste of a wonderful opportunity," he said, fixing his gaze upon her. His eyes appeared to sparkle, the corners of his mouth creeping into an appealing smile.

"But no talk about work," she said, raising her forefinger suggestively in front of her.

"Scout's honour," he said, grinning.

"You don't seem like the scouting type," she said, narrowing her gaze.

"Am I that obvious?" Max said, gesturing towards the barman that they required their drinks to be transferred to the dining room. They both stood up and Max offered Tamara the lead and they headed for the adjoining room.

"Only to those of us skilled at reading people," she said over her shoulder.

"Damned human resources," Max said, drawing a laugh from her.

CHAPTER TWENTY

TAMARA GREAVE WOKE WITH A START. For a moment she couldn't remember where she was. Glancing across the room, the floor to ceiling nets, drawn across the bay window, billowed gently in the breeze. She must have left the sash window cracked open before falling asleep. Was it a noise outside that had woken her?

The knock sounded again, only this time it was louder and more forceful. Glancing at the clock on her bedside cabinet, she cursed inwardly. Having not set an alarm the previous night, she'd overslept. That could only be Tom calling on her. The memories of the previous night flooded into her mind, along with recognition of the dull ache that only came from over indulging. She looked to the other side of the bed and found it empty. Tossing the duvet aside, she slid from the bed. The breeze coming in through the window felt cold on her skin. She noticed the hotel's landline telephone was resting on its side on the floor, the receiver was on the floor alongside it. That answered the question of why no one had called through.

She scampered across the bedroom and found the door to the bathroom was open. The interior light was on but the room was empty. Shivering, she picked up one of the bath robes hanging on the back of the door, calling out as another knock sounded.

"I'll be right there," she said, her voice resonating in the fully tiled space and greatly increasing the impact of her throbbing headache. Inspecting her reflection in the mirror, set behind the basin, she shook her head. Her hair was all over the place and she still had on yesterday's make-up which had run, leaving streaks across one cheek and resulting in panda eyes. There was little she could do about it right now. Tightening the belt around her waist, she made for the door. Passing the toilet, it was almost an afterthought to push both the seat and the lid down. Tom was an observant man and she didn't want to face any judgement.

Coming to the door to her room, she first raised herself up on her tiptoes to look through the peephole. It was indeed Tom Janssen, waiting patiently for her in the corridor. He looked up, seemingly eyeing the peephole himself, as if he sensed someone was watching him. She withdrew and checked herself out in the full-length mirror of the wardrobe before turning the latch and opening the door. Janssen smiled.

"Good morning. Sorry," he said, the smile fading a little, "did I get the time wrong?"

She shook her head, drawing the door wider and beckoning him to enter. "No, sorry. It's on me. I slept through my alarm."

She turned and walked back into the room, expecting him to follow and then hearing the door close. Looking around, she couldn't see her bag. Just the clothes she had been wearing the day before which were strewn across the floor. If Janssen thought anything about her levels of tidiness, he said nothing, hovering at the end of the adjoining corridor between bathroom and bedroom.

"Sorry, I'm really not quite with it yet."

"That's okay," Janssen said, his eyes drifting to the occasional table by the sofa at his end of the room. Two empty wine bottles were there, one had fallen over alongside two dirty glasses. She saw his lingering gaze, followed it and felt her face drop. Exhaling deeply, she bit her lower lip.

"I... erm..." she stuttered, the embarrassment bringing a knot to her stomach. He turned to her and smiled.

"I think you need a few minutes. I'll head downstairs and grab a coffee in the lounge," Janssen said. His expression was as normal, completely unfazed and equally unreadable. She nodded, appreciating the offer and adjusting the belt of her robe ever closer to her waist. Although, if it wrapped around her any tighter then it would arguably cut off the circulation. She ran a hand through her hair as he headed for the door. "I'll see you downstairs," he said over his shoulder.

When the door closed, she let out a sigh of relief and began scooping up her clothes, tossing them onto the sofa before heading for the bathroom. Her suitcase was in the corner of the hallway, set down alongside the entrance to her room. Lifting it up, she returned to the bedroom and laid it down on the bed. Unzipping it, she retrieved her toiletries bag and went for a shower. The day wasn't starting as planned but she had to admit, it could have been much worse. From here, it could only get better.

TOM WAS SITTING in an armchair in the lounge, next to one of the windows overlooking the front of the hotel. The chairs were of a reasonable size but his height and physical stature made it appear as if he was sitting awkwardly. He had his back to her, coffee cup on a small table in front of him and he didn't hear her approach. Looking out of the window and beyond the hotel grounds, the skies carried only the slightest hint of cloud cover and the morning sun promised a pleasant day ahead.

"That's better," she said in lieu of a formal greeting to get his attention. Janssen looked round, smiling. "Thanks for that."

"No problem at all," he said. "Do you need to get anything to eat before we leave? I'm afraid we have an unexpected call to make before heading to the station."

Tamara looked around. The lounge was empty, without even a staff member in sight. She looked towards the dining room where several of the guests were having breakfast and her stomach rumbled. She considered ordering something to take with them but quickly dismissed the idea. What with Janssen being with her, the last thing she wanted was to bump into Max over breakfast. The thought made her nervous and she offered Janssen a dismissive shake of the head.

"No. I'll pick something up later. Are you ready?" she said, looking at his coffee cup. He sat forward, lifted it to his mouth and drained it in one fluid motion.

"Now, I'm done," he said, setting the cup down and standing. Reaching for the jacket on the adjacent chair, he pulled it on.

"Where is it we have to go?" Tamara said, her eyes flitting nervously around the room. A staff member entered. It was the barman who had been on shift the night before. He smiled at her, dipping his head by way of greeting and for a brief moment she felt a touch of paranoia threaten to pick at her. She pushed it aside, turning her attention back to Janssen. She found him gazing on her. Meeting his eye, he raised both eyebrows in query. Only then did she realise he'd been talking to her and she hadn't registered a word of it.

"Is that okay?"

It didn't sound like it was the first time of asking either. "Sorry. What did you say?"

"The concierge, from over at the Beaconsfield, called earlier. He says there was a break-in at the apartments overnight. I figured we could swing by and check it out."

Another person entered the lounge. Tamara felt a flutter in her chest and was relieved to see it wasn't Max.

"Yes, of course. Absolutely. Let's make a move."

She set off and Janssen had to move quickly to catch her up. No one was on the reception desk and they stepped outside into a fresh breeze drifting in off the sea. Janssen unlocked the car, Tamara looked back at the hotel, relieved to be leaving for the day. Janssen caught her eye as she lingered by the door.

"Are you sure you're all right?"

"Yes, of course," she said. "Why do you ask?"

"You seem a little…" he said, glancing back towards the hotel entrance, "distracted."

"I'm fine."

She opened the passenger door and got in. Janssen did likewise. He pressed the engine start button with one hand as he dragged his seatbelt across his chest with the other. Tamara looked over to him.

"What did the… concierge, was it, say had happened at the apartments?"

Janssen engaged the car in gear and pulled away, checking over his shoulder as he did so.

"He said one of the apartments has been vandalised but I have to admit, I didn't get all of the details."

"Is it Devon's?"

"That's what I'm assuming, otherwise why would he call us specifically. Cassie left him with her telephone number."

"Speaking of whom, is she on her way to London with Eric?"

"As we speak."

The drive across town didn't take long. Janssen appeared to know the best route, unsurprisingly, and he took them down several narrow streets into the heart of the town which ensured she lost her bearings almost immediately. After a couple of minutes, they rounded a tight ninety-degree corner and the sea appeared before them, the sun glinting off the waves. Janssen pulled into the kerb. They got out and Tamara eyed the apartment block. It stood out from those surrounding it. It was stunning. Looking around, this area didn't appear to suffer from antisocial behaviour. An expanse of lawn, situated across from the buildings lining the street, was well tended and there was a substantial playground for young children. Each property faced the sea offering uninterrupted views of the water and the coast in each direction.

"Nice place," she said absently.

Janssen nodded his agreement without a word and directed her to the building behind them. They entered the lobby and Ewan Dixon looked up from his desk. He stood up and intercepted them before they had covered half the distance towards his desk.

"Thank you for coming," he said, looking between them. Tamara could almost see his grey matter turning over in an attempt to remember if they'd met before. She guessed it was part of the job for him.

"What seems to be the problem, Mr Dixon," Tamara said, only adding to the man's dilemma by addressing him directly. Dixon's gaze flitted between them for a moment longer before settling on her. She paid attention to the reports others wrote. At this point, she chose not to introduce herself. The fact he had neglected to mention the visitors to Devon Bailey's apartment, visitations he should and would have been well aware of, ensured a question mark was put against him. If he was unsettled by her presence, then that was a bonus at this time.

"Somebody broke into Mr Bailey's apartment last night. I'm afraid they've done a terrible amount of damage."

"You had better take us up," Tamara said. Dixon nodded, turning on his heel and heading for the lifts. She glanced at Janssen and he raised his eyebrows, tilting his head to one side. *Why would someone wish to trash Devon's apartment?*

CHAPTER TWENTY-ONE

THE LIFT DOORS parted and they stepped out. Ewan Dixon led them to the left and the first door they came to was Devon's. There was no need for Dixon to unlock the door. It had already been put in. Where the latch met the frame, the wood was splintered and split. By the looks of it, the damage appeared similar to that of a ram used by the police when required to take down a locked door. When wielded in the hands of a competent person, it only needed one swing and impacting at the right point to gain entry. This clearly wasn't the work of a mindless vandal. Janssen stepped forward, placing a restraining hand on Dixon's forearm.

"It's probably best if you wait out here," he said. Dixon nodded.

"You don't think someone's still in there, do you?"

Janssen shook his head. "Unlikely, but we wouldn't want you in there corrupting a crime scene, would we?"

"Oh, I see," Dixon replied, averting his eyes from Janssen's gaze. "In which case, I think we may have a problem."

He looked to Tamara. By the look on her face, she also realised what the concierge was implying. Janssen took a deep breath.

"Have you been inside the apartment already?" he asked.

Dixon flushed with embarrassment. "One of the residents called down... I thought I should investigate." He looked between them. "I'm afraid I didn't think."

"Which part of *no one goes in there* didn't you understand when we spoke yesterday, Mr Dixon?" Janssen said. The concierge didn't answer. "Did you touch anything?"

"Not much."

"Wait here," he said firmly, indicating to Tamara that they should go inside. She nodded and came to join him. The sound of another door opening further along the corridor made him look. The face of an older man appeared, the neighbour Janssen realised from Cassie's description must be Geoff Scott, casting a curious eye over proceedings. Janssen indicated the neighbour with a flick of his head and Tamara nodded.

"I'll take a look around. You can join me in there," she said.

Janssen moved out of her way and she entered the apartment. Janssen raised his finger pointedly in front of Ewan Dixon, and jabbed it towards the floor where the man was standing.

"You wait here," he said. Dixon nodded solemnly.

By the time Janssen reached the door to Geoff Scott's apartment, the man himself was nowhere to be seen. The door was still ajar and he knocked on it lightly with his knuckles, easing it open. The apartment was a mirror image layout of Devon Bailey's, the door opening into an open-plan living space. Geoff Scott was standing inside with his back to the door, looking out through his folding doors at the sea beyond. Janssen entered, pushing the door closed behind him.

"Mr Scott?" he said. "My name is Detective Inspector Janssen."

"I know who you are," the man said, turning to face him with his hands in the pockets of his flannel trousers. "I saw you here yesterday, along with that nice pretty lady."

"DS Knight?"

"Cassandra, yes," Scott said, smiling. "She's not here today?" He sounded disappointed.

"I'm afraid she is required elsewhere," he said. "Can you tell me anything about what happened next door last night?"

Scott shook his head emphatically.

"You didn't hear anything?" Janssen asked, looking over his shoulder in the direction of Devon's apartment, as if he could see through the walls. "Are you certain? They would have made something of a racket putting the door in."

"Well... I heard a loud bang... and I thought it odd, but then there was nothing, so I figured I'd misheard and went back to sleep."

"What time was this?"

Scott thought about it. "I was already in my bed, so it must have been after eleven but I couldn't say for sure."

"Did you see anyone hanging around yesterday? After we left for the day perhaps?"

Scott shook his head. He appeared agitated, as if there was more he wanted to say but was reticent. *Was it a matter of trust?* Maybe Cassie would have better luck. Janssen took out one of his contact cards. Scott seemed reluctant to move from his position by the balcony and he appeared even less likely to add anything further. Janssen placed the card down on a small occasional table by the door, tapping it with his forefinger and tilting his head towards it.

"If anything comes to mind, please do give me a call, would you?"

Scott nodded firmly, his body language was stiff, rigid. Janssen thanked him for his time before turning and stepping back out into the corridor. Ewan Dixon was exactly where he'd left him and he walked past without saying a word, entering Devon's place in search of Tamara. The apartment was in disarray. Whereas the previous day it had been immaculately presented, well ordered and almost too clean to appear lived in. It was now the total opposite. The wraparound corner sofa had been shredded. The cushion liners had been torn apart and the feather stuffing was strewn all around. The cupboard doors of the kitchen cabinets hung open and several had seen their contents emptied onto the floor. He moved through the apartment, picking a path of least resistance endeavouring not to trample any potential evidence. Although, at this point he was unsure what the perpetrators were up to. He called out to Tamara and she appeared from the master bedroom.

Looking beyond her, he saw the doors to the wardrobes were also open and their contents suffered a similar fate to those of the kitchen. He could also see that the double bed had been slashed in much the same way as the sofa. Fibre filling and feathers were everywhere.

"They've pulled the bathroom apart too," Tamara said. "Taken the panels off beneath the wall-hung sanitary ware and the built-in bath as well. They didn't leave anything to chance."

"This must have taken quite some time," he said, looking around. "It sounds like the neighbour heard them making entry but nothing afterwards. Or so he says."

"They were definitely looking for something," Tamara said, scanning the living room.

"But the question is: did they find it?"

She scanned the interior, searching the room for what might have been missed.

"You say CSI haven't been able to get here yet?"

"No. They were tied up at the cliffs and then processing the car. At that point we didn't know whether it was a simple accident or a suicide."

She nodded. There was no hint of criticism from her.

"If you ask me, someone wanted to get in here before we did. They knew we'd be coming."

He found the suggestion logical. That meant whoever did this was probably watching them. Either that or, his thoughts drifted to Ewan Dixon, the concierge, someone who had inside knowledge of a forthcoming search that would be taking place.

He found his frustration rising. With hindsight, he should have sealed the apartment off properly yesterday. But, then again, anything was possible with hindsight.

"We'll need to get a statement from the jobsworth to see what it was he touched," he said, referring to Dixon.

Tamara lowered her voice. "What do you think the odds are that he touched an awful lot?"

Janssen turned and went back to the corridor. Dixon was still there. He hadn't moved a step. There was nothing wrong with his hearing today.

"Can you pull up the CCTV from last night?" he asked.

"Yes, of course," Dixon said, apparently pleased to be useful. "What time period are you looking at?"

"Start with around ten o'clock last night and then we can go forward or back. Do you have screens downstairs?"

"Yes, I'll get it ready for you."

Janssen allowed him to leave and then returned to Devon's apartment. Tamara had taken one of the chairs from the dining table and positioned it against one of the far walls of the living room. She was standing upon it and he noticed she had donned a set of blue latex gloves.

"What are you doing?"

She remained focussed on where she was and what she was doing for a moment longer before beckoning him over with a flick of an open palm. He crossed the room, pulling on a set of gloves himself. As he came closer, he realised she had a small pen knife in her hand and was working at a grille plate on the wall. It must have been a warm air heating duct or air conditioning. Either way, when he approached, she reached out to him. He held up his palm and she dropped several screws into his open hand. Returning to what she was doing, she released the grille from its place on the wall and passed that down to him as well. Tamara then closed the blade and took out her mobile phone. Holding it up to the hole in the wall, roughly the width measuring wrist to elbow, she illuminated the interior and he heard the sound of her mobile camera taking a burst of shots. Pocketing her mobile, she then reached into the ducting and the sound of rustling plastic carried to him.

From the ducting, hidden behind the wall, she dragged out a blue plastic carrier bag. Whatever was contained within the bag bore some weight as she visibly struggled to pull it clear. She passed it down to him and then he offered her a hand to steady herself while she got down from the chair. Crossing the room to the dining table, he carefully put the bag down. The handles had at one time been taped over, suggesting the contents had previously been sealed up. Tamara produced her mobile once more and took several photographs of the bag from different angles before they widened the opening to photograph the contents. Finally, Janssen was able to reach into the bag and pulled out a handful of notes. They were shrink-wrapped in bundles of five, with each one still secured together with a paper band. All were twenty-pound sterling denominations. He placed them down on the table next to the carrier bag. Reaching back into the bag, he produced another clutch of notes, only this time they were fifties but still wrapped and sealed in the same way.

"How much do you reckon?" he asked, glancing between the fifties in his hand and Tamara. She blew out her cheeks, eyeing the remaining notes.

"Fifteen, twenty grand... maybe more."

He was inclined to agree.

"Someone was looking for Devon's money."

"Or wanted theirs back," she countered.

"True," he said, putting the fifties down alongside the other bundle. "Odd decision, though."

"What's that?"

"If you're after Devon's money, or want yours back, it seems a little odd to throw him off a cliff before having him give it to you."

He looked over to her and Tamara met his eye. She was about to reply when someone knocked on the door. She indicated for him to see who it was. He walked to the door and opened it. Ewan Dixon was waiting there for him. He appeared agitated, nervous.

"What is it?" Janssen asked.

"It's the CCTV. It's gone!"

"What do you mean, *gone*?"

"There's no recording from last night," Dixon said. "It's not there."

CHAPTER TWENTY-TWO

"ARE you sure we're in the right place?" Cassie asked, turning to Eric before glancing about the surrounding area. The traffic noise was significant enough for her to feel the need to raise her voice to ensure she was heard. The sound was a continuous drone only punctuated by noise from the nearby construction site.

Looking in that direction, Cassie saw the site was closed off from pedestrian view by wooden boards lining the perimeter. Many of these had become impromptu advertising hoardings for such varied offerings as the nearby marketplace to theatrical productions at a local venue. Eric stepped back, craning his neck to see beyond the chain link fencing barring their way and to the building beyond. Like much of the area where they were standing, it also appeared closed for access.

"This is the address given," he said, sounding bereft of confidence. "I'm pretty sure of it."

Cassie let out a deep sigh at the sound of a pneumatic drill. "Well, we're here, so let's go and take a look."

Each fence panel was tied to the next with a metal clasp and all were held in place by fixing into portable concrete blocks. Where they were standing was the entrance to the site, a small collection of brick buildings, two storeys high with retail units at the base and either flats or storage rooms located above. The panels in front of them were secured with a padlock and chain but with some effort, she was able to lever them aside just enough for her to slip a leg through to the other side. Eric came to help and between them, she managed to force her way through the gap. They then repeated the process for Eric and he joined her on the other side. The detective constable's expression conveyed his concern as he looked around the site.

"Don't worry, Eric. It's not like we're going to be caught doing something wrong."

Eric seemed less than convinced. She didn't comment further. He was young, inexperienced. Ideological. The thought shook her. He could only be five years her junior at most. Maybe her decision to remain in the job wasn't in her best interests after all. She hadn't always been this cynical or disillusioned. Or maybe she'd just hidden it better.

She looked around, assessing the site. There were several signs indicating the area was closed to the public and demanding correct clothing be worn on site but by the looks of it, nothing much was happening here. Some of the nearby buildings were boarded up. Those with exposed windows, mainly on the upper floors, had been the target of vandals who'd had some measure of success with either stones or other projectiles. Even the ground beneath their feet, poured concrete in many places, loose gravel in others, bore the hallmarks of abandonment. Grass and weeds grew sporadically all around them, some reaching almost to knee height.

Cassie set off towards the building, unsure of whether they would find anything useful. There were no businesses operating from here anymore and there hadn't been for a long time.

"Do we know when this logistics firm was registered here?" Eric asked as he joined her.

"Not at this address, no. Companies House has it registered for years, though. It's not a new company listing. It may have been the offices once but there's no way they were doing any distribution from a place like this," Cassie said, raising a hand to shield her eyes from the glare of the sun.

They'd made it into central London by half past nine that morning before heading across the capital to the south east and the borough of Lewisham in search of AMK Logistics and its registered company offices. Despite the lack of cloud in the sky, the sun was shielded from them as they were in the shadow of a number of nearby tower blocks that were either recently finished or undergoing construction. Approaching the nearest building they found it secure. There was no visible signage to identify what may have once traded from it or who owned it now.

"It doesn't look like anything traded from here in a while," Eric said. "Is it cynical of me to wonder if it's just a shell company?"

The honest answer was that she didn't know. Maybe the company was just poor when it came to updating its admin. She didn't answer as a newcomer caught their attention. The fence panels they'd squeezed between were currently being unlocked by a heavy-set man in a high visibility jacket. He glanced in their direction as he lifted one of the fence panels clear, allowing him room to bring his vehicle, a white four-by-four pick-up with a luminous streak down the side, through from the highway beyond. They watched as he clambered into the cabin of the pick-up and drove towards them at speed. He pulled up near to them, his expression akin to a scowl. He seemed to find getting in and out of his vehicle something of a challenge. Unsurprising, Cassie thought, judging by the size of his frame. He looked like a mobile site security guard or something similar.

"You can't be here," he said, in a gruff East End accent. "This is private property."

"Police," Cassie said, effortlessly brandishing her warrant card in one smooth motion. "Who owns this site?"

The newcomer lost an element of his brusque demeanour but the scowl remained fixed in place.

"It's part of the Gateway project," he said, as if that answered everything.

"Gateway?" Eric asked.

"Yeah. The Lewisham Gateway rejuvenation scheme. You aren't from round here, then?" Both Cassie and Eric shook their heads. "Look around you," he said, making a sweeping gesture with his arm. "This is the next phase of gentrification. You've got Hither Green, Ladywell and Forest Hill surrounding us. We've got the hipsters moving in on Deptford selling their breakfast cereal at eight quid a box, and Blackheath with their Range Rovers which is proper posh. A bit like Hampstead, just south of the river. Even bloody Catford has a gastro pub now."

"Is there a point in there somewhere?" Cassie asked, although his displeasure at the speed of change appeared obvious.

"They reckon these ugly flats and a few shops will turn this place around," he said. "Bring the money in from those who want to live here and commute into the city. Open up some artisan bakery or something while they're at it."

"Sounds nice," Eric said. His smile faded when the man shot him a dark look. Apparently, he didn't agree the change would be positive.

"It all started to go wrong when Chiesman's closed down in the 90s, if you ask me." Cassie was pretty sure she hadn't. Neither did she care whatever Chiesman's was, but assumed it was a local business at one time. "They won't be happy until this place is unrecognisable."

"I feel for your loss," Cassie said flatly. Eric met her eye. He seemed unsure of her sincerity. He was right to question it.

"Well, police or not, you can't be here." The guard had lost patience with them, or maybe Cassie in particular. "This is a construction site. It's not safe."

Cassie looked around. The nearest construction work was at least two hundred metres away and taking place in a different compound altogether.

"Not much going on, is there?" she said, unable to keep the

sarcasm from her tone. Not that she made much of an effort to do so.

"This here will be phase two," the man said with a shrug. He interpreted her unasked question from her quizzical expression. "I don't know when it's due to start."

"Ever heard of a company called AMK Logistics?" she asked. "They used to operate out of one of these buildings."

He thought about it very briefly. There didn't appear to be a spark of recognition at mention of the name.

"Nah. Never heard of them. Come on, you need to leave now."

Cassie glanced at Eric and indicated for them to do so with a nod of the head. There was nothing more they could glean from the site anyway. The security guard adopted a smug expression which may or may not have made him less annoying, but that was something of a judgement call. He got back into the cabin of his pick-up, started the engine, and accelerated around them in order to get back to the highway first.

He was already waiting for them when they reached the pavement with one hand on the fence panel. As they passed from the site back onto the footpath, he followed them, levering the panel back into place and wrapping the chain tightly between the two. He secured the padlock in place, only this time it was far tighter than when they'd first arrived. There was no way they'd have squeezed through now. The guard got back into the pick-up and drove away without another word.

Eric looked to the left and right. "What do you want to do now?"

She followed his gaze up to the nearby construction site. A tower block, standing at least fifteen storeys high, was rising in the foreground of a completed building behind it. Much of the construction appeared to be centred around the train station. She looked in the other direction towards what she thought was the high street, gesturing that way with a flick of her hand.

"Eric, what did your mam tell you to do if you ever got lost as a kid?"

Eric thought about it. "Ask a policeman."

"Ah... strange how people differ. Mine always told me to ask the local newsagent."

"Why?"

"I'm not sure," she said, setting off with him a half-step behind. "Maybe because they do the newspaper deliveries and so know the streets or maybe," she stopped for a second, looking to him, "because there's always a local newsagent around."

Eric frowned. "Sure as hell won't always be a policeman around these days."

She laughed and resumed their walk. It turned out that she was right, they were on course for the high street. It was bustling with people. In the central pedestrian precinct they found an open market selling anything from fruit and vegetables to mobile phone cases and fresh fish. There was even one woman of note, sitting at the outer edge of the stalls, who appeared to be selling prawns from a bucket. Eric shuddered as they passed her. Cassie noticed and found herself smiling at his discomfort. She wondered how much time he'd spent outside of Norfolk. Some of the food markets in Thailand would most likely blow his mind.

To either side of the market were the shops. There were many of the usual high-street brand names but often located in between were some interesting independent premises, an Italian delicatessen and several small cafés could be seen in between a multitude of pound shops and those selling fried chicken. The general impression was of a place that could be argued as either on the up or on the slide, depending on what your motivation was.

"I don't see a newsagent," Eric said, looking past the various stalls in the direction of a large building at the end. It was modern, squat and seemed out of place. It was the local police station.

"What about that one?" she said, pointing across to the far side of the market.

Eric narrowed his eyes. "I think that's a Turkish supermarket."

"It'll do."

Cassie set off in between stalls and Eric had to scamper after her to catch up. Entering the shop, it turned out Eric was right. From the outside it looked like any other convenience store but on the inside they found a narrow building stretching some way back and selling a wide range of products from meat to laundry detergent and newspapers. The shop was quiet with only a handful of customers.

Approaching the counter, Cassie displayed her warrant card to the man standing beside the till. He appeared nervous at first until she explained they were only looking for local information. He was young, early twenties, well presented and broadly disinterested in his job but polite enough. She wondered whether this was a family enterprise and he was one of the owner's children. It seemed that kind of place.

"No, sorry," he said, shaking his head. "I've never heard of that company. If it was around here, then I never saw it."

"Never mind," Cassie said, taking a folded sheet of A4 paper from her coat pocket. "Have you ever come across this man around here?"

She unfolded the paper and laid it on the counter for him to see. The cashier immediately looked away, shaking his head. The image was that of Devon Bailey, a pencil sketch drawn up by a police artist. The mugshots taken from his youth would be next to useless as they were decades old. In her mind, he'd been too quick to dismiss the image. She tapped the paper gently with her forefinger, leaning forward and meeting the young man's eye. She smiled, trying to keep her body language and tone warm and friendly.

"I'm sorry, what was your name?" she asked. He hadn't given it and she hadn't asked.

"Amir," he said, smiling weakly.

"Amir, do you think you could look again? Only this time, really take a good look. It's important."

He studied the sketch once more, only this time his gaze hovered over the image. She watched closely, seeing his lips part slightly. She guessed his mind was working overtime but for what reason she couldn't say.

The entrance door opened, drawing Amir's attention in that direction. Hers followed. Three black men entered, she guessed they were in their mid-thirties. They were dressed casually, or at least it was a casual image they sought to portray, along with a great deal of bling. Each of them sported gold chains, diamond studded earrings along with impressive watches on their wrists. Whether any of it was genuine, she couldn't tell. They first eyed Amir, then her, his gaze lingering on her which made her feel uncomfortable. She broke the eye contact and he wandered off into the shop with his friends. If the impact of their presence on her was discomforting, on Amir, it was stark. He was now adamant, as well as pushy.

"Don't know him," he said flatly, pushing the paper back towards her.

Cassie met his eye and he immediately averted his gaze from hers, looking into the shop. The three men were wandering around, picking up items in something of a random manner. Other shoppers quickly made way for them as they passed.

"You're sure?" she asked.

"Yes. Never met him," Amir stated. "Sorry."

He was nervous. No, it was more than that, rattled. She took out a contact card, reversing it, she scribbled something on the back and then passed it to Amir. He read the front and then flipped it to see the other side. She'd written the name of the hotel they were booked into for that night.

"If you want to talk, you'll find me there," she said, angling her head to ensure they made eye contact. She smiled. "Anything you know might be useful."

He nodded, glancing to his right. He was agitated. It was obvious. Gesturing to Eric, she indicated for them to leave.

"Thank you, Amir," she said warmly. He nodded again and they left.

"What was all that about?" Eric asked once they were walking back through the market.

She shook her head. "This is the type of place that still hasn't changed much despite everything going on around it. Everyone knows everyone else... and their business. People around here will know Devon Bailey."

"But they don't want to talk about it," Eric said.

"It looks that way," Cassie said, looking back at the supermarket. The doors opened and the three men they'd seen entering were now leaving. Two of them were eating some snacks they'd just purchased, she hoped, and the last one out caught her eye. Again, she found a sense of disquiet wash over her as they eyed one another. Then, he smiled, taking two sideways steps and holding her gaze until he then turned and walked away. Even then, he afforded her a quick glance over his shoulder, accompanied by a broad grin. She watched him until he caught up with the others, taking a left turn into an alleyway and disappearing from view. "Come on, Eric. Let's try Devon's last known address."

"You think we'll find anything there? It was years ago."

"No harm in looking, Eric. No harm at all."

CHAPTER TWENTY-THREE

SHE PRESSED the doorbell once more, only this time held it in place for long enough to draw an inquisitive look from Eric, standing alongside her. She leaned closer, trying to see through the wire reinforced pane of glass set in the front door but it was no use. The glass was obscured and even if she could see through it, the interior was shrouded in darkness.

"Looks like no one's home," Eric said, adopting a glum expression.

Her eyes narrowed as she looked at him, resisting the urge to roll her eyes. Turning back to the door, she hammered the flat of her fist on the door as if she had the need to wake the dead. It was the middle of the afternoon and it had taken them hours to find the address. The post code held on file for the flat turned out to be wrong, sending them on a detour into a part of south London that could have been a rabbit warren of sorts. Had it not been for the help of some locals, they would likely never have found this place. They were on the third of four floors of a small block of flats. They were probably built in the mid to late fifties, constructed from brick with open walkways running the length of the building from a communal stairwell in the middle. So far, their journey into London had been a total washout. Cassie had no intention of going back to Norfolk empty handed. She'd had to lobby hard for two days, feeling that one day with the associated travel constrained their ability to achieve a result. Tom Janssen agreed, in the end, but to deliver nothing tangible for the time of two detectives wouldn't look good this early in her new role.

"What should we do?"

She didn't look at Eric, remaining fixed on the barrier before her. He was a nice lad, Eric, and she thought she would end up liking him but right now, he was bugging her. Did he always need someone to take the lead or was he capable of independent thought?

"How about we smash the door down."

"We can't!"

Cassie looked at him, her brow furrowing to accompany the look of disdain. "No, Eric. Of course we can't. I was taking the piss."

"Oh, right. Got yer," Eric said. "So… what are we going to do?"

Before she had a chance to reply, a door opened further along the corridor. A face peered out, eyeing them warily. Cassie took a step back, looking over and smiling warmly as she took out her ID.

"Nothing to worry about, love," she said. "Police."

The woman emerged a little further from inside her flat, still with one hand on the door frame as if it was both steadying and comforting. Cassie took her measure. She was black, elderly, easily into her eighties and appeared frail. Crossing the short distance between them, she indicated the flat over her shoulder with her thumb.

"My name's Cassie."

"Evelyn," the woman said.

"I don't suppose you know who lives next door, do you?"

The woman scowled. "I wish that I didn't. Nothing but trouble. You'll be lucky to get them out of bed before the sun goes down. What have they been up to now anyway?"

Cassie shook her head. "Nothing as far as I know. We're actually looking for someone who we know used to live there. Devon Bailey. Do you remember him?"

The woman's expression softened, if only a little, turning more to surprise. "Devon? Now, there's a name I've not heard in many a year."

Cassie wasn't great at placing accents, ironic bearing in mind her own was so pronounced and easily identifiable as from the north east. She thought this lady's was Jamaican but edged with a cockney intonation. She must have lived here for years.

"You remember him, Devon?"

"Oh, yes. I remember Devon all right," she said bobbing her head and raising her eyebrows in a knowing way. "He's not the kind of boy you forget, let me tell you."

"What do you mean?" Cassie asked, although she already had a pretty good idea.

"Challenging boy," she said, tilting her head to one side. "Ran his poor mother ragged."

"His mother. Did she live here too?"

"Yes, yes, yes," she said, waving a hand in front of her in a circular motion. "The two of them lived next door. Iriya and her little boy, Devon."

Cassie looked back towards the flat, Eric flicked his eyebrows and followed her gaze.

"But she doesn't live there anymore?" Cassie asked.

"No. Bless her. Iriya moved on some time ago. The council let the flat to… I shouldn't say. The Lord will not care for what I say about those who followed."

"And what about Devon? Has he been around?"

She shook her head. "Not seen the boy for years! And I wouldn't have anything to say to the likes of him if I did."

"Fair enough," Cassie said. "Any idea where Iriya moved on to? It would be good if we could have a word with her."

"That will take some doing young lady... you'll have to speak with the Almighty first."

"She's passed away?"

"Mmm... yes, that's it," she said, making the sign of the cross in front of her heart. "Bless her."

"Anyone around who might remember Devon or Iriya?" Cassie asked, hoping she got the pronunciation right.

"No, I think I'm the last one," she said with a proud smile. "They've been moving us on in the last couple of years but I'm still here," she said, wagging a finger in the air, the smile broadening into a grin.

"More people dying?" Eric asked.

Evelyn's smile faded. This time Cassie did roll her eyes.

"What a thing to say! I was talking about the council, you daft lad" Evelyn said.

Eric glanced at Cassie and then averted his eyes from her gaze, looking to his feet and chewing on his lower lip.

"You could always try St. Mary's," Evelyn said, looking to Cassie.

"St. Mary's?"

"The hospice. That's where they took Iriya before she passed."

"Thanks. We will."

Evelyn retreated to her flat, hovering at the threshold and turning back to them as they made to leave. "Lovely lady, Iriya. She deserved better."

Cassie acknowledged the comment, unsure of exactly what it was meant to imply. Evelyn disappeared from view and as the front door closed, she called out.

"And have a word with them next door. Ask them to keep the noise down."

She didn't wait for a reply and the door closed, the sound of a security chain sliding into place. Cassie allowed herself a hint of a smile. Eric followed suit but it faded as Cassie frowned at him.

"*More people dying?*" she said with a frown and a shake of the head. "Geez, Eric. What are you like?"

"Sorry," Eric said as they set off for the stairwell. "I'll look up St. Mary's on my phone."

THE HOSPICE WAS LOCATED NEARBY. It was a converted Victorian house and located at the end of a row of similar terraced properties, across from a small park. Some construction work was taking place nearby. It seemed like the whole borough was either being refurbished or rebuilt. A sign indicated this particular project was bringing back the Quaggy, a local river that ran through and emptied into the Thames. Artist's impressions suggested it would have something of a Parisian flavour to it. Cassie couldn't help but think they'd be working some magic for that to be the reality. They entered the hospice and identified themselves. After a few minutes of waiting, they were ushered through into the office of the general manager, Mrs Reid. She was a bubbly woman in her early fifties, who seemed concerned about their presence. Cassie moved to reassure her immediately.

"We're looking for information about a former resident of yours, Iriya Bailey. Are you familiar with her?"

The woman relaxed, her shoulders dropping. "Ah, yes. Iriya was a resident here. She passed away some time ago, I'm afraid."

"Do you remember when?"

"Last year," she said, her brow fixed in concentration. "In the late summer, I think. I can check for you. Cancer. Bless her. She was a lovely woman. As you can imagine, we see a lot of our residents pass on. That is what we provide here, palliative care for those who have nowhere to go and no one to care for them. Even so, Iriya left something of a hole in our hearts. Why do you ask?"

"It's more her son, Devon, that we are interested in. Did he ever visit his mam?"

Reid shook her head. "No, I can't recall Devon ever setting foot here. If he did, I'm sure I would know about it."

"But you were aware of him?"

"Oh, yes. Absolutely. Iriya used to speak of him all the time. For someone who expressed so much love for her child, I would have expected him to but alas, he didn't."

"Any idea why that might be the case?"

Reid smiled but it was one borne out of politeness rather than warmth. "There isn't much I haven't seen in this job when it comes to people, Detective Sergeant. But I will say this, when a parent speaks so glowingly about a child who never comes to visit, only one of two things is true. Either they're unable to visit by way of being stationed overseas or, as is often the case, they are incarcerated. Or, alternatively, the apple of their parent's eye is not quite as tasty as we have been led to believe."

Cassie smiled. "That is a very cynical view, if you don't mind me saying so?"

"Like I say, I've met all kinds."

"Which camp would you place Devon in?"

Reid pursed her lips, choosing not to answer.

"Was Iriya married?"

"Not as far as I know. She never spoke of a husband. She only ever mentioned Devon. I always had the impression it was just the two of them."

"I see."

Cassie was deflated. Each lead was turning out to be a waste of time.

"Come to think of it, though. I think we still have some of her things packed away somewhere."

"What type of things?"

"Just some special items she brought with her. Not much, pictures and sentimental keepsakes that she couldn't bear to leave at her flat," Reid said, thinking hard. "I think she realised she wasn't going back there and the thought of leaving them behind was something she couldn't face. I don't think anyone came to collect her effects." She got up from behind her desk, moving to a filing cabinet positioned against the adjacent wall. "Usually, we destroy things or send them to charity shops if they are not collected within a month or two." She glanced back to them apologetically. "Otherwise we would be overwhelmed."

"I understand," Cassie said.

Mrs Reid rummaged through her folders, eventually opening one and triumphantly declaring, "Aha! Knew it."

"You have something?"

"I'll be right with you," she said, heading out of the office.

Cassie looked to Eric, who smiled as he spoke, "Perhaps this won't be a washout after all."

"Unless it's a shoe box with a bus pass and ticket stub from a Pink Floyd concert," she replied.

They didn't have long to wait. Mrs Reid returned with a small box in her hand. She set it down on the desk and pushed it towards them. Cassie smiled, noting it was in fact a shoe box. She lifted the lid. The contents weren't particularly inspiring. There was a wooden set of rosary beads with a small crucifix, a few black and white photographs that were dogeared along with a miniature figurine of what she guessed was the Virgin Mary. Cassie replaced the lid, glancing at Eric.

"May we keep hold of these?" she asked.

"Please do. They will only end up being destroyed if they stay here. I'm amazed I still have them as it is. Do you think it might help?" Mrs Reid asked.

Cassie smiled warmly. "You never know. Thank you for your time."

"WELL THAT WAS a colossal waste of bloody time," Cassie said once they were clear of the hospice.

"Let's go to the hotel, get checked in and have a drink," Eric said. "Maybe we can find a way to sell this to Tom that doesn't make it sound like we've been on a jolly down here."

She smiled warmly at him. That was the first decision she'd heard him make, and it was a good one.

CHAPTER TWENTY-FOUR

CASSIE KNIGHT'S gaze drifted towards the television mounted on the wall of the bar. The sound was off and she wasn't convinced the match was live. Hardly anyone present was paying the game any attention and the other screen, above the bar, was set on a twenty-four hour news channel. It, too, was silent although someone had ensured the subtitles were on. There was a fire in an industrial building somewhere across the city. The locals probably knew where but to her, London was London and she had no idea of the geography.

Eric was tapping out a message on his mobile, head down, bearing an expression of focussed concentration as his thumbs furiously navigated the keyboard. He paused momentarily, sweeping up his pint glass and taking a mouthful of beer. For some reason, she found it odd that Eric drank. He was so fresh-faced and innocent, she wasn't sure he was old enough.

"Are you going to eat those?" she asked.

Eric looked at her quizzically, following her pointed finger to the basket that sat alongside his empty plate.

"Nah, I've had enough."

"In that case, do you mind?" she said, referring to the contents.

He shrugged. "Help yourself."

She didn't need a second offer and reached across the table, picking up the basket and tipping the chips onto her plate. She put one in her mouth, then gestured for Eric to pass over the bowl containing the condiments. He did so and she rummaged through it, eventually picking out two sachets of mayonnaise.

"With chips?" Eric asked, taking a break from the essay he was writing and scrunching his nose up in mock disgust.

"Yeah. You can't beat it," she said. Eric looked less than convinced. "I went over to Holland on a friend's hen-do a couple of years back. That's the way the Dutch eat chips, with lashings of mayo. Trust me, you never go back."

"That's just wrong," Eric cut back, shaking his head. "Where do you put all that, anyway?"

She looked at her plate. She'd plumped for the curry off the specials menu, with both side options of peshwari naan and rice, obviously. Eric had gone for the steak and chips. She half considered whether he'd done that just to come across more manly as his initial choice of the risotto had been met with such derision. She hadn't meant anything by it, merely suggesting that a bowl of warm rice and mushrooms wasn't suitable for a growing boy. Eric could take a joke but those made at the expense of his youth or inexperience seemed to cut a little too close to the bone. She felt bad when he amended his order. Having seen off her own meal, she was now picking at the remains of his. That wasn't unusual. She was well known in her family for being able to tackle more food than anyone might expect for one so small. It was a gift, her father used to say.

"It's a talent," she said, swiping a chip through a small mound of mayonnaise. Covering her mouth with her hand as she chewed, she winked at him. "Stick around. You haven't seen anything yet."

Eric grinned, finishing his pint.

"Do you want another?" he said, looking to the bar.

They'd checked into their rooms and gone for food. Cassie

texted Janssen, avoiding a phone call on the pretence of weak mobile signal and promising to check in first thing in the morning. He hadn't replied yet. She didn't know if that was a bad thing or not. She hadn't figured him out yet and Eric's conclusion didn't deliver more detailed an analysis than *he's a top bloke*, whatever that meant.

"I'm all right for now," she said. Eric stood up and she immediately picked up her pint glass, saw off the contents in one fluid motion, replacing the glass on the table and wiped her mouth with the back of her hand. "Looks like I do."

Eric grinned. "I've just got to duck outside and make a call. I'll go to the bar on my way back. Reception's lousy in here."

The irony of poor signal in the lounge bar wasn't lost on her, imagining Janssen reading her text message with that ever-present unreadable expression that seemed chiselled into his features.

"Checking in?" she asked, careful to avoid any suggestion that she was mocking him.

"Yeah. Becca's a worrier, you know."

With that, he stood up, leaving the table with his mobile in hand as he scrolled for the number in his phone book. Cassie was pleased he wasn't calling his mother because, admittedly, that had been her first thought. Rather than wait for him to return, he might be a while, she decided to get the drinks in. She reached into her pocket for her purse, searching fruitlessly for a minute. They'd placed the food orders against the room but alcohol had to be kept separate. These days, they were getting hot on expenses. Too many people taking the piss, ruining it for everyone else.

Realising she must have left her purse back in her room, she got up. She could wait for Eric to come back but the lounge wasn't busy and they were unlikely to lose their table to other patrons if she left it for a few minutes. Looking to the entrance to the lounge, she couldn't see Eric. He would be pacing around the car park or lingering in the outside seating area, chatting to his girlfriend. It was sweet. She remembered what that was like, almost. It had been a while for her and she was realistic enough to know that wouldn't change any time soon. She could easily nip up to her room and be back before Eric returned.

The barman looked up as she headed across the lounge towards the lobby and the stairs up to the next floor, and she mouthed *two minutes*, signalling with two raised fingers. He nodded and smiled. Slipping out past reception which was unmanned, she went through the doors and mounted the stairs. They both had rooms on the first floor and Eric's words echoed in her mind. The extra steps would help burn a few calories. Not that she was in bad shape. It was as much a mystery to her as anyone else that she never appeared able to put on more weight than she already carried irrespective of what she chose to eat.

The corridor was empty as she walked to her room, passing through a set of fire doors that were difficult to push open. The hinges groaned as the mechanism snapped it closed once she released her grip. Swiping her key card on the access panel, the green light flashed and she entered the room. The one and only window on the far side of the room was cracked open and the net curtain rocked gently back and forth in the breeze. Her purse was where she expected it to be, on the desk beneath the wall-mounted television. She took a quick bathroom break before picking up her purse and stepping back out into the corridor. Closing her door, she tested the handle just to be sure it was locked and confident that it was, she set off back to the bar. This time she put some weight behind her attempt to open the fire door. The door to the stairwell was alongside the lifts on the first-floor landing and she considered taking the latter but dismissed the idea as lazy.

Pushing the door to the stairwell open, something made her hesitate. Whether it was a sound or a flicker of movement in the corner of her eye, she couldn't say but she reacted too late.

Turning to look, she felt something strike the side of her face and she stumbled backwards into the stairwell, partly in shock and partly due to the inertia of her recoil from the attack. Trying to right herself, she reached for the balustrade as the nearest anchor only for a dark blur to advance on her.

She was struck again in her chest. Had someone kicked her or was she punched? Falling to the carpeted floor, she tried to scream but the wind escaped her lungs as a boot smashed into her stomach. Her lips moved with the pain but uttered no sound. Doubled over on the floor, she rolled and scrambled away from her attacker on all fours but she didn't get far. One hand roughly took hold of her hair, hauling her head upright so fiercely that she yelped in pain and struggled to draw breath. The pain was only channelled to another area of the body as she felt another blow, probably from a knee, to her ribs as he dropped his weight onto her back. Her efforts to escape ended right there. Someone leaned in close, snapping her head to one side.

She was so close to him that she could feel the warmth of his breath on her face, recognise the smell of stale cigarettes on his clothing. She felt his grip tighten on her hair, as if that was possible and all the horrific memories that she'd spent months burying came rushing back. She felt a surge of panic rising within that was bypassed quickly by desperation.

"No… please…" she all but whispered, her eyes tearing.

ERIC SMILED at Becca's joke. She always made him laugh with the most terrible of puns. She knew they were awful, not even good enough to make it into anything but the lamest of comedy shows but that was the beauty of it; Becca didn't take herself too seriously. That was one of the things he loved about her the most, her ability to remain grounded no matter what was occurring around her. That might be one reason she managed to tolerate a relationship with him. It was fine when things were quiet but CID had a habit of making him change plans at the last moment or keeping him out until all hours, sometimes with barely a moment's notice.

He was certain some women wouldn't stand for it. Not that Becca didn't get annoyed with him. Not just Becca, many people did but, arguably, that said more about him than others. He glanced at his watch. He'd anticipated making a quick call but he missed Becca, missed hearing her voice even though he'd seen her only the night before. The idea of not talking to her daily, let alone not seeing her, was something he hadn't given much consideration to recently. Now, the thought was very much at the forefront of his mind.

"Becca, I'm really sorry but I should go," he said, failing to hide his disappointment at saying so.

"Oh, okay. I understand. Duty calls and all that."

"Yeah, that's right. We're just discussing what our next move should be," he said. His thoughts drifted to Cassie. That discussion was largely over. They had no more leads to follow. The trip to the capital had been a waste of time.

"My boyfriend," Becca said, "chasing criminals across the country. That's pretty cool."

Eric felt like he should correct her because the reality was far less exciting but, in truth, he liked her admiration even if he felt undeserving of it.

"I'll be back by lunchtime tomorrow, I expect."

"Will you text me later?" Becca asked.

"Yes, of course," he said, the corners of his mouth creeping into a smile in anticipation. "I'll see you tomorrow."

He waited for the line to go dead as she disconnected the call but it remained open. He had no intention of being first to hang up.

"Are you going to hang up?" Becca asked.

"No. You hang up."

"No, you should."

They both laughed before agreeing to hang up at the same time. They did it on the count of three, only for Eric to stay on the line, his smile broadening to a grin. The line went dead. His smile faded as he fell flat. She'd hung up. That wasn't what he was expecting. Slipping the mobile into his pocket, he set off back inside, only now feeling the cold. How long had they been chatting? Cassie would be annoyed for sure.

Back inside the lounge bar, he looked to their table. Cassie was nowhere to be seen. Glancing at the clock, he hadn't been gone as long as he'd thought. She can't have gone off in a strop. More likely that she was in the toilets. He did as he'd said he would and headed to the bar for another round of drinks. The barman came over and he ordered another two pints of beer. Becca didn't drink pints. Her drink of choice was gin or wine if she fancied it. The barman placed both drinks down and Eric handed him a ten-pound note. The barman glanced at it and back to Eric, raising his eyebrows. Eric had forgotten where he was. Exhaling heavily, he took out a fiver from his wallet and passed it across. The barman smiled and rang it up. Over five quid a pint. London was taking the piss.

The barman handed him his change and Eric inclined his head towards where they'd been sitting.

"Have you seen my friend?"

"Yes. She said she'd be back in a couple of minutes."

"Great, thanks," Eric said, pocketing the coins and picking up the drinks. One had overflowed and he felt it running across his fingers as he turned to walk away.

"Mind you, that was some time ago," the barman said. Eric hesitated, glancing up at the clock on the wall again, before nodding his appreciation and walking back to the table. He sank into his seat, wiping the flats of his fingers on his seat, first checking to make sure no one was watching. He took a mouthful of beer and turned his gaze to the football match. It was one all but he was a fan of neither side and it didn't hold his interest.

Glancing to Cassie's seat, he wondered what she'd gone to do. Maybe Tom had called and she'd gone in search of better signal. He thought about texting her but remembered he had no signal in the bar and dismissed the idea. Returning to his pint, he settled in to watch what remained of the match.

CHAPTER TWENTY-FIVE

CASSIE KNIGHT FOUND herself struggling for breath, fighting to free herself from the vice-like grip of her assailant. She sensed that her attacker found her struggle amusing, allowing her just enough movement to think that she was making progress before he would assert his control once more. He was strong. Far stronger than her and he was in absolute control. She tried to arch her back, to put some distance between them, but that only served to make him laugh. It was a laughter borne out of twisted pleasure.

He manhandled her so that her face was half-turned towards his. All of her instincts were screaming at her to look away from his face but her training taught her the opposite; to search for anything distinctive. She saw his mask, thick and black with holes for eyes and mouth. His teeth were stained yellow and all she could note were his brown eyes and dark skin. He spoke, his voice was heavily accented, rasping and gravelly.

"You've been sticking your pretty little nose into things that don't concern you," he hissed.

She grimaced as he clamped her face with his hand across her mouth, gripping the flesh of her cheeks between his thumb and fingers.

"Please… I don't…" she started to say, the words almost unintelligible.

"Shut up!" he said, gripping the back of her head with the other hand and dragging her up onto her haunches. "Take this as a warning—"

Cassie brought her balled fist up into his groin with as much force and determination as she could muster. He squealed, indicating she'd struck the intended mark, and doubled over, momentarily loosening his grip. It was the fraction of a second she needed and she channelled all her energy from her feet and launched herself forward head-butting him squarely in the face. Already off balance, he keeled over to one side with Cassie applying a little assistance and shoving him away.

"Oi!" a voice shouted from below her in the stairwell. "What the hell are you doing?"

The challenge sounded as if the voice was coming closer, running up the stairs. Her attacker rolled away from her, much to her immense relief, and came to his feet. He barged through the door back into the corridor and within seconds Eric was kneeling alongside her. He appeared to hesitate, placing a hand on her shoulder.

"Are you… okay?" he asked, looking her up and down.

"I'll be fine," she croaked. "Just get after him, will you."

Eric nodded, rising and running for the door. He clattered through it, turning left and disappearing from view as he gave chase. Cassie slumped backwards against the wall and drew breath. Emotions cascaded through her, fear, anger, relief all coming unbidden in a haphazard fashion and each threatening to overwhelm her. She ran a hand through her hair, feeling a painful sensation in her scalp. He'd dealt with her roughly and aside from that discomfort she felt the side of her face throbbing from where he'd struck her. She inspected her face with the tips of her fingers. There was no blood and didn't appear to be anything other than superficial damage. Using the wall to steady herself, she levered herself upright. Holding out her hands before her, she saw they were shaking. She knew it was nothing to worry about. It was the adrenalin. It would pass soon enough.

Gathering herself, she took a step towards the corridor, planning to join Eric. The first step felt shaky but she steeled herself and pressed on. Pushing the door open she stepped into the corridor and looked to the left in the direction they'd run. There was no one in sight and she listened, trying to hear where they may have gone but it was no use. The door to the stairwell opened, startling her. Spinning on her heel, she glared at the newcomer. The man was dressed in a suit and he seemed just as surprised by her reaction as she was with his appearance.

"Excuse me," he said, moving to one side and walking past her. She remained where she was, watching him with a wary eye, lips parted and breathing heavily. He continued on, a quizzical expression on his face. He rounded the next corner and disappeared. She leaned against the wall, exhaling heavily and looking to the ceiling.

"Get a grip, woman," she said under her breath, drawing her hands down across her face.

There was movement at the end of the corridor and Eric honed into view. He was alone and trudged his way back towards her, with each step his feet appeared more leaden. Coming to stand before her, he shook his head apologetically.

"I'm sorry. He made it to the fire escape. I couldn't catch him. He was too damn fast!"

She forced a weak smile. "That's all right. Don't worry."

Her attempt to relieve him of guilt was genuine but it failed all the same. She was, however, extremely grateful for his opportune arrival.

"Are you okay?" he asked.

"I'll be fine, Eric. Thanks," she said, bobbing her head.

"You sure?"

He was genuinely worried about her, she could tell. She held up a hand between them. "Honestly, I'll be okay. It looks like this trip wasn't a wasted effort after all."

"How so?"

"That was a warning. Someone didn't like us asking questions earlier today."

"Yeah, but who?"

She shook her head. "I don't know, but right now I need a drink."

"Already lined up," Eric said. "Are you sure you're—"

"Eric! I am fine," she said, immediately regretting the harshness of her tone. She smiled, choosing a lighter response, "Come on. Let's have that drink."

Eric held the door to the stairwell open and she passed through it, avoiding looking at where she had been restrained on the floor. It was almost as if she was willing it to not have happened, as if she could distance herself from the memory. That hadn't worked for the previous year, so there was no real expectation for it to work now. They entered the hotel reception and Cassie saw him standing there. He was loitering at the entrance, barely a half-step inside the building. Eric almost walked into her as she stopped in front of him. Then he, too, saw the newcomer.

"Amir?" Cassie asked. The young man looked ready to bolt as soon as she addressed him and she moved to intercept. "Amir, are you here to see us?"

He bit his lower lip, his eyes flitting around the lobby as if fearful of being seen talking to her. He nodded.

"Yes. But now… I'm not so sure."

He was assessing her, his gaze not meeting her eyes but reading her facial expression. Only then did she realise he was looking at the side of her face which was stinging. The marks of the assault must be visible, no doubt her cheek was inflamed and her hair must have been a state.

"Come on, I'll buy you a drink," she said, gently ushering him towards the lounge. He nodded and they set off. Cassie glanced to Eric and he flicked his eyebrows up. He was obviously in agreement; this trip was definitely not a waste of time.

They returned to the table that they'd previously shared. The empty glasses had been cleared and one full pint remained in situ; the one Eric bought for Cassie. Amir wouldn't accept the offer of an alcoholic drink, choosing a glass of coke instead. Cassie wasn't sure if this was a religious abstention or just that he wanted to keep his wits about him. He looked like he could do with one. His eyes wouldn't cease scanning the room. He was clearly agitated and jumped when startled by the barman putting a tray of glasses down on the counter. She wanted to reassure him that he was quite safe and that they would protect him. Bearing in mind what just occurred upstairs, she was unable to do so. Eric returned with three soft drinks, sliding into a seat next to her.

"Why did you come here?" she asked.

Amir glanced around as if concerned they would be overheard. Cassie did likewise but no one was within earshot.

"I'm thinking I shouldn't have."

"Well, you're here now," she replied, placing a glass of coke in front of him. He nodded his appreciation. "This afternoon, you recognised the man in the sketch, didn't you?"

Amir's eyes wandered, eventually lowering to meet hers. Again, he nodded. "Yes. I know him. Everyone knows him."

"Tell us how?"

"Like I say, everyone knows Devon. Or at least, anyone who does probably wishes they didn't."

"Devon's dead, Amir," she said. He stared at her long and hard, his eyes narrowing. For some reason, she had the feeling he felt threatened by Devon Bailey and knowing that he wouldn't be around to deliver any form of retribution might loosen Amir's tongue a little. Amir glanced towards Eric, asking the question with his eyes.

Eric nodded. "It's true. Devon died a couple of days ago."

"How?" Amir asked, relief in his expression.

"We're looking into it," she said, reluctant to offer any more information. "So, tell us how you know him."

Amir gently pressed thumb and forefinger to his eyes, taking a deep breath. "Things are changing around Lewisham. It's become a place to really make money."

"You're talking about the regeneration?"

"Yes, exactly. I mean, don't get me wrong, people have always been able to make money here. My father's shop for example. We've been in that place for decades. He started it when he first arrived here. Built it up from nothing. Back in the 90s, when everyone was shutting down, he stayed, serving local residents, employing local people. Then, the high street chains started to leave, handing the streets over to the bookies, pound shops and fried chicken shops. We all cracked on as the surrounding areas changed, adapted. Locals were moved out, encouraged with the quick offer of cash or forced to… one way or another." Amir sank back in his seat. It was as if the retaining wall of his reticence had been breached and he was free to let rip. "Now there's the Gateway Project. We knew it was coming. They began it back when I was starting high school, so it's not a shock. New shops, flats, a refurbished train station. They're really smartening the place up. All good and that, but it's not just the developers or the council. Other… interested groups are seeing what they can make from it."

"Devon Bailey?"

Amir met her eye. He nodded.

"What was your involvement with him?" Eric asked.

"Not me directly but my parents," he said, lowering his voice. "Look, you said you wanted information on Devon, but just so you know, I won't be repeating any of this on the record. I'm not stupid."

"Devon *is* dead," Cassie reiterated.

"He may well be," Amir said, sitting forward, "but he's one man."

"Then what are you prepared to tell us?"

Amir exhaled heavily, closing his eyes for a second. "Devon moved with some pretty heavy hitters locally. You already know that, though. It's obvious." Cassie looked sideways, neither wishing to confirm or deny what they knew. The more he thought they knew, the more relaxed he would likely be.

"Are you talking about the gangs?" Cassie said.

Amir nodded. "Yeah. When I was younger, the talk around town was all about the Yardies. Now it's the Russians."

"Devon?" she pressed.

"He was in with one of the former," Amir said, lowering his voice to a conspiratorial level. Then he released a short laugh but one of little genuine humour. "Growing up, we all knew that the Yardies were tied into the local drug scene. Every mate of mine who was knocking out skunk or whatever had a Jamaican friend, you know. I remember how loads of people started talking like they were from Kingston when they'd never left Lewisham in their lives. It was cool to appear associated with them. Personally, I think talk of Jamaican gangs was just that, talk. It was nonsense."

"Yeah, we still see that," Cassie said.

"Let me tell you, these guys aren't cool. They're scary as hell."

"You seem knowledgeable," Eric said, drawing a dark look from Cassie. They were getting somewhere and Eric sound accusatory.

Amir stared at him, but it was without animosity. "I've lived all my life here. People talk. Drugs are one thing but they like their respect almost as much as they like their money."

"What do you mean?" Cassie asked.

"What's the fastest way to make money in London these days?"

"You tell us," Cassie said.

"Property," Amir said. "Particularly in an up and coming area. We've got the second phase of the Gateway starting, plus extensions to the Bakerloo Line coming in the next decade. Easy money if you have the sites."

"Where does Devon fit into this?"

"My father bought his shop a long time ago, when no one else was investing in this town. Now, it's looking valuable. People want him to sell. Devon... was one who repeatedly encouraged him to do so. Not that I've seen much of him recently. That job's fallen to others."

"Those guys in the shop earlier?" Cassie asked.

Amir averted his eyes from her gaze. He wouldn't say so but it was obvious.

"Can I take it that your father is less keen to sell than they would like?"

"The shop is his life," Amir said. "If he sold up, where would he go? What would he do? My parents have built a life here, it's not just about the business. If Devon's dead... then, I feel for anyone who loved him but, as far as I'm concerned, it's not a bad thing. He was a nasty piece of work. The likes of him will always get what they deserve in the end, whether in this life or the next."

"If you talk to us on the record, we might be able to help—"

Amir cut her off with a dismissive laugh and a swipe of the hand before she could make any commitment. "I doubt that. Your lot have never been able to get a handle on the gang culture. You can't even deal with a bunch of kids on scooters. Nah," he shook his head emphatically. "It's most likely too late for my old man. He'll have to sell up sooner or later. One way or another, one of these gangs will take it from him. The question is whether he walks away by choice or is unable to walk at all."

Amir stood up, finishing the drink set in front of him. He wiped his mouth with the back of his hand.

"I'm sorry. There's nothing more I can do for you."

"Then why come," Cassie said, "if you aren't prepared to take a stand?"

Amir fixed his gaze on her. Any attempt at laying a guilt trip on him wasn't going to work. "You asked. I told you. My parents bust a gut to make something of themselves, to give me and my brothers a decent start. I graduated with a law degree last summer and now I'm back here, supporting them any way I can." He pursed his lips, looking beyond across the lounge. "For as long as I can until my father jacks it in. If whatever you're investigating takes the pressure off them, off my family, for a while then I'm all for it but if you want me to stoke the fire then you can forget it," he said, turning and walking away. "Thanks for the drink," he said without looking back.

Cassie leaned forward, placing an elbow on the table, inclining her head to one side and gently scratching the back of her head as she mulled his words over. Amir left the lounge without a backward glance. She sighed deeply. Looking to Eric, she guessed his expression was one mirrored by her own.

"Where to go from here?"

Eric exhaled deeply and shook his head. "Do you want a proper drink? I need one."

She glanced towards the bar. She didn't. Amir's visit and subsequent conversation was a valuable distraction but his departure saw the return of her anxiety. She wanted to retreat to a place of security, somewhere with a physical barrier between her and the world. She shook her head.

"No. I think I'll just head to my room. Call it a day."

Eric seemed disappointed, then the realisation dawned on him and his expression changed to more thoughtful.

"Yeah. You're probably right," he said, meeting her eye before averting his to the table. "I think I'll do the same. I'll walk with you upstairs."

It was a poorly disguised attempt at chivalry; a protective act from someone with empathy. She smiled.

"It's okay, Eric. I don't need a bodyguard."

"No, no…" he shook his head. "That's not it at all. I'm tired."

His explanation lacked sincerity, widening her smile. She reached across the table and gently patted the back of his hand. "Thank you, Eric. It would be lovely of you to do it."

He smiled, an expression highlighting his youth, similar to that of a proud school boy praised for a homework project.

"Are you going to be all right?"

"Eric, if you ask me that one more time I'll be giving you a slap of your own."

His smile faded. "I'll take that as a yes."

CHAPTER TWENTY-SIX

TOM JANSSEN SAT QUIETLY, arms folded, listening to Cassie and Eric's recounting of their brief visit to the capital. It was now late afternoon and they'd returned to Norfolk following their efforts that morning to learn more about Devon Bailey and his associations. To find the dead man had gang affiliations wasn't much of a surprise. An illegal firearm along with a stash of bank notes stuffed into an air-conditioning duct tend to imply a criminal connection.

He was unnerved to hear they had been followed back to their hotel. Tamara in particular, sitting beside him in the ops room, appeared deeply alarmed when Cassie described being challenged in the stairwell. Eric, perched on the edge of a nearby desk, made to speak at one point but a glance towards him from Cassie seemed to stop him in his tracks and he thought better of it.

The information supplied by the local, Amir, pushed Devon Bailey towards association with serious organised criminal gangs. For him to have dropped off the radar for so many years, it was reasonable to assume he'd elevated himself away from the actions of mere foot soldiers and further up the hierarchy. It still didn't answer the question as to what he was doing in Sheringham though.

"Are you okay?" Tamara asked, concern edging into her tone. Again, Janssen noted Eric cast a brief glance towards Cassie but she didn't reciprocate. The right side of Cassie's face was darkening and bruising was beginning to show. She must have taken a knock at some point but other than that, she seemed all right.

Cassie looked at Tamara. "Yes, I'm okay. It's just one of those things."

"Yeah," Eric said, "I just wish I'd been able to catch him."

Tamara's attention remained focussed on Cassie and, to Janssen, it was as if something unsaid passed between the two of them. Again, he felt a flutter of irritation inside his chest. The two of them knew each other, had worked together before, and yet, officially, he was still unaware of the fact. Why Tamara would choose to keep the nature of their relationship something of a secret, if that was what she was doing, he couldn't understand. Had he been prone to bouts of paranoia, he would probably see Cassie's appointment as Tamara's eyes within his team. The thought still popped into his mind but he cast it aside almost immediately. Tamara was certainly not one to be labelled as a control freak, far from it. Not once since she took up her role had she ever overturned any of his decisions or made him feel that she had anything other than complete faith in his judgement. The arrival of a new DS with links to her past shouldn't change that; and yet he was perturbed by the omission of their history. Tamara broke the eye contact with Cassie and turned to him.

"I think the superintendent was really hoping that this would be concluded as a suicide," she said, before adding, "as soon as possible."

"Murder is never a good look," he said with a wry grin, "particularly this close to the start of the season. The local power brokers will start pushing hard to have this cleared up before it has the chance to damage business."

"They already are," Tamara said, clearly unwilling to elaborate further. Maybe she would in private when it would be just the two of them. "So, let's recap." She took a deep breath, rising from her chair and crossing to stand before the information boards on the wall. "What do we know about Devon Bailey's local connections?"

Janssen cleared his throat. "The word locally is that he was into property. We've had that confirmed by Sandra Leaford. Although the car he was driving is leased to a logistics firm that may or may not be something of a front for another enterprise as yet undetermined."

Tamara glanced sideways towards him, interlocking her hands in front of her face with her forefingers forming a point which she tapped against her lips as she thought things through. "From what Eric and Cassie learned in Lewisham, there's a strong possibility that Devon and his associates were looking to make money from property but… pressuring locals to sell up in order to profit from a regeneration scheme has no bearing on what he might be doing here in Norfolk."

Janssen had to agree. The property connection was plausible but plans in the capital appeared unrelated. Cassie knitted her eyebrows together in deep concentration.

"Geoff Scott pretty much stated Devon was knocking off Sandra Leaford."

Janssen looked in her direction. His expression must have been disapproving.

"Sorry. Having an affair." Janssen found himself smiling. She was direct. He would say that for her. "Maybe the property interest goes no further than Sandra's underwear."

"By all accounts he was also seeing Helen Kemp," Janssen said.

"Which brings us onto her husband, Shaun," Tamara said, pointing to the board depicting both Kemp brothers.

"And his brother, Jamie," Janssen said. "One who has major addiction and financial problems along with the other who, we're presuming, has a wife who may well be carrying another man's child. There's one hell of a motive right there. And I also wouldn't remove Shaun from the financial problems just yet either."

"Why would you say that?" Tamara asked.

"Instinct as much as experience. I know the family, remember? Years back, as a teenager, I helped work Frank Kemp's boat for a time. I know the business, not an expert I'll grant you, but well enough to recognise a skipper who's struggling to keep it all together. He near as dammit said that he couldn't afford a crew and that boat of his is falling apart. I'd venture it's in need of an extensive overhaul and Shaun hasn't got the funds. Not even close."

Tamara took a deep breath, weighing up the information. "So, he's in financial difficulty and his wife's bed hopping while he's out at sea. And her chosen love interest has ready cash floating around. There's a couple of motives right there. Didn't you say Shaun had accounted for himself at the time Devon fell from the cliff?"

"Yes," Janssen said. "His brother stated he was due back into port but had engine trouble of some description, putting in further along the coast to have it seen to. If that's true, we need to know where he was, where he slept and if anyone can verify his whereabouts. That goes for Jamie too."

"His motive would be purely financial, wouldn't it?" Cassie asked.

Janssen wasn't so sure, staring at the pictures of both Kemp brothers. "Not necessarily. Those two will always stand by one another. They always fought like animals with one another but believe me, when push comes to shove, they'll be standing side by side, whatever the other has gotten themselves into."

"Enough to kill?" Tamara asked.

Janssen thought on it. "I don't know about murder… but I have no doubt they'll both help the other to cover one up."

"How likely are Jamie or Shaun to know about Devon's hidden cash?"

Janssen shook his head. "Impossible to say. If they knew about it, wouldn't they have gone for it prior to killing Devon?"

Eric piped up. "And it's taking one heck of a risk to break into the apartment after the event, especially when they know we're on the case. Are they as bold as that?"

"Good question," Tamara said.

All eyes fell on Janssen. The truth was, he didn't know. How could he? He hadn't spoken to these two for years.

"I don't know," he said following a period of reflection. "But people will go to great lengths to get their hands on money. Whether they would have the foresight to ensure the footage from the CCTV was destroyed the night the apartment was broken into bothers me."

"Yes, where are we with that?" Tamara asked.

Janssen shook his head. "The concierge says the office containing the camera system is never locked. They've never felt the need. Anyone in the building could have got in and accessed the hard drive. It makes a nonsense about the security though."

"And who's to say the money you found in the apartment was all of it?" Cassie said. "I mean, we are assuming that was all of it but maybe not. Maybe what was in the ducts was what they missed?"

"Then the Kemps will be cash rich right now," Janssen said. "We should have another word. It would be nice to assess the dynamic between Shaun and his wife. It might give us an idea of where they are at."

Conversation was interrupted by Tamara's ringing phone. She returned to the desk and picked it up. Looking at the display before answering, Janssen was almost sure he saw the corners of her mouth forming into a smile as she turned and began walking away.

"Excuse me, I have to take this," she said over her shoulder before answering the call. She lowered her voice into a hushed tone as she stepped out of the ops room and into Janssen's office. Closing the door behind her with her free hand, she was indeed smiling as she turned her back to the room and spoke to the caller.

"I think the next steps for us should be to revisit Helen and Shaun Kemp but also to try to establish a timeline for Shaun and Jamie's movements. If he put in along the coast due to mechanical problems, then he did so to have someone take a look at it. I want to know who that is. Start calling round and speaking to anyone Shaun may have asked to inspect the boat. There won't be too many that would be willing to handle that boat on short notice. Likewise with Jamie. Let's light a fire under them and see what happens. In my opinion we can't trust either of the Kemps and unless they have a rock-solid alibi for where they were when Devon took a fall, they aren't coming off the list."

"What should we do about the property angle and Sandra Leaford?" Cassie asked.

"Sit on it for the moment. Leaford isn't going anywhere. Leaving her to sweat on it for a while might prove advantageous," Janssen said.

Seeing Tamara finishing up her call, he indicated for the two of them to crack on and stood up. Eric hesitated, as if he still had something to add. Janssen waited but Eric first glanced to Cassie who met his eye. The DC looked back to Janssen and shook his head, turning and sliding off the desk to fall into step with Cassie. Janssen crossed the ops room to his office, seeing Eric and Cassie have an exchange in something of a huddle before he met Tamara at the threshold of the office. Cassie seemed to dismiss something Eric said, much to his displeasure. He turned his attention to Tamara. She smiled as he entered, closing the door. There was something about her; be it a relaxed facial expression or her demeanour, he couldn't say.

"Everything all right?" he asked.

"Yes, of course," she said, smiling broadly. "It was a personal thing. All good."

Her smile slipped away behind an imposed mask. He was intrigued but didn't press her on it.

"I've tasked them with establishing the strength of Jamie and Shaun's whereabouts when Devon was killed," he said, flicking his head towards Cassie and Eric over his shoulder.

"Good idea," Tamara said, the smile returning. "What do you plan to do?"

"I was going to speak with Helen Kemp, and Shaun if he's there. Now he's back on dry land, it will be interesting to gauge the state of their relationship. If she was having an affair with Devon, there might be a fracture there that we can widen."

"Great idea."

"Do you want to tag along?"

She glanced at her watch, frowning as she carried out a mental calculation before shaking her head. "Do you think you could handle it alone? I've just... got a thing."

He was surprised. It was unusual for her to not want to be at the vanguard of a case once she was directly involved.

"No, not at all," he said. Looking out of the office, his gaze fell onto Cassie. She was multi-tasking, typing information into her computer with a land line telephone clamped between her ear and shoulder. "You know Cassie?"

"Yes. What about her?"

He hesitated. Should he ask the question or not?

"You never told me you'd worked with her before. Why not?" he said, fixing his eyes on hers and being careful not to make the question sound accusatory. If he was expecting a denial or a defensive rebuttal, he didn't get one.

"What of it?"

He was taken aback but didn't show it. "I'm just curious as to why you didn't mention it, if only to give me an insight into my new DS."

"Is it not better to form your own opinion rather than have me shape it for you?"

She had a fair point.

"I'm just surprised, that's all."

Tamara's body language had shifted now. She was visibly tense, in stark contrast to a few moments ago.

"Anything else?" she asked. He shook his head. "Good. Then I'll see you in the morning." She walked to the door, turning back to him with one hand on the frame. "There's no ulterior motive, Tom. I don't work that way."

He smiled. "I know."

"Pick me up first thing?"

He nodded. "Of course. Do you need a lift back to your hotel now?"

She shook her head, smiling and tapping the door frame with the flat of her hand before making to leave. "No thanks. Already sorted."

CHAPTER TWENTY-SEVEN

TOM JANSSEN'S mobile rang as got out of the car. It was Eric and he answered as he walked, locking the car with his key fob as he crossed the road. It was a bright end to the day. The wind had dropped, leaving a stillness in the air that was pleasant. The waves crashing onto the pebble shore at the foot of the nearby cliffs could be heard but, other than that, all was calm.

"What can you tell me, Eric?"

"Jamie Kemp doesn't appear to have returned home. His wife is there, I saw her come home from work but I'm pretty sure she's alone."

"Looks like Kerry-Ann was telling the truth," he said.

"What's that?"

"Never mind," he said, glancing at a car that passed by him on the street. It wouldn't be long now before commuters started coming home. Cliff Road would fill up soon enough. Coming to stand before the Kemps', he turned his attention back to Eric. "Stay where you are for a bit, would you. You've got eyes on the house?"

"Yes. I'm parked a little way up the street and from here I can see if anyone comes or goes."

"There's a rear door as well—"

"I know," Eric cut in. "It opens into an alleyway at the back but there's only one way in and out of there and I can see it from here."

Janssen smiled. Eric was developing nicely as a detective. Not too long ago he might have needed some input to avoid possible errors. He wasn't there yet, but there was certainly progress.

"I'm at Shaun's place now. I imagine my visit might shake things up a bit, so stay alert and keep your eyes open. You never know what the reactions could be."

"Jamie and his missus are separated though, right? I mean, you know her don't you?"

"Yeah, but it was a long time ago," Janssen said. "People change, as do our recollections of them. I'm no more infallible than anyone else. I'll give you a shout when I leave."

"Okay, I'll hang on here until you tell me otherwise."

Janssen hung up, slipping his mobile into his coat pocket as he knocked on the door. Shaun's car wasn't parked out front. He'd checked the DVLA database to see what was registered to him and it had come back with an old Corsa. It can't be valued for much more than scrap. It wasn't necessarily a critical factor but it was certainly another indication that Shaun was struggling financially.

He saw a flicker of movement through the obscured glass but it disappeared again almost as soon as he saw it. Raising his fist, he thumped on the door three more times and waited. Whoever was inside knew he was there but they seemed disinclined to come to the door. He thought about heading around to the rear but knew they could just as easily ignore him there as well. He knocked again, only this time more aggressively, leaning to his left and peering into the front room in an effort to see through the net curtains. He couldn't, but that wasn't the point. He had to make them realise he wasn't going anywhere.

A few moments later, a figure appeared in the hallway and unlocked the front door. It was Helen, Shaun's wife. He could tell from the mass of curly hair hanging to her shoulders. She cracked the door open, half her face peering out at him from around the door. He narrowed his eyes, trying to read her expression. She was sullen, withdrawn.

"Helen," he said by way of a greeting. "Is Shaun here?"

She shook her head. "No. Sorry."

Her speech was stilted, her expression fixed. Something wasn't right. He angled his head further to see around the door but she pushed it closed a little more so that he was unable to. He gently placed the flat of his hand on the door to stop her from closing it fully, just in case that was her aim.

"May I come in and speak with you?"

Up until now, she'd made no real effort to meet his eye, choosing to look at his feet rather than him. Now she did so and he saw much in her eye. She closed her eyes, drawing breath and nodded, releasing her grip on the door and allowing it to open inward. Janssen felt a flicker of anger surge in his chest as she revealed herself. The right side of Helen's face was heavily discoloured. The bruising around her cheek and jawline was coming out in shades of deep blue and yellow. Her right eye was also heavily bruised and almost completely shut with a cut in the path of her eyebrow. Now he understood both her reluctance to come to the door and the nature of her speech. She stepped back from the door allowing him to enter, turning and trudging back towards the kitchen. He followed, closing the front door behind him.

"Has anyone seen to that?" he asked, as she sat down at the small table in the corner of the kitchen next to the back door.

She shot him a look of disdain, her one good eye narrowing. "What difference would it make?" She reached for a packet of cigarettes that lay on the table, taking one out and reaching for a lighter. Helen Kemp was dressed in jogging bottoms and a vest top. The latter was tight across her midriff and even though she was sitting down, he could easily tell that Cassie was right. Helen Kemp was starting to show.

"Do you think you should?" he asked, gesturing to the cigarette as she struck the flint of the lighter, igniting the flame. She held off lighting the cigarette, shutting off the gas supply and removing the cigarette from her mouth. Her lips remained parted in something of a dismissive pout. "I mean, what with your condition."

"It's not against the law," she said but he could tell from her tone that she knew she shouldn't.

"No, of course not but… "

He left the words hanging and she tossed the lighter back to the table, held the cigarette aloft in front of her for a moment before putting it back in the box.

"Happy?"

He chose to ignore the comment, glancing at the packet and wondering how long the cigarette would remain in there once he was out of the door.

"When will Shaun be back?"

"No bloody idea," she said, sinking back into her seat and gingerly raising both legs to the chair opposite. "And I couldn't care less either."

"He do that to you?"

She scoffed, shaking her head. "No, I fell down the stairs."

He was irritated by her attitude. He understood the power and control domestic abusers had over their partners but, at the same time, her belligerence annoyed him.

"I think you and I both know that isn't true," he said, placing his hands behind him and leaning against the counter. He took great care not to come across as intimidating. Sometimes, with his size and build, it was almost unavoidable but he knew he would be unlikely to be able to help Helen if she couldn't be at ease in his presence. He wished now that he'd brought either Cassie or Tamara with him. Either of them would be better able to approach this. "We can help, if you'd let us."

She laughed. It was a sound without genuine humour and more than a little mocking.

"Really? You could help me? What are you going to do, take the Kemps off the streets?"

"That's quite possible, yes."

"For how long?" she said. He got the impression she had thought about this before. "A month, three maybe? And what do you think would happen once he's out… or his psychotic brother? What then?"

"There's help available."

"Don't make me laugh," she said, dismissing him with a flick of the hand. "Besides, I deserved it."

"No one ever deserves that," he said, experiencing a sinking feeling. "Think of your baby—"

"What do you want, Tommy?" she said, averting her eyes from his gaze. Her expression went hard and her demeanour cold as she stared straight ahead.

"I would like to know about your relationship with Devon."

Her head snapped round and she looked at him. She was steeling herself, he could tell, but her one good eye glazed over. She sniffed loudly, bringing the back of her hand to her face and touching it to her eye.

"What about it?"

"You said you met him at the food bank. Is that right?"

She shook her head. "No. I met him one night in town when we were out for a drink. He was with Jamie."

"They were friends?"

Again, she shook her head. "I'm not sure Jamie has friends, so to speak." She ran a hand through her hair, moving it away from her face and tucking it behind her ear. "He looked like he knew him quite well."

"And Shaun, did he know him too?"

She fixed her gaze on him, shaking her head almost imperceptibly. "Not as far as I know."

"And he came to help at the food bank? From what I've learned about him, it doesn't sound like something Devon would have been involved with."

"You think?"

He wasn't sure if she was intending to be sarcastic or not.

"Did you ever go to his place, Devon's apartment?"

She looked away from him, nodding slightly. "On occasion."

"Nice place," he said, looking around the kitchen. "Bit of a change to this."

She chuckled, shaking her head. "Yes it was."

"That kind of lifestyle, flash digs, nice car... plenty of ready cash to throw around... can certainly turn a person's head. Wouldn't you say?"

"Is that your polite way of asking if Devon and I were seeing each other?" she said with a condescending sneer.

"Were you?"

She fixed him with a stare, running her tongue across the edge of her lower lip.

"Yes. I was banging him every chance I got."

Janssen exhaled slowly, breaking the eye contact. There was a razor-sharp edge to Helen Kemp and he was sure it was a barrier she erected in order to protect herself. She reached for the cigarettes. This time she sparked up without hesitation, taking a steep draw and exhaling the smoke to the ceiling.

"As you see, Inspector. It's my mouth that gets me into trouble."

He raised his eyebrows. "Did Shaun know?"

"Not at first. After all, it's pretty easy to get away with when your husband's out at sea most of the time."

"When did he find out?"

She took another drag, this time exhaling the smoke via her nostrils. She sniffed again, wiping her nose on her forearm before shrugging.

"Don't know for sure," she said, absently toying with the lighter in her free hand. "Let me know how he felt about it last night though."

"I guess he wasn't pleased with Devon either."

"No, doubt he was," she said. "Luckily for him, Devon isn't around."

"Meaning?"

"Shaun wouldn't go up against someone like Devon. Not even with his weasel of a brother backing him up."

She made a strong point. It also stood to reason that Devon would be on his guard when around the husband of a woman he was having an affair with, making it all the more surprising that he went to his last rendezvous without the gun he kept at his apartment. If that meeting was to be with either of the Kemps, it was a fatal misjudgement. Somehow, though, Janssen figured Devon must have felt safe with whoever killed him. The body had no signs of defensive wounds and Devon would have put up a fight if he'd seen the attack coming, which was yet another indication that he didn't feel threatened.

Another thought occurred to him as she spoke. By all accounts, Devon was also seeing Sandra Leaford. Were the women aware of one another? If either woman was under the impression of exclusivity, then there were two more suspects with credible motives for them to consider. He found himself assessing Helen's capability as she sat across the kitchen from him. She was slightly built, but athletic, and it was conceivable that she could manhandle Devon's body over the edge of the cliff top. The gentle slope towards the edge would make things easier to get the body rolling. However, Devon Bailey was a big man and it would be a stretch to have got him in and out of the car by herself but certainly possible. Likewise for Sandra Leaford.

"What are you thinking?" she asked, breaking his train of thought. He'd zoned out for a moment but had been looking in her direction. "Are you wondering if the baby is Devon's?"

"I'd be lying if I said it hadn't crossed my mind."

She smiled weakly. "Yeah, mine too."

"Do you know where I might find Shaun?"

She looked up at him. "On his boat, I expect. Either there or with his brother somewhere."

"Do you know where Jamie's staying at the moment?"

"With anyone who'll have him," she said, making no attempt to disguise the lack of regard she held him in.

"Right. Thank you for your time," Janssen said. He made to leave, Helen remaining where she was. He turned back to her. "I meant what I said. I can help you, if you'll let me."

She stared at him. He felt certain she was calculating the credibility of the offer. It was genuine. He would do everything within his power to get her out of this situation regardless of whether it helped his investigation. Whether he passed the assessment or not, he couldn't tell.

"I'll bear that in mind, Inspector Janssen."

He walked to the front door and let himself out. Despite the sun falling away behind the buildings of the town, the evening was still bright, if a little cold. He walked back to his car, taking out his mobile phone, he called Eric.

"Hi Eric. I'm leaving the Kemps now. There's no sign of Shaun here, he may be with his brother or on his boat. Hang on there for another half hour. Let me know if anyone shows but after that, head home and I'll see you in the morning."

"Will do," Eric said, hanging up.

Janssen reached his car. Leaning on the roof, he touched the mobile to his lips and looked back towards the house. Domestic violence was something he wouldn't put past either brother, and the threat of it would be magnified by addiction or financial stress. A damaged mind capable of doing that to his pregnant wife, regardless of the justification he might seek to use, would make him more than capable of murder. His desire to know where both Shaun and Jamie were on the night Devon died was heightened now. If Shaun couldn't prove he was out of town, then he'd be moving up the list of suspects. He thought about calling Tamara and sharing his thoughts but changed his mind, putting his mobile away and getting into the car. He had the feeling she wouldn't appreciate the call tonight.

CHAPTER TWENTY-EIGHT

TAMARA STOOD BACK, observing herself in the mirror of the bathroom. The outfit wasn't the best fit but so late in the day, half an hour before most of the shops closed their doors for the day, there was little other option. She drew her shoulder-length hair up, wondering whether she should tie it up or leave it loose. Letting go, it fell to more or less how she usually wore it. That is to say, without much intervention. The other night, having returned early from the conference in London, she cut quite a different figure to usual. Was that what had appealed?

She took a deep breath, reaching for her make-up bag and rummaging through it to see what lipstick options she had. Yet again, she didn't usually bother. The thought occurred to her that she was making this effort, presenting herself as someone she wasn't. That would only end one way.

Examining her reflection, she considered cancelling but it was a fleeting idea that she dismissed. Ever since she'd called it a day with Richard, her fiancé, she'd doubted herself, doubted her decision making. The wedding had been on the horizon, a long way off, but all of a sudden it had been drawn into sharp focus barely a few months away. The magnitude of her life choices was overwhelming. Surely it was normal to be hesitant? But that wasn't the issue. Nerves were one thing but when she found herself questioning whether her life would just be far easier if Richard was dead, she realised she was making a mistake.

That's not to say she wanted him dead, merely that it would be easier to extricate herself from their life together if he was. She wasn't fair to him. They may have had different views on where their relationship was heading, and how they should go about getting there, but he loved her. Of that, she was certain which only made her judge herself harder. Even when she called an end to the relationship, he had tried, been patient and caring.

That was all a few months ago and she hadn't spoken to him recently. Aside from a brief flirtation with Tom Janssen, which, although tantalisingly appealing, would have been potentially catastrophic professionally, she'd kept clear of men. Until now. Not that she was looking. Far from it. Her relationship status had been nothing other than anxiety-inducing for as long as she could remember. The absence of a wedding ring on her finger was something her mother would mention with alarming frequency, particularly in light of her split from Richard. These were conversations that only amplified the negative view of herself that she held so strongly.

She chose a dark red colour. It wasn't too glam but sophisticated with a hint of danger. The thought of danger excited her. She wasn't averse to taking risks. In her personal life she often gave in to impulse, a trait she couldn't replicate in her work. There was no room for that. Besides, she told herself, she was due some fun. It had been a rough year.

Turning her thoughts to Max as she applied her make-up, he was just what she needed. He was charming, intelligent and could hold a conversation. The fact that he was handsome was an added bonus. After she woke the previous morning to find he'd left without a word, she figured that was it, even harshly judging herself for being so carefree. Tom's appearance at the hotel to pick her up added to the awkwardness, the feeling was similar to when she'd crept back into her bedroom via the window long after curfew, to avoid being caught by her parents only for them to knock on the door moments later.

Max hadn't left town. Maybe his business meeting was rescheduled and he'd stayed on. She doubted he'd done so for her but the idea that he may have excited her.

Her mobile beeped and she glanced down at the screen. Max was in the lounge waiting for her. Pulling herself upright, she turned sideways to the mirror and eyed the contours of her dress. She needed to get out more. The winter had been wet and cold. At least that's what she told herself was the reason for adding some weight. She'd forgone her usual hiking routines, having lost interest a few months back, these days more inclined towards a bottle of wine and a film.

Smiling at her reflection, she left her hair down and told herself she wouldn't get much better than this. By all accounts, she still looked great and Max hadn't objected the other night. Vowing not to look beyond this evening, she picked up her mobile and stepped out of the bathroom, switching off the light as she went. As an afterthought, she put the mobile on the desk in her room. Tonight, she wasn't on call, and headed for the door.

She went down in the lift, checking herself in the mirrored wall as she descended. Reception was empty aside from the lady on the front desk. She was on the telephone and paid her no attention as she passed by and into the lounge. Max was sitting at the bar nursing a drink. As soon as he saw her, his face lit up and he slid off the stool and crossed to meet her. He was as she remembered, only perhaps better looking. He moved with the same grace and confidence, coming to stand before her and offering her a seat at the bar.

"Would you like a drink... or shall we head straight through for dinner?"

She glanced at the bar and then over her shoulder towards the dining room. "I'm starving. Do you mind if we eat?"

"Not at all," Max said, gesturing towards the dining room

with an open hand. He held out his forearm in an emphasised formal manner, accompanying the action with a warm smile. She returned it, looping her own through his and they moved off in tandem. All of her neuroses were forgotten in that moment.

———

SHE WASN'T sure what had woken her. Shafts of silver light streamed in from outside. Tonight was almost a full moon and the skies were evidently clear. The window to her room was cracked open as normal, no matter what the weather, she preferred fresh air over stuffiness, and the curtain swayed backwards and forwards on the breeze coming in off the sea.

Reaching out beside her, she found the bed empty although the sheet was still warm to the touch. Hoping Max hadn't slipped out as he had done previously, Tamara propped herself up on one elbow. Her eyes felt dry and gritty and despite the wealth of natural light it took her a moment for them to adjust. A figure stood at the end of the bed with his back to her.

"Max? What are you doing?"

The sound of her voice startled him, and he looked over his shoulder. He was naked, the sheen of moonlight reflecting from his muscular figure.

"I couldn't sleep," he said softly. He appeared to stretch his arms out in front of him before turning to face her, resting his hands on the foot of the bed. "Insomnia is a real pain."

She gently patted the bed next to her with the palm of her hand, smiling. "Come back to bed."

He returned her smile and walked around to the empty side of the bed and slid in between the sheets. She shuffled over and lay her head on his shoulder, placing her right hand on his chest. She absently stroked his skin while he stared up at the ceiling.

"What's on your mind?" she asked.

He exhaled deeply, before drawing breath and turning his head to meet her eye. "I didn't plan this, you know?"

"Nor did I," she said. "For a moment, I thought you'd taken off again."

He smiled. "Not this time. I thought it would be good if I stuck around for a while."

Something in his tone worried her slightly. It didn't feel like he was about to give her the brush off, quite the opposite in fact but even so, he was troubled. He edged himself closer to her and kissed her gently on the forehead. Tamara angled her head and he leaned in and they kissed passionately, Max rotating his body and looping an arm around her, drawing her to him in a strong embrace. She felt the recurrence of excitement and at the same time his arousal became apparent. She was pleased he had chosen to stay the night. They made love once more only this time, in stark contrast to earlier, it was gentle but no less passionate. Soon after, Max fell asleep with her arm draped across his chest and this time it was Tamara who couldn't sleep.

She lay alongside him, listening to his breathing and watching the rise and fall of his chest. Listening to the rhythmic sound of the waves breaking on the shore, she pictured them in her mind's eye. Reaching across to the bedside table, careful not to disturb Max, she picked up her phone. The glare of the screen hurt her eyes as she unlocked it she saw the text message from Tom. She opened it. It was timed at nine-thirty the previous evening.

CASSIE FOUND SHAUN'S MECHANIC... *there's some debate surrounding the time he was supposed to be working on the boat. I'll pick you up early. T.*

SHE HELD the phone out in front of her face and reread the message. For some reason she felt guilty, which was of course utter nonsense. She had nothing to feel guilty about, and yet, she couldn't dismiss the sensation. Max's breathing became irregular and he coughed twice before rolling onto his side. Tamara removed her arm, giving him the freedom to settle.

She gently loosened the sheets around her and slipped out of bed. Moving around the room, she headed for the bathroom, pausing as she passed the foot of the bed. Her shoulder bag was on the chair, the case files she had brought home visible inside. One of them appeared to have been stuffed in at an odd angle. Had she put them in there like that? She couldn't remember. She'd left the office in a hurry, needing to find a local clothing shop before they closed. Glancing at Max's sleeping form, she found herself doubting him. That swiftly progressed to questioning of herself, her motives, and why she was already looking for ways to sabotage something good that had only just come into her life.

Shaking her head, she resumed her course to the bathroom. The cool breeze on her skin made her shiver and her thoughts turned to Tom Janssen. Entering the bathroom, she flicked on the light above the mirror and carefully closed the door so as not to wake Max. Standing in the same place she had been only a few hours earlier, she found herself looking at her reflection once again, only this time, her thoughts were clouded by images of Tom. She tried to force to mind a picture of Max but it was rapidly beaten away by the imposing form of Tom Janssen. Tamara sighed, disappointed in herself and, somewhat strangely, disappointed in Tom.

"Damn you, Tom," she whispered quietly, staring hard at herself.

CHAPTER TWENTY-NINE

TAMARA GREAVE WAS WAITING in the hotel reception when Tom Janssen entered the lobby. He almost walked past her, as she was reading one of the complimentary newspapers the hotel left out for both guests and visitors. Max had risen and left her before six in the morning. He had an early meeting with clients and needed to set off. It was a shame. She would have enjoyed having breakfast with him. There was something about the anonymity that staying in a hotel afforded you that allowed her to set aside any inhibitions she might have had.

Where this relationship, if that was what it could even be described as, might lead she had no idea and wasn't giving it much thought. Max was an interesting man who'd walked into her life at an opportune moment, the first since a certain detective who was standing before her now at any rate. And he was unavailable.

"Sorry. I nearly missed you," Janssen said. "Are you good to go?"

"Yes. Absolutely."

She folded the paper and put it down on the coffee table in front of the sofa she was sitting on. Picking up her bag, she looped the handles over her shoulder and the two of them went outside. The sky was clear and the air had a crispness to it that signalled the approach of spring wasn't far away. In the meantime, when standing out of the sun, it was still chilly.

"You implied in your text that Shaun's alibi might not stack up," she said, walking to his car parked in front of the hotel.

Janssen nodded. "Possibly. Eric did some digging for me last night, made contact with some of his local connections. Shaun uses a boatyard along the coast for all of his maintenance, be it mechanical or when he needs to dry dock. Seemingly, he doesn't have many alternative options because he's got such a bad reputation."

She stopped walking, thinking it through. "Because he doesn't pay?"

"Yes," Janssen said with a knowing flick of the eyebrows. "No one else will touch him because they're all expecting him to go under at any point. The word is that he's hanging on by his fingertips at the moment. Judging by the state of his boat when I visited him on it the other day, I'm not surprised to hear it."

Tamara resumed her walk to the car and Janssen unlocked it. Climbing in, she pulled on her seatbelt and as she was clicking it into place, she looked across and met his eye. "What is it with you and the Kemps? I don't think you hold a candle for either brother but Shaun in particular seems to rub you up the wrong way. Reading about the two of them, I would have figured it was Jamie who you'd take issue with the most."

Janssen started the car, staring straight ahead but not looking ready to move off. He took a deep breath and then glanced across to her.

"It goes back a bit," he said.

"We have time."

Janssen chewed on his lower lip for a moment. She wondered whether he was formulating the words to the story or thinking of a way that he could brush her off.

"My father died when I was a teenager," he said, his gaze

fixed on some point in the distance. "It was a heart attack, very sudden. None of us saw it coming."

"I'm sorry," she said, regretting asking the question as she saw the change in his expression. Usually, Tom Janssen was very difficult to read. He was sensitive, emotional, but guarded when it came to expressing those feelings. It was unlike him to appear so vulnerable.

"That's okay," he said, glancing at her and smiling. "It was a long time ago. I was only fifteen, three weeks shy of my sixteenth birthday."

"That's... harsh," she said. The words sounded hollow and inadequate and she should have managed better.

"It was harsher on my father, I assure you," he said with a wry grin. "Anyway, my father was a good friend of Frank Kemp, Shaun and Jamie's father. They used to go fishing together. Not often but when they found the time. He looked out for me after my father died. My mother too. It counted for a lot. My dad was the rock that everything in our house was tied to, you know?"

She nodded. In her family, the world revolved around her mother but the sentiment was the same.

"So you must have spent a great deal of time with the Kemps then?"

"Yes," he said, inclining his head to one side. "Unfortunately."

"You didn't share the same friendship with the sons as your respective fathers did with one another?"

Janssen laughed. It was tinged with a bitter edge.

"We did... for a while at least. You see, Shaun and Jamie were close in both age and bond. They didn't leave a lot of room for anyone else and always preferred each other's company to that of a wider peer group. At school, most of us thought they were pretty weird but not so aloof that we didn't mix. After Dad died, Frank would haul me out of the house to come and join him and the boys on his boat. I think it was to give my mother a break just as much as it was to draw me out of myself. You'll probably be surprised to hear I was a little insular back then."

"You? No, don't believe it," she said, smiling. He returned it.

"At first, it was odd jobs, cleaning up or basic maintenance. I was pretty good with my hands and enjoyed time out on the water."

"Hence why you live on a boat?"

His smile broadened, meeting her eye. "I've always wanted to live on a boat but yes, being out on the water is one of the few things in life I really enjoy. It's the calming nature of being out there, being one with the sea. You know what I mean?"

"Not so much," she said. "Wide expanses of water scare the hell out of me. Pretty much my worst nightmare."

She considered asking him more about what the *few* things were but figured now wasn't the time. This was the most information she could remember Tom ever offering without it being pulled from him kicking and screaming.

"I think Frank saw something in me after a while, I'm not sure what... maybe a kindred spirit, someone he could save. So, he would pay me in the school holidays to work with him. I'd be out on trips bringing in the catch. Looking back, I'm not sure how legal it all was but I enjoyed it. It gave me purpose. I don't think his boys took kindly to my presence after a while."

"Do you think they were jealous?"

Janssen thought about it. "Jamie? Not really. I don't think he was ever bothered about much aside from himself. The notion of delayed gratification is not something that would ever enter his mindset. Besides, he couldn't stand being on the boat. It played havoc with his life. Shaun, on the other hand, didn't like it one bit. I think he saw me as driving a wedge between him and his father."

"Justified?"

He thought about it, eventually bobbing his head slightly. "Maybe he had a point." Janssen looked over and she read the pain that he still carried in his expression. "It's nothing I've thought about in many years. I missed my father very much."

She pursed her lips, her instinct telling her to reach out to him, tell the teenage boy inside that it was okay. It would all be okay. She didn't. She just smiled weakly, a response that felt sorely inadequate. Janssen didn't say any more, reaching forward and pressing the engine start button. The car fired into life and he put it into gear.

"So where are we going?" she asked.

"To nail down Shaun's alibi once and for all."

JANSSEN PULLED the car to a stop just inside the gates. He had been inside a number of those with more modern facilities. This yard was no such operation. He was well aware that it had been in business for well over a century, its name well known locally, and one of the last independent facilities offering services to local operators.

The decline in the fishing industry along with the increase of larger commercial fleets moving in their operations meant smaller businesses struggled to compete. Larger fleets meant larger ships and these required expanded workshops, hoists and quays to berth at that required significant investment; investment that traditional operators just couldn't hope to finance. Every few years a newspaper article or local appeal for investment would be heard and Janssen was surprised that the place was still going. The very fact that they were one of the few apparently willing to extend Shaun Kemp a credit line was possibly indicative of their need for business.

Glancing around the cramped yard, he saw a number of boats up and out of the water but the visible moorings were less than half full. There was very little by way of quay heading and the wooden walkways of the bank looked to be in a poor state of repair. He got out, Tamara doing likewise, and they turned their attention to the workshop. It was wooden and rickety. Janssen doubted much had changed there in decades. No one was around and he pointed towards the interior, the sound of a radio playing carried to them. Tamara nodded and they crossed the short distance. The ground was uneven. The weather was good but Janssen could see how the surface would be churned up once a period of wet weather set in.

Only one figure was inside, a man in his late thirties. He was dressed in blue coveralls and wore a respirator mask as he wielded a mechanical sander along the hull of a wooden skiff. It looked like a full restoration project was underway. Momentarily he saw them, meeting Janssen's eye, holding it for a few seconds, before switching off the machine. The shrill sound dissipated as the motor wound down. He gently placed the tool on a nearby workbench, slowly removing his mask. The grime and sawdust were ingrained on his face around the edge of where the mask was set across mouth and nose. He rubbed at the latter with the back of his hand, all the while watching Janssen with a wary eye.

"Been a long time, Tom," he said, nodding a curt welcome.

"Yes, it has, Tony," Janssen replied, casting a quick glance around the workshop before his gaze returned to his childhood acquaintance. "How have you been?"

Tony shrugged, his expression remaining fixed, intense. "Been better, been worse. You know how it is."

"How's business?"

"Shite."

"Sorry to hear that."

"Yeah, well," Tony said, taking a deep breath and perching himself against the bench behind him. "Get a trade, they said. Back in the day, you remember?" Janssen nodded. Tony's face split a rueful, sideways grin. "You'll never be out of work if you have a skill."

"You're working," Janssen said.

"Yeah. For now. I should have followed your lead, Tom. Even when there's a downturn there are still scumbags to chase."

"More so in a downturn," he concluded.

"Somehow, although admittedly it is nice to see you, I doubt this is a social call, Tom."

"It's not, no. One of my officers spoke to you about some work you did on Shaun's boat."

Tony folded his arms across his chest in a casual manner but his body language was tense.

"What of it?"

"What did you do for him?"

Tony fixed his gaze on Janssen, his eyes narrowing. He then flicked a glance at Tamara before pulling himself upright.

"He had a problem with the hydraulics, couldn't deploy his nets properly let alone draw them in."

"I see," Janssen said, glancing sideways to Tamara. "And you're sure about when he docked... and you spoke to Shaun?"

"Of course," Tony laughed, dismissing Janssen's question. "Known him for years haven't I. Hardly likely to forget, am I."

"Well, you forgot that you got yourself nicked for that fight inside the Baker's Arms, over Cromer way, on the same night, so you'll have to forgive me for asking the question."

Tony's face dropped, his lips parting slightly as his mind appeared to go into overdrive. He averted his eyes from Janssen's gaze, and absently chewed on his lower lip.

"Nah..."he said eventually, "you must have the dates wrong."

"That's the thing about us, though, Tony. We do this for a living. Perhaps you should have stuck to fixing boats and left Shaun to fend for himself," Janssen said. "You know we're investigating a potential murder here, right?"

That information appeared to be news to the mechanic and his arms dropped into his lap as he sat bolt upright. "Now hold on a minute," he said, his tone elevating in pitch. "No one said anything about murder. I don't know anything about a murder."

"What do you know about fixing Shaun's hydraulics?" Janssen countered.

Tony stared at him hard. Janssen figured he was calculating what he should say, how he could extricate himself from the hole he'd dug for both himself and for Shaun.

"Nothing. I never looked at it."

"Now we're getting somewhere," Janssen said. "And Shaun?"

Tony held Janssen's eye for a moment longer before, then he looked at his feet, shaking his head. He was clearly disappointed to be landing his friend in trouble.

"No. I never saw him."

Tamara took a deep breath, shooting Janssen a brief look before asking her first, and very pertinent, question. "Where *was* Shaun that night?"

Tony exhaled, staring straight at her and splaying his hands wide, replying in a dejected tone. "How the hell would I know?"

CHAPTER THIRTY

BACK IN THE CAR, Janssen drummed his fingers on the steering wheel while playing the conversation over in his mind. The temptation to arrest Tony and detain him at the station for as long as humanly possible was very strong. It wouldn't have been an action motivated by spite, although assisting in the fabrication of an alibi for a murder suspect would be reason enough, but more from a desire not to tip their hand in Shaun's direction. He was still unaware that his makeshift alibi was no longer in play. How long that might last was anyone's guess, however, once they drove away from the boatyard.

How strong was the connection between Tony and Shaun? Somehow, he figured it wouldn't be as unbreakable as Shaun might like. They were old school friends and such ties should never be underestimated but the Kemp brothers were always very focussed on themselves. In all likelihood, Tony was another useful tool to be manipulated.

If Tony was telling the truth, hard to discern when considering a recent track record of lying to the police, then Shaun hadn't confided in him why he needed an alibi. If he was in Tony's place, he would feel mightily aggrieved at being drawn into such a serious situation. With that in mind, there was a possibility that Tony would retreat and hunker down, wait for the storm to pass, rather than have it out with his friend. In which case, Shaun would no doubt carry on oblivious to the change in his position. That might give them the edge they needed.

However, the possibility that the moment their car pulled out of the boatyard would trigger Tony to reach for his mobile was just as likely. They still had no direct evidence with which to tie Shaun to Devon's murder, even if he seemed to inadvertently be doing his level best to draw the investigation in his direction.

"Shall we go and have another word with Shaun," he said, looking over as Tamara fastened her seatbelt, "or leave him be and keep an eye on him?"

Tamara was about to reply when her mobile rang. She glanced at the screen.

"It's Cassie," she said, answering the call.

"I've been doing some digging around Devon Bailey and his business interests, trying to work out what he's been up to in Norfolk."

"Go on."

Janssen started the car, putting it in gear and making ready to set. Tamara put the call on loudspeaker so they could both hear it and Tom waited.

"Right. We know Devon's car was registered to a logistics firm that turned out to be something of a bust when Eric and I went to London. I looked into their accounts. All have been filed on time with HMRC and the company has a solid financial position despite having an address that is nothing but a brownfield building site. I couldn't find any evidence of any actual contracts that they carry out, which suggests only one thing when taking into account the nature of the man himself."

"Shell company," Tamara said.

"That's what I reckon," Cassie said. "So, where there's one shell company, you usually find several more with contracts and money passing between them to help make them appear more legitimate. So, I thought I'd delve a little deeper. There are two more companies registered to that particular site and a third that has Devon Bailey named as a director."

"What do these companies do?" Tamara asked.

"One tips its hat towards the logistics firm attached to Devon and is imaginatively titled AMK Holdings, whereas the other two are equally vague as to what services they offer. But this is where it gets interesting. One of the firms has a history of flipping property."

"Flipping?" Janssen asked.

"Yes, that's where you buy a property and then sell it on in quick time for a higher price."

"Didn't they bring in regulations to counter that after the last financial crash?" he said.

"Only for residential properties that require a mortgage for the purchase," Cassie said. "After a sale is recorded at the land registry the property is not mortgageable for the following six months, but that does nothing to hamper a cash purchase. I doubt you will be surprised to hear that Sandra Leaford's company brokered several of the deals according to the internet history I've seen on the addresses."

"Interesting," Janssen said, "but we already know Devon and Sandra had some manner of a business relationship. She confirmed it with you."

"She did, yes, but she also said they were nowhere near completion and were only at a very early stage. She was quite insistent on that point," Cassie said. "From what I'm looking at, she's been involved with Devon in one form or another for the past year, at least. But there's more. From what I can see, a finance company was used as an intermediary in several of the purchases, arranging bridging loans and acting as guarantor."

"How is that related?" Tamara asked.

"Sandra Leaford is named as a director of the firm."

Cassie said nothing, further allowing both of them the time

for the information to sink in. Janssen exchanged a quick glance with Tamara.

"Sounds an awful lot like a laundering operation to me," Tamara said. "I think we'll have to have another word with Sandra. Thanks, Cassie. Outstanding work, young lady."

"Anytime," Cassie replied. "I'll gather as much info as I can and email it to you."

She hung up. Tony appeared at the entrance to the workshop. He eyed them warily, wiping his palms on a rag. Janssen looked to Tamara and she nodded, confirming they should head off. He reversed the car and headed for the entrance to the yard. Tamara exhaled slowly.

"Buying and selling of property, renovation and development in particular, are very effective for washing money," she said as Janssen pulled out into traffic on the main road. "There's plenty of scope to inflate costs, miss deadlines and incur financial penalties or take out high interest loans. It's simple… and pretty smart."

"I guess the more layers in the process you control, the easier it is to avoid detection," Janssen argued. "If Sandra is involved in the financing and the purchasing, she will find it very hard to claim ignorance of Devon's business. I'm looking forward to hearing what she has to say."

THE ESTATE AGENCY was closed when they got there. Speaking with the manager of the shop next door, no one had seen Sandra or her staff for a couple of days. Her house was in Thornham, further along the coast, and they drove straight there. It was an impressive house. A former manor house, set in extensive well-landscaped grounds and only a short walk through the nearby nature reserve to the deserted beaches beyond Holm Dunes. The electric gates parted and Janssen took the car up the winding driveway to the front of the house.

"Estate agents are well paid," Tamara said as he stopped the car.

Janssen cast an eye around the building. "Successful ones are, and around here there is certainly no shortage of people with money but I very much doubt all this came from her business in Sheringham."

"I think we should press her pretty hard. So far, no one has been particularly forthcoming and it's starting to annoy me," Tamara said. He nodded his agreement.

He turned off the engine and they both got out. The front door opened as they approached it and a woman, dressed in a sharp trouser suit appeared from within. Janssen hadn't met Sandra Leaford before but he knew it was her waiting for them under the cover of the porch. The voice they heard over the intercom had been matter of fact, detached, and he guessed that was a member of staff. A house like this would need many people just to maintain the grounds, let alone the upkeep of the property itself. The way she carried herself, the attention to detail of her appearance as well as the quality of her outfit suggested she was the owner.

Sandra Leaford's face split a welcoming smile as they introduced themselves but Janssen saw something beyond the forced, superficial expression. It may put potential clients at ease but he could see through the facade. Sandra Leaford was on edge and the warm smile did little to mask it from him. He wondered if Tamara thought the same. They introduced themselves, Sandra leading them back into the house and turning right into a large drawing room. The walls were lined with mahogany panelling, an ornate chandelier hanging as a central focal point of the room.

"I didn't expect to be seeing anyone from the police again so soon," Sandra said as the three of them sat down on two large sofas facing one another. "I'm not sure what your junior colleagues told you but, like I said, Devon and I had a passing business relationship. I don't see how I can help."

"That's interesting that you think so," Tamara said, taking the lead. "Our enquiries show you have been directly involved in not only the sale of several properties to corporate entities with direct associations to Devon Bailey, but you are also a director of Arkon Financial. Is that correct?"

Sandra's shoulders appeared to sag for a moment before she took a breath, drawing herself upright. Her eyes never left Tamara.

"I have many corporate clients," she said flatly. "The nature of Devon's professional relationships are nothing to do with me. Devon was looking to make investments, so it is no surprise if our paths crossed."

"It is a little coincidental, though, wouldn't you say?" Tamara said.

"But not unsurprising," Sandra countered. "And regarding Arkon… yes, I am a named director, although it is my husband's company. To be honest, I have little to do with the business; it's more of an advisory role."

Janssen took that to mean she was a co-owner on paper and wondered what benefit her involvement brought to the company's trading position.

"But you are aware of the company's activities?" Tamara asked.

"Yes, of course I am," Sandra said curtly. "I fail to see the relevance, however—"

"Arkon provided financial loans to enable several of those purchases."

Janssen could feel the tension simmering between the two women. He had seldom seen Tamara Greave irritated, except possibly by himself on occasion, but Sandra Leaford was a person who appeared to have quite a knack for triggering her. Tamara had the bit between her teeth whereas Sandra was trying very hard to appear casual.

"Well… I would need the details in order to refresh my memory," Sandra said after a moment of reflection.

"I think that would be a good idea because almost everything you've told my officers so far as turned out to be... how can I put this politely, economical with the truth?"

"I don't think I like your tone, Inspector," Sandra said haughtily.

"Chief Inspector," Tamara replied. "And whether you care for my tone or not makes no odds to me. We have credible witness testimony that places you in Devon's apartment on repeated occasions, often staying there overnight. To suggest that you and Devon barely knew one another is quite frankly insulting."

Sandra Leaford's mouth fell open. Evidently, she wasn't used to being spoken to in that manner. He'd expected her to push hard but, even taking that into consideration, Tamara genuinely didn't seem bothered about Sandra's sensibilities.

"My... my... personal relationships have no bearing on this matter," Sandra said.

"They do when your lover is murdered and you do your level best to distance yourself from him."

"I... I..."

"Might like to revisit your earlier statements?" Tamara asked. "Or perhaps we need to speak with your husband."

At mention of her husband, Sandra's face fell and she averted her eyes from the scrutiny of both detectives. Her lips moved but words didn't follow. The door to the drawing room opened and someone entered. Janssen stood as the man approached them, a look of concern crossing his face as he caught sight of Sandra's expression.

"Darling, whatever is the matter?" he asked.

Sandra shook her head in reply, putting a balled fist to her mouth. Janssen guessed he was Sandra's husband. This conversation was about to get interesting. He glanced at Tamara who appeared to have lost her train of thought, perhaps thrown by his arrival. The man's concerned gaze flicked between his wife and Janssen, then to Tamara and back again. Janssen extended his hand.

"DI Tom Janssen," he said. The man met his hand. His grip was strong, making eye contact as they shook hands. "This is my colleague, DCI Greave."

The man nodded to him, glancing briefly at Tamara still sitting on the sofa. She was staring straight ahead and Janssen couldn't fathom what had gotten into her.

"Max Harcourt," Sandra's husband said in introduction. "What can we do to assist the police?"

"They're asking questions about Arkon," Sandra said, finding her voice.

"Whatever for?"

Again, Janssen looked to Tamara whose face appeared drained of all colour. Sandra was staring at Tamara now, her expression cold and hard. He answered the question.

"It is specifically related to financial loans to a man by the name of Devon Bailey," he said.

"Devon?" Max repeated, tilting his head to one side. Janssen nodded. "Terrible business. Poor man. Are you any closer to figuring out what happened that night on Sheringham cliffs? Gossip has been in overdrive since the chap died."

Janssen fixed Max with a stare. "I believe we aren't far off making an arrest."

"Good to know."

The man didn't flinch. If he knew something, he wasn't letting on.

"Now, about Arkon's dealings with Devon Bailey, we have numerous questions we—"

"And I will be more than happy to address each and every one, Inspector," Max said, holding up a hand and interrupting him, "once you have documented them in writing to my solicitor and arranged a mutually convenient time for us to meet."

Max held Janssen's gaze. His expression was open and warm, but it didn't carry to his eyes.

"If you feel it necessary for such a formal approach," Janssen said. "Might it not be best to have this cleared up immediately?"

Max nodded firmly. "I'm sure you will understand the need for discretion when it comes to investments, Inspector. People use businesses such as mine because they do not wish their affairs to be a matter of public record and if this is related to a murder inquiry, which I believe has been conveyed to the press, then I think formalities are important. It is for the avoidance of my clients' doubt as much for transparency."

"As you wish," Janssen said, looking to Tamara, Max's gaze followed. She didn't look up.

"Is there anything else we can help you with today?" Max asked.

Tamara shook her head. Janssen found himself annoyed by the switch in her approach but said nothing.

Max smiled warmly, looking between the two detectives. "In which case, we will hold you up no further. I'm sure you have much to do."

Janssen returned the smile. It was forced. He didn't like this man, finding his charm and easy manner disconcerting. They were being brushed off. Either the man saw them as insignificant or he was hiding something. If he was a betting man, he'd put good money on it being the latter.

The front door was closed on them almost before they'd set one foot on to the gravel-lined driveway. Tamara increased her pace, reaching the car first. Coming to the driver's side, he looked across the roof at her but, feeling his gaze upon her, she looked away. He unlocked the car and she got in. He looked back towards the house and thought he caught a glimpse of Max Harcourt in the window of the drawing room, watching them. It was fleeting and, within a moment, he was gone. Janssen got in, shutting the door and glancing at Tamara in the passenger seat.

"Are you okay?" he asked, genuine concern replacing the earlier confusion.

"I'm fine."

"Are you sure? Back there, you—"

"I'm fine, Tom! Just leave it will you," she said, glaring at him.

He held her eye for a moment, something had gotten to her but for the life of him, he didn't know what. The colour had certainly returned to her face but that may have been due to his irritating her. He thought about responding, asking again, as she faced forwards seemingly in her own little world but a quick glance at his mobile phone saw he'd missed several calls. They were all from Eric. He tapped the screen, raising the handset to his ear as he turned away from Tamara.

"What can I do for you, Eric?" he asked, keeping half an eye on Tamara sitting alongside him.

"It's Jamie Kemp," Eric said. Something in Eric's tone piqued his curiosity. "I'm at the Norwich University Hospital. I think you need to come down here as soon as possible."

CHAPTER THIRTY-ONE

JANSSEN AND GREAVE were met by Eric at the entrance to the critical-care complex of the hospital. The thirty-mile drive had been done in almost total silence, Tamara unwilling to engage in any conversation beyond the most basic of interactions. The longer it went on, the more concerned he was. Any thoughts as to why were put on the back burner as Eric bounded over to meet them.

"He's in a hell of a state," Eric said, lowering his voice part way through the comment and running a hand through his hair, looking behind him towards the waiting area. Janssen followed his gaze, catching sight of Kerry-Ann. She was sitting on the edge of her seat, rocking gently backwards and forwards, staring straight ahead. Eric indicated her with a flick of the head. "That's Jamie's wife," he said to Tamara and then looking to Janssen. "You know her, I believe. She called the office from here, this morning. She was looking for you," he said to Janssen.

"I left her my contact card," he said. "And I know her."

Tamara glanced up at him quizzically.

"We were at school together," he said and she nodded. Turning to Eric, he asked, "What's happened to Jamie?"

Eric sucked air through his teeth, shaking his head slowly. "He's in a bad way, taken a right hammering. He's been in surgery for the last couple of hours. We're waiting on the doctors coming to speak with us but it doesn't look promising. After his wife called, I checked the reports. It came across the wire at three this morning. He was found unconscious in the street, in the early hours."

Kerry-Ann looked up and over in their direction. When her eyes fell on him, she got out of her chair and came towards him. Her movements were stiff, halting, as if she'd been locked in the same position for quite some time. Her eyes were bloodshot and red-rimmed. She was clutching a scrunched-up tissue in her right hand.

"How are you?" he asked.

She looked nervously between the small group, Tamara and Eric backing away slightly in order to give her space. She reached out and took his hands in her own, looking straight into his eyes. They were silently pleading with him but for what he didn't know, perhaps to offer her some hope.

"Tom, thanks for coming."

Tears welled and he steered her back towards the waiting area. It was still early in the day and no one else was present aside from the staff buzzing around the nurses' station. Tamara and Eric lingered a few metres away, heads together in discussion.

"I must admit I was surprised to have the police knocking on my door before the sun came up," she said as she sat down. He took a seat alongside hers. "Even more so when they said he was on his way to hospital. Do you know anything?"

"About his condition? No," he said.

"No, I mean about what happened. Do you think he was drunk and got run over or something?"

He found himself in an odd position. Unwilling to speculate, he found it very coincidental that a peripheral figure in the investigation would have such an accident but it was possible.

He did his best to keep his tone measured. "Let's see what the doctors say first, yeah."

They didn't have long to wait. The double doors at the end of the corridor opened and a doctor appeared. He glanced in their direction, first visiting the nurses' station before coming over to them. He introduced himself as Dr Hopkins, the lead consultant in Jamie's care. Janssen read his expression. The man looked tired but projected confidence.

"Mrs Kemp," Dr Hopkins said, "your husband is in a critical but stable condition." Kerry-Ann smiled weakly, buoyed by the news. The consultant moved quickly to convey the gravity of Jamie's condition. "However, he is still gravely ill. We've carried out an emergency procedure to alleviate the pressure on his brain and stabilise him but the next twenty-four to thirty-six hours will be critical in terms of his prognosis."

Kerry-Ann appeared ready to ask a question but thought better of it. Instead, she forced a grateful smile and bobbed her head slightly. The doctor was clearly unable to predict the future and, from what he said, it was purely a waiting game. Dr Hopkins excused himself and Janssen signalled to Kerry-Ann that he would return, falling into step alongside the departing doctor. He touched his forearm and Dr Hopkins stopped, turning to him.

"Doctor, could you tell me the nature of Jamie's injuries?"

Hopkins eyed him warily, glancing past him towards Kerry-Ann, still seated and clasping her hands in her lap before her. "Are you a relative?"

"No. Police," he said, taking out his warrant card and discretely showing it to him. Dr Hopkins nodded.

"Mr Kemp has been through something… rather disturbing. His catalogue of injuries," he lowered his voice, "are quite severe. Both of his legs are broken at the knee, as are the bones of his hands and his ribcage has also suffered multiple fractures. And believe me, those are the least serious of his injuries that we're tackling. The trauma to the brain is the greatest threat to both his chances of recovery... and indeed survival."

"He was found alone in the street. Are the injuries consistent with a hit and run?"

Hopkins shook his head emphatically. "I don't tend towards speculation, Inspector, but I find that very unlikely indeed. My field of expertise is not in forensic medicine but I would suggest these injuries, by and large, are not accidental."

Janssen thanked him and returned to where Kerry-Ann was sitting. Tamara joined them as he retook his seat. Kerry-Ann glanced up at him, a brief smile crossing her face before it rapidly dissipated. He fixed her with a stern gaze.

"Kerry-Ann, have you had any contact with Jamie since we last spoke?"

She met his eye, nodding almost imperceptibly. "Yes. Last night. He came round... I'm not sure when, but it was late on. I was getting ready for bed."

"What did he want?"

"For the most part, it was much the same as usual," she said, her eyes flicking towards the ceiling as she thought hard. "He was full of the same promises, telling me how things were going to work out. I didn't really want to listen, I never do. There's only so many times you can hear the same tune before you get bored of listening to it."

Janssen nodded his agreement slowly. "You said for the most part."

"Yes," Kerry-Ann said.

"What was different?"

Her lips parted and her expression changed before her brow furrowed. "He was sober for starters. Believe me, that's not happened for a while. I don't know," she said absently rubbing at one side of her face as she sought to remember the previous night's events, "he seemed upbeat, positive. It's not what you'd usually say about Jamie. Cynical... stubborn and lazy, yes, but not positive. He was talking at a million miles an hour. For a bit,

I thought he was on something but now, looking at it, he was just really excited about something."

"Do you know what?"

"He didn't say exactly, only that him and Shaun had something big they'd been working on that was going to solve everything. I was sceptical, as always. I mean, who wouldn't be when those two get their heads together, eh?" She sank into her chair, visibly deflating. She flicked her eyes to Tamara, who had so far remained silent, and then they passed back to him.

"Did you see or hear anything unusual last night or in the last couple of days for that matter?" he asked.

"Not really," she said, her eyebrows knitting together as she thought hard. "Although, I did see a guy sitting in a car parked further up the street recently. It's been a bit odd, the same guy, same car. I know that sounds odd but he stood out. You don't see people waiting there very often. The road's too narrow really. Caught my eye, you know?"

Janssen thought about it, casting a brief sideways glance towards Eric. Maybe he hadn't been as discrete or careful in his surveillance as he should have been.

"What car was it, do you know?"

"No, sorry. I'm not great with cars but it was a big black thing. One of those four by fours... not a pick-up type but a Chelsea tractor."

Janssen exchanged glances with Tamara. That wasn't a CID car she was describing.

"I know Jamie and me... have our differences," Kerry-Ann said. "God knows, they are massive, but I do love him. If he could just sort himself out... "

She let the thought hang unfinished in the air, dropping her head and rubbing fiercely at her cheeks with the flat of both hands.

"I know," Janssen said, chewing on his lower lip as he indicated for Tamara to join him. He gently touched her shoulder in a friendly gesture of support as he stood up. She looked up at him and he tried his best to offer a reassuring smile as he stepped away with Tamara. They were joined by Eric who had been holding back so as not to overwhelm Kerry-Ann. Once Janssen was confident they were out of earshot, he relayed the doctor's thoughts about Jamie's condition.

"Sounds like they were watching Jamie's house for him to put in an appearance," Tamara said.

"And the Kemp brothers have got in way over their heads this time."

"Who are they?" Eric asked.

Janssen exhaled, glancing back at the dejected form of Kerry-Ann. "That's the question, Eric. Is it possible Devon Bailey brought some of his more salubrious acquaintances with him from London?"

Tamara didn't look convinced. "Devon's been in Norfolk for months. Why now?"

"Was he hiding?" Eric suggested. "It would stand to reason. Sheringham is out of the way. Who would look for him out there?"

"Throwing money around on property and sleeping with anyone who'd have him is hardly keeping a low profile though, is it," Janssen said.

Eric shrugged.

"Whatever Jamie and Shaun were planning, they expected a large pay-off. Devon had a lot of cash stashed at his place, maybe elsewhere too," Tamara said. "What was Devon using the money for and why did he have it here in the first place? I can see how he might be laundering money through property investments... money that has been generated through nefarious means but where the Kemp brothers fit in, I'm not sure. Eric, I want you to track down Shaun. We still don't know where he is and bearing in mind what's happened to his brother, we should make it a priority to locate him. When you do, don't make contact just sit on him and call us, okay?"

"Is he a suspect?" Eric asked. "In the attack on Jamie, I mean."

"Doubt it," Janssen said with a shake of the head. "From what the doctor said, I imagine what happened to Jamie was more like torture or punishment rather than a falling out between siblings. Shaun can be just as much of a loose cannon as his brother but this is beyond him. No, whoever did that to Jamie is an experienced hand. They could have killed him... he might still die, but killing him wasn't the intention."

"Then what was, do you think?" Tamara asked.

Janssen fixed her with a concerned expression. "I imagine it was two-fold. They wanted something from him... and at the same time they wanted to send a message."

CHAPTER THIRTY-TWO

TAMARA STARED out of the window at the passing landscape. They were passing through mile upon mile of open countryside on their way back to the coast having left the hospital. Before they left, she'd made a call to the locals and arranged for a uniformed presence to be subtly maintained in the complex-care unit. It wasn't beyond the realms of possibility, albeit unlikely, that whoever attacked Jamie Kemp might return to finish the job.

She repeatedly tried to figure out the link between Jamie, Shaun and Devon but no matter how many times she replayed the connections in her head, she still fell short. She wanted Shaun or Jamie Kemp to be Devon's killer. More than that, she needed it to be one or both of them. The alternative sent a chill down her spine.

In the corner of her eye, she caught Tom Janssen surreptitiously studying her. It was to be expected. Her behaviour would have raised more than just an eyebrow with him. He was able to read the slightest change in those around him and she'd been less than subtle. But how could she explain herself? How could she tell him that she'd potentially compromised her position, let alone the entire case?

The thought brought with it a wave of anger at herself;

anger that she could be foolish enough to put herself in this position. Still, there was doubt. She hadn't asked Max what he did for a living, she hadn't really cared, and was only too happy not to discuss her own work. Had he deceived her? In fairness, she wasn't exactly truthful when he'd asked questions of her.

The anger passed to guilt. If Max was playing her, then he was very good at it. The fact that he was married would probably have affected her the most in the past, but not now. Life was complicated. Relationships more so and it wasn't as if she'd set out to wreck a marriage. Had she known, she would have stayed away from him, not allowed him into her world. *But he is in your world,* she chastised herself. Letting out an involuntary sigh drew Janssen's gaze to her once more. She recognised a house at the upcoming junction, it was a modern design set back from the road beyond a copse of established trees. They were nearly back at the station.

"Something on your mind?" Janssen asked, turning his attention back to the road.

She glanced across at him, weighing her words carefully. There was no option. If she allowed him, or one of the team, to stumble across it, it would only make matters worse.

"I think I... might be in a bit of trouble," she said. That was something of an understatement bearing in mind the consequences.

Janssen's expression changed to one of concern. He pulled the car into the side of the road, mounting the grass verge. They were on an interconnecting road cutting through farmland, used predominantly by locals or agricultural traffic to move between fields. She hadn't seen another car for several minutes. Janssen engaged the hand brake, leaving the engine ticking over and the gear stick in neutral.

"I thought so," he said, inclining his head to one side and turning to face her. "What's going on?"

She took a deep breath, averting her eyes from his gaze,

feeling a flush of embarrassment. "I think I might have compromised the investigation."

Janssen frowned, his expression one of puzzlement.

"And myself, come to mention it."

Letting out a controlled release of breath, Janssen reached out and switched the engine off. "I think you'd better start at the beginning."

She described her first meeting with Max Harcourt in the lounge bar of her hotel, how they'd struck up a conversation and enjoyed having dinner together. She left out the details of how the night ended, with Max returning to her room. Initially, they had exchanged telephone numbers on the off chance they would meet again but, having first walked her to her room, things escalated. She remembered Janssen's expression when he'd come to her room the following morning to pick her up, seeing the two glasses. She'd remembered to put the toilet seat down but missed the more obvious.

She knew by his expression that he'd twigged, only he was far too gallant to mention it, then or now. For the most part, he listened to her explanation in silence, nodding and making encouraging sounds when required. She was grateful that he didn't ask questions or seek to break up her telling of the story; to do so may have damaged her will to continue. As it was, she felt vulnerable in the retelling. More than that, she felt shame. The opinion held of her by those around her was important, particularly Tom's. She didn't want to be lessened in his eyes.

Having described the phone call from Max, the one taken in the ops room, along with the subsequent dinner date, she fell silent, feeling both relieved and humiliated in almost equal measure. She hoped for reassurance, for a sign perhaps that her error in judgement wasn't as significant as she'd thought. Reading Janssen's expression, she realised she wasn't going to get it. He leaned back against the head rest of his seat, running a hand across his jaw, contemplating all that she'd said.

"But you didn't know who he was and nor did you tell him

what you did, right?" he said at last. She shook her head. "Do you think it is a coincidence that you met?"

Up until that moment, she hadn't considered that their meeting was anything other than a coincidence. How would Max know what case she was working on or why she was in town, until that first night she had been in London? Viewing the situation from a cynical mindset sent a cascade of thoughts through her mind from the moment she received the call to head back to Norfolk immediately to the booking of her accommodation. When Tom challenged her on why she was dispatched so suddenly to the investigation, his fear of her doubting his ability, she had accepted the order without question. Now, her chance meeting with Max seemed like anything but. That would mean he had connections, at least one of a significant rank within the Norfolk Constabulary who could have passed on her name and details, whether deliberate or by happenchance.

"You think someone may have tipped him off?" she asked, not quite believing the words were coming from her mouth.

Janssen was thoughtful before his expression split into a rueful smile. "The way senior local figures have reacted to this murder... people talk, often saying far too much and speaking when they have no business to. Speaking too freely in the wrong company can have consequences."

There was sinking feeling in the pit of her stomach as those words sank in. "I didn't think it could get any worse."

"Well, we don't know that that's what happened," he said, in a clear attempt at reassurance. It wasn't enough, his expression did little to enhance the attempt.

"I should remove myself from the investigation."

The words hurt as she spoke them. Janssen shook his head.

"Let's not jump the gun."

She studied him. Was he humouring her?

"If you do that, you'll have to say everything you've just told me to the chief super… and I don't think that'll do your position much good."

"What choice do I have?" she asked, knowing the words were true but desperately wanting him to shoot her down. "If it comes out that… that I—"

"That you're a single woman who had dinner with a man she just met," he said, fixing his gaze on her. "Yes, truly shocking."

"You know that's not how it will be presented."

"However it is presented, whether it's this afternoon or after we've closed the investigation, is how it will be. That doesn't have to happen today. As of right now, we need to manage the situation. You never know, if it's the worst-case scenario and Max used you to try to get the inside track on the investigation, we might be able to turn it to our advantage."

He had a point but why didn't it make her feel any better. "Max told me he hadn't planned any of this to happen." She met his eye, the sense of embarrassment returning. "At the time, I believed him."

"It's your call," he said, sweeping his head back to face forward, flexing his grip on the steering wheel. "But I see no positives from you falling on your sword right now. None at all." She was about to protest but he continued. "Besides, you've no idea who offered you up to Max, *if* that's what happened. You might end up tipping our hand by speaking up now."

"So, you think I should sit tight?" She recognised the tinge of hope in her voice. Her throat was dry and an odd sensation could be felt in her legs, a disembodiment of sorts.

He nodded. "We need to sit tight."

She held his gaze, reading the sentiment in his comment. Janssen wasn't about to abandon her.

"Thank you."

He smiled but his eyes narrowed at the same time. "But if there's going to be real trust between us, then we need to be open with one another."

She gently bit her lower lip. "Where are you going?"

"I don't appreciate being kept in the dark."

"I've told you everything that happened," she said, genuinely confused.

"Not about Max. I'm talking about my team," Janssen said. "What is it about Cassie you're not telling me? And believe me, I know you're holding something back."

She pursed her lips, turning to the front and staring straight ahead. She could feel his eyes upon her. She chose her words carefully.

"I would never recommend, or force anyone onto your team who I didn't think would be of benefit to you," she said, turning back to face him. "Do you believe that?"

He met her eye and they maintained the contact while he weighed up an answer to the question.

"I do believe that, yes."

"Then I ask you to trust me… and to trust in Cassie and her abilities."

They remained fixed in a silent embrace for a few moments longer before he broke the eye contact, looking out of the window and drawing a deep breath.

"So, you're not going to tell me then," he said with a wry grin. She didn't reciprocate it.

"I don't feel it's my place to say. I'm surprised you haven't done some digging of your own."

"That's true, I could make some calls. It wouldn't be hard to find out," he said. "Don't think it hasn't crossed my mind either."

"Then why haven't you?" she asked.

He clicked his tongue against the roof of his mouth.

"To be honest, I think there's a reason why you haven't said… and it's probably a good one."

"But it's still bugging you, isn't it?" she asked, smiling.

He tilted his head to one side and then bobbed it in agreement, pouting at the same time.

"Damn right," he said, starting the car before engaging first gear.

The remainder of the journey back to the station was made in silence. She found herself wondering what Janssen made of it all. There was no judgement or disapproval of her actions and he didn't appear thrown by her somewhat cavalier approach to her personal life. Not that that was how she saw it herself but others might disagree. She wasn't in the habit of making such flirtations with men she hardly knew; after all, she had been with Richard for years and had expected to be married by now. The decision, made on a whim, to throw caution to the wind on this occasion was not her finest moment.

Thinking about it, it was very much the type of situation she often advised her teenage nieces not to find themselves in. When they rolled their eyes at her, she felt old and yet here she was, making the very mistake she cautioned them against. Would she ever be old enough to learn from her own mistakes? Probably not.

Entering the ops room, Cassie immediately stood up from her desk, waving frantically to get their attention. Janssen joined her as she crossed the room to Cassie's desk. Eric was nearby and he indicated with a shrug that he didn't know what she wanted.

"Okay, thank you for calling me. I really appreciate it," Cassie said, nodding along to whoever she had on the line. "Yes, one of us will need to take a statement from you… no, no, it might be one of my colleagues who does that. Yes, I'll be in touch."

She placed the receiver down, looking between the senior detectives and maximising the drama.

"What is it?" Tamara asked.

"That was Geoff Scott on the phone."

"Devon Bailey's neighbour?" Janssen clarified.

Cassie nodded. "And the resident curtain twitcher of the Beaconsfield apartments, by all accounts. It seems he wasn't quite as forthcoming with you the other day while Eric and I were down in London. He told you he heard a noise, probably when someone put the door in to Devon's apartment."

"Around eleven, I think, after he went to bed as I recall," Janssen said.

"Yes, but that wasn't all of it. He's now saying that he saw some shady looking characters entering the apartment earlier in the evening, around half six."

Tamara was puzzled, her eyes narrowing. "Why change the timing? I don't understand."

"That's just it," Cassie said excitedly. "The door was probably put in as he described but these guys were let into the apartment... by none other than Ewan Dixon. He watched it through the spy hole of his door. Saw it clear as day."

"Then why the hell didn't he tell me that?" Janssen asked.

Cassie smiled. "Apparently, you've not got a pretty face."

Tamara glanced between them, Janssen shaking his head in despair. "Well," she said with a grin, "that's only a matter of opinion."

CHAPTER THIRTY-THREE

TOM JANSSEN PRESSED the buzzer on the intercom and waited. The door to the communal entrance was locked and much of the apartment block appeared deserted. Many people will still be out at work. It was a small block of half a dozen apartments that, by the look of the exterior, would appeal to young professionals starting out. They were compact and modern. Cassie Knight stepped back, looking up at the upper floors in search of signs of movement or occupation.

"None of the curtains are drawn, so he must be up and about," she said.

Janssen nodded and pressed the buzzer again, only this time he held it for an inordinately long time.

"Maybe he's just avoiding us."

They had failed to locate Ewan Dixon at the Beaconsfield Apartments. The concierge desk was unmanned and no one they spoke to could remember seeing him that day, nor the previous one. If Geoff Scott's revelation proved accurate, then Dixon had questions to answer.

Janssen cast his mind back to when the concierge entered Devon Bailey's apartment when he'd specifically been told to remain outside. He had touched the door frame, irritating

Janssen and thus contaminating the scene with his fingerprints. At the time it was seen as an innocent error but now, it looked altogether different. Whoever it was that Dixon let into Devon's apartment, their vandalism of the contents left him in quite a predicament. Had they gone about the search, presumably for the cash he had hidden, in such a way as to allow their presence to pass unnoticed, then his involvement may never have been brought into question.

Once the apartment was trashed however, it made the question of how they gained access a real problem for him. Deciding to break down the door must have been the only solution available to him once the obvious carnage of the interior became clear.

The concern for Janssen was that Dixon, realising he was unable to keep clear of the investigation, had panicked and chosen to flee, taking with him the names of the perpetrators.

Scott's description of those entering Devon's place was very vague. He only saw them from the rear as they entered. The only identifiable person was Dixon, the man he saw on a daily basis.

There was no answer despite repeated attempts and Janssen was about to consider alternative options when a figure appeared from within, descending the stairs into the lobby. The man hesitated as he approached the door but then opened it anyway. Janssen understood his reticence, security doors were there for a reason and people attempting to gain entry without being buzzed in by a resident should be viewed with scepticism.

He brandished his warrant card, identifying them as police. The man immediately stepped aside, holding the door for them and offered a weak smile.

"I don't suppose you've seen Mr Dixon today by any chance?" Janssen asked.

"Ewan? No, not for a couple of days. Is everything all right?"

"Yes, nothing to worry about," he said, taking the weight of the door from the man, allowing Cassie to pass through before following on.

They mounted the stairs, heading up to the second floor where Dixon's apartment was located. There were two on this floor, one on each side of the stairwell. Janssen knocked on the door but, just as before, there was no answer. He exchanged a glance with Cassie who seemed equally frustrated.

"Do you want to come back or…"

"Or what?"

"Or you could kick it in," Cassie said with a mischievous smile. "I mean, it doesn't look reinforced. A bloke of your size should be able to handle it."

He eyed the door. She was right. In stark contrast to the communal doors downstairs, this one looked flimsy. He leaned in closer to the obscured glass of the window in a vain attempt to see inside. He couldn't. All he could see of the interior was a light blur.

"It's not like he's a prime suspect or we think he's in a life-threatening position, though, is it?"

Cassie leaned in to the door herself, turning her head to one side as if straining.

"What was that?" she asked.

Janssen listened. He couldn't hear anything. "What was what?"

"That noise. I thought it was someone calling out," she said, raising her eyebrows as she looked at him. "I could have sworn it was a voice calling for help."

He narrowed his eyes, biting his lower lip and shaking his head.

Cassie feigned ignorance. "What? The neighbour said he hadn't seen Ewan for days. He seemed genuinely worried to me," she said with an exaggerated look of concern.

"He did seem upset. Maybe we should check," he said.

Cassie smiled, withdrawing a radio from her coat pocket. She contacted the control room and received a crackled authorisation to carry out a welfare check. She nodded to Janssen, indicating to the door.

He smiled, wagging a cautionary finger at her as he stepped back, ushering her to one side. "Don't make a habit of this, Detective Sergeant."

"I wouldn't ever," she said. "Whenever you're ready."

Janssen took a breath and then stepped forward at speed, raising his foot and driving it against the lock plate. The door flexed but didn't open.

"I thought you were in shape," Cassie said, inclining her head off to one side. Janssen shot her a dark look before making a second attempt. The first had been to gauge the pressure required and, at the second time of asking, the lock gave way and the door flew inwards, the frame splintering under the force of his assault.

"See. I am in good shape," he said, drawing breath and bringing himself upright. Cassie grinned but it soon faded as a familiar smell was brought to them on a draught from the inside.

"Is that what I think it is?" she said.

Janssen nodded, stepping forward and covering his mouth with the sleeve of his coat. Even in the hallway of the apartment, the air was oppressive. It was incredibly hot. Janssen put the flat of his hand against the radiator and it was hot to the touch. Although the warmth of spring was yet to come fully upon them, and the wind coming in off the North Sea could cut through you, it didn't seem cold enough to warrant this level of heat. He read the dial on the thermostat mounted on the wall alongside the entrance to the kitchen. It was turned around to its maximum setting, well beyond the highest printed number of thirty degrees. The heat inside must have been closer to forty-five degrees or higher.

Passing the kitchen, being careful not to touch anything, they left the hallway and entered the living room. It was an open-plan living and dining room. The television was on, the volume set at an unpleasant level, far too loud for anyone apart from the hard of hearing. Ewan Dixon was in the dining area. He lay across a table, flat on his back.

Janssen approached, choosing carefully where he put his feet. When he came to within a foot of the body, his presence disturbed a cluster of flies. They rose up, at least a dozen or so, some circling the body whereas others settled down upon Dixon's face moments later. Dixon's right hand was pinned to the dining table with a carving knife, blood had run from beneath the hand and dripped from the surface to the floor, pooling on the laminate. The man's face appeared to have been pulverised, so much so that he was barely recognisable. The golden name badge pinned to the lapel of his blazer suggested he'd not long returned home from his shift before he'd met his fate.

"I don't think it was him you heard calling," he said, almost gagging from the stench permeating the room.

"No. I think he's a bit past saving," Cassie said. "If it wouldn't mess with the forensics, I'd open a window."

"I think it'd take a bit more than that," he said.

Turning his attention back to Dixon, he analysed the man's skin colour. He'd seen enough dead bodies over the years, both a result of natural causes as well as premature deaths, to realise Dixon had been dead for a while. Covering his mouth, he leaned in closer and examined the one eye that wasn't swollen shut as a result of the beating. He saw it was bloodshot with small red spots.

Lowering himself, he examined his neck above the collar line of his shirt and wasn't surprised by what he saw. He would have loved for Cassie to have opened every window in the apartment to their full extension but it was a crime scene and they had to minimise the impact of their presence.

"What have you found?" she asked.

He raised himself upright again, indicating towards the neck. "They beat him and then strangled him to death. There's a ligature mark around the neck, looks like wire as it's cut into the skin. The petechial haemorrhaging in the eye balls is indicative of asphyxiation."

"They bribed him to get in," Cassie said, thinking aloud, "and then killed him to ensure he kept quiet."

"That's pretty much the size of it," he agreed. "Dixon got rich."

"And then he got dead," she said, frowning. "I'll call it in."

Janssen nodded but didn't take his eyes off Ewan Dixon's body as she stepped out. He didn't blame her. The atmosphere in the room was an overbearing assault on the senses. Whoever did this knew what they were doing. This wasn't random. Dixon had been tortured but for what reason? Maybe it was to see if he'd spoken to anyone already, or perhaps they thought he'd taken the money they couldn't find. Either way, they were no strangers to this level of violence. Most people, even those prone to aggression and bouts of violence would baulk at doing this to another human being. It took a degree of wicked callousness that few people possessed.

Jamie Kemp came to mind. He, too, had been worked over in a similar fashion and perhaps left for dead. Was that an error or a calculated move on their part? Devon was dead, now too Ewan Dixon. If you've committed a premeditated murder once, it became preferential to leave no witnesses even if that meant one or two more killings. There would be less chance of getting caught.

The setting of the thermostat was further evidence of their previous experience. The high heat and humidity not only affected the determination of the time of death by increasing the decomposition rate of the body, but also sped up the breaking down of forensic trace evidence, hampering an investigation. Whoever did this was a professional. He couldn't help but think that some of Devon's associates or adversaries were in town and they were starting to clean house.

The clock on the investigation was ticking and things were escalating quickly, and time to get a result was running short.

The stench was becoming unbearable and he had to step out, joining Cassie on the landing of the stairwell. Despite being out of the apartment, the smell was equally strong where they stood. He knew it didn't matter where they went for the remainder of the day, the smell of death would cling to them, going wherever they did. This was why morticians and pathologists carry gels to apply to their noses in order to mask the odour.

Cassie hung up on her call, turning to him. "That's CSI notified and some uniform is on its way to lock down the scene."

"Good. The DCI?"

"I've just spoken to her. She thinks we need to find Shaun as soon as possible."

He agreed. Shaun would be the next target, if it wasn't already too late.

"Get a body round to Shaun's place, plain clothes. Have them keep an eye on Helen, make sure she's safe. They might try and use her to get to Shaun. That's probably how they got to Jamie, by watching his wife."

"Will do," Cassie said. She grimaced.

"What is it?"

"Just thinking about Helen Kemp. I didn't think things could get any worse in her world. Not only is she pregnant and having her husband knocking her around but now she's got to worry about all this," she said with a flick of the head in the direction of the interior.

"Yeah, true," he said. Then, indicating the side of her face where her bruising was starting to come out, "Talking of being knocked around. You said you were challenged down in London. That looks like more than a challenge. Are you okay?"

She adopted a thoughtful expression. "I may have underplayed what happened a little... but there was no point, no witnesses and I couldn't tell you who did it."

"You still should have said."

She pursed her lips, nodding ever so slightly. "I know."

"Is that what Eric said to you?"

He'd noticed an exchange between the two of them once

they'd left his office after recounting the events in the capital. She didn't want to meet his eye but she nodded her confirmation.

"Eric was annoyed with me for not saying," Cassie said, sounding regretful. "I put him in a position... and I shouldn't have."

She looked up to find him staring at her. She seemed ready for an admonishment but that was the last thing on his mind. "Are you okay?"

The relief in her expression was palpable and she smiled weakly. "Yes. I will be."

"Good. We'll need to talk about it later but I'm sure you had your reasons."

Her gaze lingered on him while she waited for him to say more but, instead, he indicated the mobile in her hand. "Better get that body round to the Kemp's sharpish."

"I'm on it," she said, turning away to make the call.

"Cassie?" She turned back to face him, mobile pressed against her ear. "Are you okay here for a bit. I've got something I need to do. Eric can come and get you."

She nodded, returning to the call. If she was curious as to where he was going, she didn't ask.

CHAPTER THIRTY-FOUR

TOM JANSSEN SAT in his car listening to the engine ticking over as he stared at the closed gates in front of him. They were solid wood, easily six feet tall and barred any meaningful view of the house beyond. He contemplated what he was doing there, what good it might do. The answer was potentially nothing but the capacity to make matters far worse was certainly in the forefront of his mind.

He should turn the car around and head back to the station. Better still, head home and spend the evening with Alice, maybe put Saffy to bed and think this through a little more. But he couldn't do that. He was wrestling with a thought in his mind and no matter how hard he tried, it wouldn't settle.

The gates began to move, the initial jolt as the electric motors engaged saw them wobble at first before they opened. His mobile phone beeped and he glanced down at the screen. It was a text message from Tamara. He ignored it, returning his attention to the gate. The headlights of a car became visible and as soon as the space was there, the vehicle emerged and pulled out onto the road. It was a small white mini-van and by the look of the two passengers in the interior, dressed in matching green jumpers, they were landscapers who'd finished work for the day.

Either he acted now or he went home.

Putting the car in gear, he moved off, crossing the short distance between where he was parked and the entrance to the driveway. The gate was already beginning to close as he passed through. The sensors picked up his vehicle's presence and they juddered to a halt, moving once again when he was clear. The gravel crunched under the weight of his wheels as he continued up the driveway and parked in front of the house, just as he had done that morning.

"This is probably a bad idea," he told himself, getting out and walking to the front door. This time there was no welcome from Sandra Leaford or any other. The exterior lights were flickering into life, the sensors detecting the darkening skies as the sun was already below the horizon. He rang the bell and waited. The front doors were substantial, double fronted and reinforced with cast-iron rivets. They appeared ancient. Whether they were or not was anyone's guess. The fabric of the building was clearly original but the building must have seen a great deal of work to bring it into the modern era.

He wasn't there long before he heard someone unlocking the door and it was pulled inward. A studious looking man stood in the entrance lobby, his eyes narrowing on Janssen. He didn't wait to be invited and walked inside. The man was set to protest but Janssen cut him off.

"Mr Harcourt. Where can I find him?" he said, brandishing his warrant card.

"He… he's in the drawing room, sir."

"No need to show me, I already know the way," he said, setting off.

Janssen entered the drawing room to find Max standing before a roaring fire set within an Inglenook fireplace, nursing a glass of red wine and admiring the dancing flames in the hearth. He was dressed in casual clothing, or what passed for him as casual clothing, with his free hand resting on the mantelpiece. He turned to look as Janssen pushed open the door to make his entrance, trailed by the man who'd let him in, protesting as he did so. Max held up his hand, offering a half-smile.

"It's okay, Sebastien," Max said. "Inspector Janssen appears to be on something of a mission."

Sebastien refrained from any further attempt to hinder Janssen's progress, stopping and allowing him to walk unopposed into the room. He glared at Janssen but made no further comment, merely looking to his employer. Max waved him away. Sebastien retreated from the room, his eyes flicking between the two men as he backed away.

"I see the constabulary have you working rather hard, these days," Max said, glancing at his watch and sipping from his glass while coming to meet him. "May I offer you a glass of wine or… will you decline because you're on duty?"

"I am on duty," he said.

"I thought so."

"And I'm also choosy about who I drink with."

Max sucked air through his teeth in an exaggerated manner, fixing him with a stare. "I see," he said, seating himself on one of the three sofas in the extensive room, leaning back and crossing one leg over another. He sipped from his glass again, before swallowing and rolling his tongue across his lower lip. He didn't offer Janssen a seat. It was no matter, he would have chosen to remain standing in any event. "Normally, I am considered quite perceptive, Inspector. It is considered to be one of my gifts and has assisted me well over the years. However, I don't need such gifts to realise you don't like me very much."

Janssen took on a thoughtful expression but didn't answer the question. Max held his gaze. Janssen considered the feeling was arguably mutual.

"What was it I said earlier today that wasn't clear to you, Inspector Janssen? I believe I instructed you to contact me through my solicitor, did I not?"

"You did," he said, breaking the eye contact and glancing around the room. "Your wife not around?"

Max's gaze narrowed before his lips parted and he broke into a broad grin. "I wonder if your hostility towards me has anything to do with Tamara?"

He shrugged. "That's none of my concern."

"Your expression says otherwise."

"I take issue with anyone who uses another to gain an advantage."

"That's just business."

He found a flutter of anger manifest in his chest and it must have been visible in his face because he saw Max tilt his head slightly, watching him intently.

"What happened between myself and Tamara wasn't about business. She was never my target," Max said. Janssen didn't believe him. "I never expected to enjoy her company as much as I did. She is… a captivating woman."

"Who just happens to be leading a murder investigation that's come close to revealing a money-laundering operation revolving around your business."

Max laughed but it was one without genuine humour. Raising his wine glass in a mock salute, Max extended his forefinger, pointing it at him. "You are very direct. I respect that. Perhaps, I like you a little more than I thought." He finished what was left in his glass and reached for the bottle on an occasional table alongside him.

"You don't seem particularly rattled?"

"Why should I be?" Max said, pouring himself another glass of wine. He lifted the bottle and angled it towards Janssen. "Are you sure I can't tempt you? It's no fun drinking alone."

"So far we have a dead man with criminal connections, purchasing property and making investments funded by your company, assisted by your wife," he said. "I should imagine you are suffering from a little anxiety under the circumstances. Everything about your world." Janssen held an open hand up in a sweeping gesture around the room. "All that you are used to could be gone in an instant, to be replaced by a brick cell, twelve feet by eight and shared with two other unpleasant characters. If it were me, I'd be anxious."

Max shook his head slowly, raising his glass to his lips but he didn't comment on the implied allegations directly. "That won't be happening."

"I wish I shared your confidence," Janssen said, coming around and taking a seat opposite. "Your trust in your abilities along with that of your associates is curious. Personally, if I was in hock with these types of people, I would be very concerned about what might be coming my way. Particularly in light of what happened to Devon and to Jamie Kemp last night."

Max's head snapped up at mention of Jamie but he lowered it soon after, focussing on his wine glass, swirling the contents gently.

"You see, to me, it appears that Devon made some enemies. Powerful ones. And for some reason, they came here to mete out some measure of punishment upon him... and also those around him. What do you make of that?"

Max grinned, wagging a finger at him. "I wouldn't be surprised by that, Inspector. Devon was a curious chap. Dangerous. Ambitious. I know he was frustrated at the lack of those qualities in the people around him. You see, everyone speaks about the Jamaican gangs, the Yardies, in hushed tones." Max lowered his voice as if fearful of being overheard. "Their reputation for brutality is well known but, in reality, it is all very much over-hyped. They care about respect more than money, and that's never been any different. When people talk about Yardies, they aren't those established back in the Caribbean. They are criminals, don't get me wrong, but these days more born and bred domestically than linked abroad. In the past, had they ever been able to come together, unify and organise then perhaps they would be better placed to counter what's now coming their way."

"Which is what, exactly?" Janssen said, sitting forward and resting his elbows on his knees.

"The pressure from those coming in from Eastern Europe," Max said, sinking back in his own seat and sighing theatrically. His brow furrowed as he met Janssen's eye. "Now they, in contrast, are incredibly well organised, well financed... and brutal with it. For years now they've been moving in on the territories that others have been unwilling to look at. These guys don't care who they piss off. You step aside or they force you to, one way or another. There is no opportunity for discussion," he said, drinking from his glass. His tone sounded resentful, almost frightened. "Now, the Devons of this world could see the writing on the wall, the need to diversify, learn from the newcomers. And that, Inspector, is where I come in. You should see me as a facilitator."

"Devon stepped outside of his circle, didn't he?"

Max drew breath. By the look on his face, Janssen wondered how much he'd already had to drink. He didn't imagine this was Max's first bottle.

"You never knew Devon Bailey, did you?" he asked. Janssen shook his head. "If you did, you would know just how bang on the money you are. Devon was... a dreadful man. Don't get me wrong, he had attributes I greatly admire, many of which I myself possess... a ruthless business acumen, single mindedness... a talent with women," he said the last, flicking his eyes to Janssen who understood the unsaid sentiment in the comment. Once again, he found his anger building but he quelled it. "But you're right, it does appear that he over-reached and that led to his downfall. You see, Devon had many plans. Plans not shared by his associates and so he sought to branch out."

"With other people's money."

Max raised his eyebrows. "Very astute, Inspector."

Janssen fixed him with a stare. "Who killed him?"

Max shrugged, raising his glass to his lips. "That, we are yet to find out which is one reason for me to get close to your investigation. Tamara seemed a logical place for me to start."

"You said we," Janssen replied, ignoring the casual manner in which he seemed to regard Tamara. "Who is we?"

Max laughed. This time it seemed genuine. "Yours is not the only investigation running at the moment."

Of all the responses he'd expected, that wasn't one he was ever likely to have considered.

"Who are you working for?" he asked.

Max's expression grew into a wide grin, revealing polished white teeth. "You see, they told me you were good," Max said pointedly. "They told me you'd be at my door at some point. I didn't see it myself. I always thought you rural folk were quite simple but I'm happy to admit I was wrong."

"Who are you working for?" Janssen persisted.

"Your colleagues at the SFO."

"The Serious Fraud Office?"

Max nodded, grinning triumphantly. "And that is why I will never see the inside of a jail cell, Inspector. But if you would be kind enough to find out who threw Devon off the cliff, that would be splendid because whoever did it has seriously put a spanner in the works."

Janssen felt a mixture of anger and professional embarrassment. Anger at another agency operating in and around his investigation without identifying themselves and also a sense of humiliation that he'd not realised earlier. There was no possible way he could have known but the revelation still stuck in his craw nonetheless. Feeling the need to stretch his legs, he stood up. Pacing the room allowed him to focus and put aside his frustration.

"So, how did they manage to get you on board?" he asked. The amused smile slipped from Max's face, his brow furrowing. His speech was starting to slur and Janssen spotted an empty tumbler sitting on the beam above the fireplace. He lifted it to his nose. It had contained scotch. Max was certainly lubricating himself, no doubt as a coping mechanism. Should his involvement with the SFO come to light, those he worked for would not take kindly to it. That knowledge would be a death sentence. His status as an SFO informant would be of no use to him.

"Perhaps I am not quite as clever as I thought I was, Inspector," Max said, raising his glass in a mock toast before drinking from it once more. "What I do now is infinitely more preferable to seeing the inside of a prison."

"Is that what they promised you?"

Max allowed his head to hang before bobbing it forward in agreement. "I have made myself almost indispensable."

"Almost," Janssen repeated. Max met his eye, his expression unreadable.

"When you next see Tamara," he said, his lips parting as he took his time to choose his words. "Do please tell her I meant what I said."

Janssen was about to respond but his mobile rang. Thinking it would be Tamara again, he glanced at the screen. The number was unknown. He tapped the answer tab.

"DI Janssen," he said. There was silence at the other end of the line but he could hear someone breathing. "This is Janssen. Who is this please?"

"Inspector. It's Helen... Helen Kemp."

He sensed her reticence, the fear in her voice.

"Hold on a second," he said, heading for the door. Max sat forwards, bolt upright.

"You will tell her, won't you?" Max said, almost pleading with his eyes. "Tamara, I mean."

"Yeah," he replied over his shoulder as he left the room. "Maybe I'll do just that."

CHAPTER THIRTY-FIVE

ONCE HE WAS out of the room, he turned left and increased his pace towards the front door. There was no sign of Sebastien and he let himself out. Clear of the house, he walked to his car.

"Helen, are you still there?"

"Yes," she said. "I'm here."

"Are you okay?" he asked, unlocking his car and getting in. Only now, certain of not being overheard, did he feel comfortable to speak freely.

"I... I'm not sure," she said. "Kerry-Ann called me. She said what happened to Jamie."

"Yeah, it's nasty."

"They're saying... he might die."

Janssen thought about what he should say. He was no fan of Jamie Kemp but he certainly hoped he would recover although, if he was honest, he didn't know why.

"Yes. Let's hope he pulls through."

There was silence again. She was hesitant and he silently hoped she was calling to take up his offer of helping her get out of harm's way. He knew that Cassie would have arranged for someone to be outside, watching over her, but he couldn't say so.

"I spoke with Shaun," she said at last. The words came with added emphasis, as if she was relieved to have gotten them out.

"When?" he asked, immediately alert.

"He called me earlier, after I'd spoken to Kerry-Ann. I said about Jamie and he already knew and that he'd seen the pictures."

"What pictures?"

"I don't know but that's what he said. He was so upset. I mean, I've heard him crying before. He always does after… after he's done something he regrets." Janssen knew she was talking about the times he'd given her a beating. Abusers were often remorseful, until the next time. "But this was different. He was different."

"Where is he, Helen?"

"I… I… don't know—"

"Helen, now's not the time to fob me off," he said firmly. "You know what happened to Jamie. Shaun's in danger. This could mean his life. Where is he?"

"I don't know! Honestly, I don't."

"Okay," he said, adopting a softer line. She was scared. He could hear the stress in her voice. "Then what can you tell me?"

"He said he was going to sort it… tonight."

"Sort what?" Janssen asked, turning the possibilities over in his mind but coming up blank.

"I don't know but he said it would all be over tonight one way or another, and that I shouldn't worry." She said the last accompanied by a derisory snort. "Like that's going to happen."

He thought it through. The only thing he could imagine was that someone had sent Shaun pictures of Jamie prior to when he was dumped in the street. They could only have come from his attackers. Jamie was a message. A pertinent and convincing one. Shaun was being forced into action.

"Helen, I want you to think very carefully. Where do you think Shaun might be right now?"

He could sense the frustration from her at the other end of the line. She didn't know. It was obvious.

"If he's not with Jamie… I would say he's on the boat."

"Thanks, Helen. Leave it with me," he said, realising he had got as much as he would from her. "I think this will be over soon enough and believe me when I tell you, I am looking out for you… and for Shaun. Try not to worry."

She thanked him and he hung up, immediately calling Tamara's mobile. She picked up within two rings.

"Tom, where the hell are you—"

"Never mind," he said, interrupting her. "Round up as many bodies as you can. This is happening tonight."

"What is?"

"Devon decided to go freelance with someone else's money. I'm pretty sure everything that's happened, to Devon, Ewan Dixon and Jamie Kemp, is all revolving around them wanting it back. Shaun's meeting them tonight."

She seemed about to argue, press him for more information but must have thought better of it. "Where?"

"Shaun's on his boat… and they don't have one. I'd say Wells… but it's a guess."

He could hear Tamara breathing and imagined her in the ops room, her expression fixed as she weighed up his theory as well as his judgement. It was his best guess but right now, that was all they had. Finally, she replied.

"We'll meet you there."

Tom Janssen gently tapped his fingers on the steering wheel. He caught Eric Collet looking at him sideways, not for the first time. He knew the question that was coming. The same question he'd asked less than twenty minutes earlier.

"How long do we give it?"

Janssen resisted the urge to offer a sarcastic reply. It felt a lot like taking a day trip with Alice and Saffy, the little girl doing what all children did and repeatedly ask *when will we be there.* The thing is Saffy was seven. Eric was decidedly older. They'd been waiting now for approaching three hours and, thus far, all they had seen were a handful of dog walkers and some of the hardier tourists, braving the cold weather ahead of the spring season, who were staying at the holiday park. This was where they were waiting, in the car park in front of the park's facilities, a short distance away from the new harbour quay at Wells.

The harbour was built to handle the upsurge in larger shipping that the traditional quay in the town could no longer manage. If this was where Shaun planned to meet, then it helped and hindered their operation in equal measure. There was only one approach road from the town, the same used to reach the holiday park and the beach that Wells was widely known for. Their ability to lock down the area with minimal police presence was therefore quite easy as a result.

The downside came from the same geographical factors. The approach road was dead straight and wide open. There was no cover offered by any buildings nor by nature in the form of trees or vegetation. They could see anyone coming just as easily as they could be seen themselves. The road was one side of a flood embankment with a footpath running parallel on the other side. Ships would arrive and dock at the quay, itself accessed via a metal bridge roughly thirty metres from where their car was parked.

Janssen and Eric waited patiently in one car with two further officers, seconded from uniform and now in plain clothes, backing them up in another. Tamara and Cassie Knight were parked up near to Wells itself watching for the approach of the suspects by car. They, too, had a van full of bodies waiting to be deployed in the take down. Once the meeting was believed to be happening, they would seal off the exit route and everyone would converge on the group. The plan was simple. The only question was whether they were in the right place. Janssen had been adamant. Now, though, he was having doubts. Seemingly, Eric was too.

"Do you think they'll be here—"

"Eric, seriously," he said shooting the younger man a dark look.

Eric seemed unperturbed. He was like an exuberant puppy, just itching to get going. From their vantage point they could see any vessels entering the estuary seeking to dock but their view of the quay itself was blocked by the embankment. He was confident he would be able to identify Shaun's boat when it arrived but they were relying on Tamara and Cassie to indicate when the others arrived. They anticipated they would do so in a dark SUV, the only vehicle that was mentioned or seen by themselves and witnesses. The more time that passed, the fewer people they saw and Janssen's intuition told him that it would happen soon or not at all. He hoped for the former. If Shaun was confident of cutting a deal or making peace with these people, then he was going to be in for a shock. They didn't appear to be leaving people behind who could identify them and he saw no reason why that would change now. Shaun was out of his depth and close to drowning.

"I'm going to take a look," he said, cracking open the door and getting out. He picked up the radio from where it lay on the dashboard and headed towards the bank. He zipped up his coat. The wind was coming in off the sea and there was heavy cloud cover tonight, obscuring the moon. The lights of Wells were in the distance off to his right with the access to the beach to his left. Walking up the incline to the foot of the bank, he could hear the sound of an engine. Confident that he was not visible in the darkness, he strained to see the approaching boat. It must be Shaun. He felt a tingle of excited anticipation in his chest as he raised his radio to his mouth, depressing the call button.

"The target is approaching," he said calmly, releasing the

button. The radio crackled momentarily before he received a reply.

"Roger that. All quiet this end," Tamara's distorted voice carried through to him.

He turned and walked away from the summit of the bank, retreating to road level. The last thing he wanted was for Shaun to eye him from his place in the wheelhouse and abandon the meet. From where he stood, he could see the boat as it passed by him at a steady pace. Moments later, the pitch of the engine changed as Kemp began the manoeuvre to bring the boat in towards the quay. The radio crackled in his hand.

"Eyes on." The simple message told him his gamble was about to pay off. They were here.

Janssen hurried back to the car as the headlights of a vehicle appeared at the end of the road, too far off for him to worry about being seen. He signalled to the occupants of the other car, both officers acknowledging they were ready. Clambering into his car, Eric met him with an expectant expression.

"We're on," he said. Eric's face split a broad grin. If he wasn't sitting in a car, Janssen was certain he'd be dancing a jig.

He could feel the adrenalin beginning to flow himself. The only concern he had was that they hadn't been able to obtain authorisation for an armed response unit to be made available to them. One was on standby in the area but, without concrete intelligence, they had to make do with the extra numbers. It wasn't ideal as they had no idea how many people they would be dealing with.

The headlight beams of the approaching car grew more intense as it came nearer, coming to a stop just short of where they waited. He knew Tamara and Cassie would be moving to seal off the beach road but they would still be some distance away, waiting for his signal to move in. The lights switched off and he waited another minute before indicating to Eric they should get out of the car. He signalled to the other officers, holding up his hand to make them aware he wanted them to stay put as he and Eric advanced.

There was a small hut at the entrance to the car park and they used that to mask their approach, keeping it between them and the car with the quay beyond the bank. Three figures were walking up the incline from the car, each of them carrying themselves with confidence, fanning out to put a bit of space between one another. Even from this distance, they looked like they could handle themselves.

Once they dropped from sight on the far side of the bank, Janssen broke into a trot, Eric a half-step behind and they covered the ground, scampering up the incline on all fours so that they wouldn't be sky-lined and visible to those on the other side. Looking down on the quayside, the three men were walking up the ramp to the gantry over the water to access the mooring. Janssen caught sight of Shaun in the wheelhouse of his boat, illuminated by the yellow hue of the interior light, gently edging the boat closer to the quay.

Janssen knew he'd be berthed shortly and then they could move in and break it up. Keeping a watchful eye on the men, now on the gantry crossing the water below them, Janssen raised the radio to his mouth. At that very moment, the man at the front suddenly stopped, reaching into his coat. For a moment, Janssen thought he might be about to draw a weapon but, instead, he revealed a mobile phone. He answered a call, immediately raising a hand and placing it on the chest of the first of his associates standing behind him to ensure they didn't move past. His head snapped up, looking around. Janssen felt a surge of dread in the pit of his stomach.

"What's going on?" Eric whispered.

He shook his head. "I don't know how... but I think we're blown."

"What?" Eric asked.

"They know we're here!" he said, meeting Eric's eye just as the lead figure pushed his associates backwards, gesturing for them to head back where they'd come from. He was certain. The operation was compromised. He contacted Tamara. "Go, go, go," he barked into the handset, rising to his feet and signalling for the nearby officers waiting to move in. They climbed out of their car and ran towards them. Janssen was already away, sprinting towards the bridge, Eric only a step behind.

CHAPTER THIRTY-SIX

AT SIGHT of Janssen's towering frame bearing down on them, the three men stepping off the ramp of the bridge split from one another and made for the SUV. Janssen heard the roar of the boat's engines straining as Shaun sought to abandon his manoeuvre and push away from the dock. He couldn't be allowed to take the boat back out to sea. Whatever he had stashed on board would be the evidence they'd need for a conviction and once clear of scrutiny he could dispose of it at will.

Flashing blue lights flickered in the direction of Wells. Tamara and Cassie were on their way. He didn't break stride, pressing on as he saw Shaun frantically attempting to guide his boat away from the quay. In the corner of his eye, he saw Eric rugby tackle one of the fleeing suspects, both men crashing to the floor. The other two were nearly at their vehicle but he couldn't grant them any more attention as he charged up the ramp and across the gantry. The metal grates shook and clattered under his weight and he made it to the quayside, briefly exchanging eye contact with Shaun. The boat was already several feet clear of the quay and within seconds would be out of reach.

Janssen powered along, both legs and lungs burning at the required exertion. He heard footfalls on the gantry behind him but he didn't dare look to see who was following on, his eyes remained trained on the departing boat. Shaun risked a glance over his shoulder and Janssen read the fear in his expression as he pulled alongside the working deck, running at full pelt. Planting his right foot, he pushed off and his momentum carried him through the air, bringing him crashing down onto the lower working deck towards the stern. He lost his footing upon landing, pitching forward and tumbling into the hatch securing the storage hold. Air exploded from his lungs upon impact and he rolled over onto his back before struggling up onto his feet.

The boat was increasing speed now, the engines straining at what they were being asked to do. For a second, he thought he heard someone calling his name over the roar of the engines and the crashing of the water against the hull, but he put it down to his imagination and dismissed it, setting off towards the wheelhouse at the bow.

Mounting the steps to the wheelhouse, he almost slipped and fell as the boat listed dramatically to one side as they approached the mouth of the estuary, the yawning blackness of the North Sea coming ever closer. Bracing himself with his right hand, he grasped the door handle and threw it open, hauling himself inside. Janssen stared at the helm, his eyes widening. No one was present, the wheel turning under the influence of the water pressuring the rudder.

The boat listed again and he stumbled forward, grasping the helm. At that moment, the door on the far side burst open and Shaun Kemp charged through, clattering into him and knocking him backwards off his feet. Both men fell to the floor, Shaun's momentum carrying him over Janssen and sending him tumbling against the wall.

Shaun was first to his feet and he took a swing, driving a booted foot into Janssen's midriff as he tried to rise. The pain was sharp and intense. He dropped to all fours, winded. The door which Janssen entered by was swinging back and forth with the swell. Shaun steadied himself with both hands and clambered out, shooting a terrified glance over his shoulder at the floored Janssen before disappearing from view.

"Shaun! It's over, where..." he didn't finish the question.

Looking at the unmanned helm, his mind solely focussed on Shaun, he tentatively rose to his feet before stumbling across to grip the wheel. Janssen killed the power to the engines. Glancing out through the windows he took his bearings. They weren't too far out from the coast and although the wind was up, along with the swell, he figured they'd be okay for the time being. Glancing to his right and through the rear window down onto the aft working deck, he couldn't see Shaun in the darkness. Grasping the VHF radio handset, he checked the main battery switch was on and selected the high-power setting before switching it to channel sixteen. Pressing the transmit button, he raised the radio to his mouth.

"Mayday, mayday, mayday..." he repeated. Then he gave the name of the vessel along with their approximate position, requesting immediate assistance. He hung the handset back on its clip and went in pursuit of Shaun, the sound of a response from the coastguard station coming through the speaker as he stepped out of the wheelhouse.

Setting foot on the deck, he looked around. Barely had he taken another step before he caught sight of something coming at him in the corner of his eye. Instinctively, he ducked and rolled forward on his shoulder just as something whistled overhead. Coming back upright, he spun on his heel and recognised Shaun, once again swinging at him two-handed with a boat hook. It was at least five feet long and Shaun wielded it as a Viking would an axe.

"Shaun, stop!" he shouted but Shaun Kemp ignored the instruction, advancing on him and swinging the weapon from left to right as Janssen backed away.

The deck of the boat was tight on space with equipment all

around them, leaving little by way of free space for him to move into. Janssen almost stumbled several times, struggling to pick a safe path of retreat as the vessel lurched one way then another.

Shaun was used to being at sea and the uncertain footing didn't seem to bother him in the least. Onwards he came, advancing on Janssen like a man possessed. All of the angst of his life, the pain and turmoil were being channelled into his assault on his former childhood friend and latter-day adversary. Janssen soon found himself backed into a place with nowhere left to go. Shaun laughed maniacally while lunging at him, red faced and wild-eyed. Janssen turned side on, narrowly avoiding the brass head of the hook which threatened to impale him only to land a glancing blow against the capstan winch, sliding off and embedding itself in the tightly wound nets.

Shaun retracted the hook but it wouldn't budge. Janssen seized his moment and stepped forward, landing a punch across Shaun's jaw. He grunted at the blow, staggering backwards and losing his grip on the pole.

Janssen pressed home his advantage and swung this time with his left fist only for Shaun to bob and weave, the punch missing and flying through empty space. The boat lurched to port and both men stumbled away from each other. Janssen braced himself against the hull only to turn just in time to deflect another blow from Shaun who launched a vicious combination of blows.

Striking back blindly, Janssen found his fist connect with a soft part of Shaun's midriff, hearing his assailant gasp in pain and seeing him stagger back. The two men squared up and Janssen felt a trickle of sweat, or perhaps it was blood, run down the side of his face. He didn't have time to check. Shaun took the moment to look around. As much as he was the aggressor, he too had nowhere to go.

"Shaun, it's over," Janssen said, trying to be assertive and calm. "Let's call it a day now, yeah, before this gets any worse for you."

"You'd love that wouldn't you, Tommy, eh?" Shaun spat at him. "Always where you're not wanted. Nothing's changed!"

"It's over, Shaun."

"No! You don't get to be in charge," Shaun hissed. "Not here. Not on my bloody boat! It's my boat, Tommy, and I call the shots."

Janssen realised how hard he was breathing. It had been a while since he'd needed such a burst of energy alongside the level of stamina required to maintain it. He was grateful for the respite. Shaun, on the other hand, seemed to be running purely on adrenalin.

"Come on, Shaun," he implored him. "Your father would never have wanted you to—"

"No!" Shaun bellowed, his eyes falling on a storage box fastened to the deck alongside him. He flicked it open and reached inside, pulling out a yellow-handled chandlery knife used for gutting the catch. He brandished it menacingly, stabbing it in the air in Janssen's direction. "You don't get to bring my father into this... he was my father, not yours!"

Janssen held both his hands up, palms flat facing him. "I'm not your enemy, Shaun. I never was," he said calmly, although loud enough to be heard over the waves that were now repeatedly hammering at the hull. They must have drifted and turned side on to the swell which was growing in intensity. He sensed their position was far less secure than he'd previously thought. They were adrift and the wind and the swell could easily drive them ashore, just as many ships had been in the coastline's history. This needed to end.

"You don't belong here, Tommy," Shaun shouted, his lower lip curling as he spoke. "And you never did."

Janssen thought he could see tears in the man's eyes but it was hard to tell in this light. The boat listed as another wave broadsided them, this time spilling across the deck but Shaun held his ground, jabbing in his direction with the blade. He advanced on him once more and Janssen sought to brace himself as the boat lifted at the bow and appeared to spin, throwing both men off balance. He tried to reach for something to hold onto but he misjudged it, his fingers grasping at nothing but air as he fell to the deck, sliding a few feet and striking his shoulder on the hydraulic boom. He howled both in pain and frustration. And then Shaun was there, towering over him, the blade glinting off the deck light swinging wildly above the pair of them. Janssen raised his hand and caught Shaun's forearm as it swept down, his brute strength halting the passage of the blade mere inches from his face. Shaun snarled as he put all of his weight behind the movement, trying to force the knife down. Janssen knew he had the power and weight advantage but Shaun was able to bring his to bear more effectively. A surge of panic flared within him. The two men were locked in a deadly embrace, one that Janssen feared he was about to lose.

THE CALL from Janssen over the radio spurred them into action. Cassie started the car and thrust the stick forward into gear, accelerating around the corner and onto Beach Road. She was unhappy to have been placed so far away, although she understood the reasons why, but was now keen to get into the thick of it. They'd watched the black SUV arrive, turn onto the road and head for the new harbour at a rather sedate pace for such an ostentatious vehicle. They briefly discussed how many occupants were inside, the interior shrouded by the wraparound privacy glass. There were at least two in the front but that was all that were visible. The van was behind them with as many officers as they'd been able to gather at such short notice. The SUV was parked on the approach road at the far end and, as they came closer, Cassie was instantly aware things were not quite going to plan. Two figures emerged over the crest of the bank, running towards their vehicle. The first to reach it climbed into the driver's seat and paused, staring at them approaching with both lights and sirens blaring.

The second dived into the passenger seat and, from his gesticulations, they had no intention of stopping. They started the car and accelerated straight towards them. There was only one road in and one out, and they were on it, careering headlong at one another at ever increasing speed.

"Block the road," Tamara instructed, sitting beside her and Cassie did so, slamming on the brakes and spinning the car sideways in order to block the full width of the narrow approach road. It made no difference, they kept on coming.

"What are they doing?" Cassie asked, watching as the SUV left the road, ploughing through the wood and wire fence splitting road from bank and mounting the incline.

"They're not stopping!" Tamara shouted, incredulous.

Cassie put the car into gear and pulled on her seatbelt, indicating for Tamara, who was about to get out of the car, to do the same.

"What are you doing?"

"Better put your belt on, boss," Cassie said, flooring the accelerator. The car jolted forwards and rapidly began to pick up speed.

Tamara wrestled with her seatbelt as the acceleration fooled the mechanism into thinking they were already in an accident.

"Cassie... what are you doing?" Tamara asked, fear edging into her tone as she finally managed to draw the belt across her and secure it into place.

The SUV was losing speed as it powered through the wild flowers and deep grass of the bank, with the driver battling at the wheel to keep them going in a straight line.

"Cassie, I want it on record that I think this is a very, very bad idea!" Tamara said as Cassie laughed, swerving the car to the right at the last possible moment, driving through the fence and up the bank just in time to connect with the side of the SUV as the two vehicles were due to pass one another. The impact threw them forward, their belts locking and clamping them firmly into their seats. The sound of the two cars slamming into one another passed them by, replaced with a loud bang and a cloud of dust that filled the interior of the cabin. Cassie felt herself hit something solid but it gave way in a split second and then all was calm as the car came to rest at the foot of the bank facing back the way they'd come.

Cassie's ears were ringing but aside from that, she couldn't hear anything else. It was like being in the eye of a storm. The windscreen had shattered, much of it was missing and a wisp of smoke, or possibly steam, drifted up from beneath the crumpled bonnet. Glancing to her left, she met eyes with Tamara who appeared dazed but otherwise okay. The DCI mouthed something to her but she couldn't hear it and looked away, not even attempting to lipread. The airbag in front of her was deflated and she figured that must have been what she hit, and maybe heard. At first, she couldn't see what had happened to the suspect's vehicle. Only when she released her seatbelt and forced open the door with her right foot, no mean feat due to it having buckled during the impact, did she see the SUV on its side a short distance away. The back-up team had already dragged the two occupants clear and they were in custody, lying face down on the ground with their arms secured behind their backs.

Turning her attention to further up the road, she saw another figure had also been detained; but of Tom Janssen and Eric Collet, there was no sign.

JANSSEN FELT HIS STRENGTH FAILING, the muscles in his arms burned like fire and the point of the blade edged ever closer. He knew Shaun sensed it as well, redoubling his efforts. A shadow emerged out of the darkness striking at Shaun and the pressure on Janssen ceased immediately as his would-be assassin toppled away from him, sprawling across the deck. Eric Collet flew past

Janssen, kicking the knife out of Shaun's hand just as he attempted to rise. He then followed that with a swift punch to the side of the head, flattening Shaun before dropping his knee onto the middle of his back. Eric wasn't tall but he was stocky and Shaun cried out in pain, Eric ignoring the protestations and swiftly drawing Shaun's right arm behind his back, pinning him to the deck and handcuffing him. There was no time to offer thanks as the boat listed dangerously to starboard, the lights of Wells flashing into view and disappearing again just as quickly.

Janssen hauled himself upright and made for the wheelhouse. Once inside, he took the helm, engaging the engines but nothing happened. He tried repeatedly but to no avail. Cursing, he screamed at the controls. The boat must be in worse shape than he thought, barely seaworthy. They weren't out of danger yet. The radio crackled into life and he recognised the call sign of the Wells lifeboat. He looked outside, towards where he thought the coastline was but in the all-encompassing darkness, he had totally lost his bearings.

Then, off the port side he saw them, the lights signalling the approach of the Mersey-class lifeboat, the Doris M.Mann of Ampthill, with its five-strong crew. Eric appeared at the door to his right, almost falling back down the steps as the boat listed violently. It had been a while since he had been out on the water with a storm front moving in on them. He'd underestimated just how quickly the situation could change, particularly given they were passengers on such a stricken vessel.

"Shaun?" Janssen asked.

"Not going anywhere," Eric shouted.

Janssen noticed Eric was wet through, from head to toe, as he clasped the radio and made contact with the lifeboat crew. He explained their position and was advised to hold tight and the crew would come alongside, attempt to fasten a line and tow them back in. At their request, he tried once more to restart the engines but it was no use. Both men took hold of anything firm as they waited for the lifeboat crew to come to their rescue. Eric's expression of excitement was no longer visible. He now looked stern, almost grown up.

"What the hell are you doing here, Eric?" he asked, smiling in an effort to relieve the tension.

Eric shrugged. "Well, I couldn't let you have all the fun, could I?"

"You took your time."

"And you left me clinging to the fenders all the way out here," Eric said. Janssen shot him a quizzical look. "My legs aren't as long as yours... I can't jump as far."

The boat jolted as the crew of the RNLI brought their boat alongside and the two vessels kissed. A figure in an orange jumpsuit and helmet appeared at the door to the wheelhouse a few moments later, sporting a sideways grin framed by several day's growth of stubble.

"Are you gentlemen in need of a lift?" he asked.

CHAPTER THIRTY-SEVEN

THE CREW of the Wells lifeboat towed the stricken trawler back to the safe harbour of Wells. Janssen lost his mobile at some point between running to make it onto the departing boat and the subsequent scuffle with Shaun Kemp. Eric's mobile was somewhere at the bottom of the estuary, a point he repeatedly grumbled about once he was sure they were relatively safe.

Once the adrenalin began to subside following Shaun's arrest and the ensuing rescue, the detective constable's previously elated mood was tempered by his complaints about being wet and cold. Tamara Greave was waiting on the quay as the boat was gently nudged into its berth. Her expression was stone-faced and hard to read. He'd been able to relay their condition via the ship-to-shore radio, confident that the message would reach the DCI. Janssen, Eric, and their additional RNLI crew member threw ropes to those officers waiting to assist them on land.

More units had arrived since they'd pulled away from the dock and Janssen cast an eye over proceedings. From his vantage point at the bow, he was able to look along Beach Road, eyeing the upturned vehicle. Uniformed officers were visible roping off the scene for the coming investigation. It would appear that the take down didn't quite go according to plan. With an operation such as this, with so many unknown variables in play, that wasn't a surprise.

He was pleased to see Cassie Knight descend the bank and walk towards the bridge. By the time he and Eric had disembarked, handing over the handcuffed Shaun Kemp to waiting officers, she had come to stand alongside Tamara. He smiled and they both returned it, Tamara then looking past him to Eric and casting an eye up and down, taking in his bedraggled condition.

"Eric, what happened to you?" Tamara asked.

He shrugged. "Got a little damp, didn't I. And I lost my phone."

Janssen sighed. "Just think about the heroics you'll be able to describe to Becca later."

At mention of his partner, Eric's face lit up. By all accounts, she already thought he was a hero, true in reality or not. On this occasion, he deserved every plaudit going.

"And I'll even get you a new phone through expenses," Janssen said, drawing a dark look from Tamara.

"Really?" Eric said, beaming.

"No, Eric," Tamara said flatly. "Tom's winding you up."

Eric appeared crestfallen but perked up when Cassie nudged him in the ribs with her elbow. "Still... hero, eh? Think about what that will get you. Wouldn't mind hearing the story myself, too."

Janssen turned his attention to her, seeing a wound to the side of her forehead. She noticed, dismissing it with a flick of the hand.

"It's nothing. We... had a bit of an accident."

"You were reckless," Tamara said, fixing her with a stern gaze. Cassie scrunched up her nose in reply.

Janssen laughed. "Makes a change from it being me."

"I still want to hear how the two of you ended up on a boat heading out to sea," Tamara said, eyeing Eric's wet clothes again, "and how you ended up in the water. But that can wait until later. What is it Shaun's been keeping on the boat?"

Her eyes moved past them to the trawler. Janssen gestured with his head for them to climb aboard.

"We've not had a chance to look but I'll expect whatever it is in the hold. Shaun was desperate to put out so that we wouldn't find it."

The four of them made their way aboard, Janssen moving to the hatch over the hold. There were two, one was mechanically operated and, judging by the condition of the vessel, he didn't fancy his chances of making it work. The other was a manhole, and he lifted that, securing it in place. Angling a torch beam down into the interior, he descended the ladder followed by Tamara. The hold was damp and smelt of fish and seawater, the latter being stronger. He didn't know when Shaun last brought in a catch but it can't have been recently.

Tamara activated her own torch, making it easier for both Cassie and Eric to join them. The hold appeared to be empty but that wasn't possible, so they split up and investigated. There was water pooling in places and Janssen theorised about the condition of both the outer and inner hulls. There was no way he would be putting to sea in this ship, it was in dire need of an overhaul and, in reality, was perhaps only worth the salvage value.

Shining his light onto the hull, he scanned the length. Tamara and Cassie followed suit and it was only Eric who seemed to continue on looking for something plainly visible. The torch's beam lit up something that caught his eye and he leaned in closer to the surface. Tapping the metal with the head of the torch, he heard a resounding clang. It didn't seem right and, holding the torch between his teeth, he felt around the edges of the panel with his fingertips. The panel flexed and then moved. Tamara, seeing he was on to something, crossed to join him and between the two of them, they managed to lever the panel aside.

Behind it were rectangular blocks wrapped in blue plastic

and secured with gaffer tape, stacked atop each other. They were packed in pretty tight and it took some leverage to prise one out. Cassie appeared alongside them, passing him a butterfly knife. He frowned as he took it from her. They were illegal, banned, and she wasn't going to be getting it back. He sliced through the tape, unfurling the plastic to reveal a block of a tan brown substance. He knew what it was, heroin. He exchanged glances with Tamara who angled her head to one side.

"Another one over here," Eric called.

They turned, illuminating his position. There were fifteen to twenty packets visible in another secret compartment beside where Eric was kneeling. Janssen shone his beam around the interior of the hold. There could be any number of false panels on display. They would need to pull the boat apart to find them all. Somehow, he didn't think it would take much to do so. The vessel was falling apart all by itself.

"It seems Devon was branching out on a solo career," he said, meeting Tamara's eye. "Only, he was using someone else's money to do so. I think they came looking for him."

Tamara frowned. "How do you know all of this? Only this afternoon we had nothing but speculation?"

He looked around, seeing Cassie moving to assist Eric in releasing some of the packets he'd just discovered. Lowering his voice so that only the two of them could hear, he leaned in to her. "Max... isn't quite what any of us thought he was."

Tamara's face dropped, her curiosity replaced by fear. He moved quickly to allay her concern, reaching out and placing a reassuring hand on the back of hers.

"It's okay. It's sorted, trust me," he said, ensuring eye contact. He gently squeezed her hand and she bobbed her head, the corners of her mouth trying for a smile. "I mean it," he said. "You've got nothing to worry about." She seemed reassured.

"What happened earlier?" she asked. "We couldn't see from where we were. How did it all go so wrong?"

Janssen exhaled deeply, then pursed his lips. "Someone

tipped them off. That's when they abandoned the meet and made a break for it."

"How do you know?"

"One of them received a call at the last moment. My guess is that was someone telling them we were probably waiting there."

"Who?" Tamara asked. Janssen shook his head, raising his eyebrows. "Max?" Tamara asked.

"Or whoever his handler is," he replied quietly. "Probably trying to maintain the integrity of their own investigation."

"Handler," Tamara repeated quietly, staring straight ahead as the penny dropped for her. "That's how he knew I was on this case… and where I was staying." Janssen nodded. "The slimy little bast—"

"He wanted me to tell you… that he meant what he said. If that makes any sense to you? For what it's worth, I think he was sorry and… he quite liked you."

She met his eye, steeling her expression. "He bloody well will be sorry if I catch up with him."

Janssen grinned and they both stood up, careful not to hit their heads and made their way back to the ladder.

"We'd better have this sealed off and have CSI get down here as soon as possible," Tamara said. Eric and Cassie came to join them. "We need this lot catalogued and secured. In the meantime, keep it between us what's down here. Understood?"

They all nodded their agreement and, one by one, set about climbing the ladder back above deck.

By THE TIME the area was secure and the forensics team had been roused, brought to the scene and broken into two teams, one focussing on the trawler and the other on the crash site, it was approaching midnight. Shaun, along with all three of the detained gang members, had refused to utter a word without legal representation. Shaun needed the on-call duty solicitor and the others summoned a team of heavy hitters up from the capital. These three were clearly not average street dealers but serious players. Whether they would be able to tie them to the murders of Ewan Dixon and Devon Bailey, or the assault on Jamie Kemp, remained to be seen. They hadn't caught them taking possession of the drugs from Shaun either. There was a chance they would be free and back on the street by lunchtime.

Janssen couldn't help but wonder if their actions tonight had managed to scupper the investigation Max was centred in. He wasn't bothered either way. Had they extended professional courtesy in his direction, then the outcome may have been different. As it was, they hadn't and if years of work fell away due to their decision, then it was too bad.

"We should all head home and get some rest," Tamara said. "We can pick this up first thing. Tom, do you want to take the lead with our three unknowns?"

He glanced up at her with a blank expression. "Sorry, what was that?"

"I don't think it's a good idea for you to interview Shaun. Not with the apparent bad blood between you, even if it is largely one sided. I figured you could take the lead with the other three."

"Yeah," he said absently, nodding. "You're probably right on Shaun but... " He glanced at Cassie, indicating her with a flick of his head. "I think Cassie should take the lead. It was her and Eric who got the information tying Devon to these characters. I think you should have the honour. I reckon you've earned it," he said to her pointedly.

Cassie smiled. "Thanks, sir... I mean, Tom."

"Okay, fair enough," Tamara said addressing Eric and Cassie. "The two of you head home and get some sleep. Cassie, do your prep for tomorrow and Eric... go and be a superhero for Becca or something."

Eric grinned. "I did call her when we got back to the station," he said, shifting his weight excitedly from one foot to the other. "She's waiting up for me... wants to hear all about it."

"No need to exaggerate this time," Cassie said.

Eric glared at her for a moment before realising she was only toying with him. His smile returned. She gave him a playful shove in the direction of the door and he feigned pain and suffering. Eric retrieved his coat, the one item of clothing he hadn't been wearing and was still dry. He had managed to change into a set of Janssen's gym gear, the only thing available to him aside from a forensic paper-suit. Standing at five foot six, Eric was dwarfed by Janssen and the jogging bottoms and sweatshirt made Eric look like a child playing dress up in his father's clothing. Tamara received a telephone call on her mobile, most likely from a senior officer judging by her tone and choice of words, signalling to ask if she could borrow Janssen's office. He didn't mind and she left him, closing the door behind her.

"I'll walk out with you," Cassie said to Eric, who nodded. "Just give me a second, yeah?"

She came over to Janssen, coming between him and the information boards he was still staring at. He glanced up at her.

"Are you okay?" he asked.

"Yes, I'm fine. I just wanted to say thank you… for having faith in me and all," she said, bobbing her head and glancing towards Eric, waiting in the doorway to the ops room. He sensed there was more and raised his eyebrows in query. She pursed her lips, turning pensive. "Before… I know you questioned my appointment—"

"Never regarding the merit," he swiftly countered.

"I know, but… Tamara and I go way back," she said, looking at the DCI who was pacing back and forth in Janssen's office, still talking on the phone. "You see, a while back, something happened to me." She paused and he realised she was building up to something and judging by her expression, it wasn't easy for her. "I was assaulted," she said, meeting his eye, "by a colleague." Cassie averted her eyes from his and he looked away, ensuring she wouldn't feel the weight of his gaze upon her. An image flashed back of her hesitation when he suggested she come with him into his office. Now, he understood why.

"I'm sorry that happened to you," he said. The words sounded hollow but he felt the need to say something.

"Me too," she said. "I wanted to walk, quit the job and hide myself away. The DCI... she brought me back."

Janssen nodded, turning himself to see Tamara watching them through the window.

"Anyway," she said, turning to leave, "I just thought you should know, that's all."

He smiled warmly. "Thank you for sharing that with me," he said. She started to walk away, Eric was agitating to leave and had no idea what they were discussing. He almost didn't ask the question, but decided to in a snap judgement. "Did they get him?"

She stopped, her back to him. She didn't turn. "No" she said quietly. "He was my DI... and he's still in the job."

Cassie resumed course without looking back, Eric grinning as she came alongside him and excitedly ushering her out of the door. He watched them leave, feeling immense sympathy for her while admiring her courage. Cassie Knight didn't strike him as a fantasist and her word was good enough for him. He returned his attention to the information boards, reading them over for what must have been the hundredth time.

"What's on your mind, Tom?"

He looked up. Tamara was hovering at his shoulder following his gaze to the boards.

"Ah... probably nothing."

"Come on, I know you well enough now. Out with it."

He sighed, sinking back in his chair. "I don't get it. Devon. I just don't understand why they did it."

"I would say that was pretty obvious," she said with a half-smile, dropping her eyes to him.

Janssen absently stroked at his chin, slowly shaking his head. "Don't get me wrong, I can see the motivation; retaliation, punishment or sending a warning to others... but to do so before they got their money or drugs back. That doesn't sit right with me."

Tamara looked to the ceiling, thinking hard as he looked up at her. "I see what you mean. Maybe they got ahead of themselves or didn't realise the lengths he'd already gone to and were then scrabbling around to catch up. Perhaps they're the thickest gang members known to man... who knows?"

Janssen drew breath, resigned to not answering every question this night. The interviews tomorrow might fill in some of these gaps. He had the feeling they wouldn't.

"Maybe you're right," he said but he remained unconvinced. Tamara laid a hand on his shoulder.

"Tonight, can we just celebrate the positive result and worry about the rest in the morning?"

"Sure," he said, smiling at her.

Tamara returned his smile and crossed the room to retrieve her coat from the back of her chair.

"Don't stay on this too long, Tom," she said over her shoulder, heading for the door. She paused, turning back to him and leaning against the door frame. "Tom?" she called. He looked round. "Thanks."

"What for?"

"Dealing with Max... and seeing that I didn't make a bad situation worse."

"Anytime," he said, nodding in her direction. With that, she was gone and he sat alone in the ops room. Rising from his seat, he went into his office and opened the top drawer of one of the filing cabinets. Inside, he found the evidence bag containing Iriya Bailey's personal effects that Cassie and Eric brought back from London. Sitting down at his desk, he laid the contents out in front of him and flicked on his desk lamp. Something wasn't right and he was determined to figure out what it was that troubled him.

CHAPTER THIRTY-EIGHT

THERE WASN'T much to show for a lifetime. Iriya Bailey left behind a wardrobe full of old clothes, a handful of grainy black and white photographs and some religious iconography. Janssen picked up the rosary, dangling the crucifix before him. The strap was aged leather and each of the beads appeared to be crafted by hand rather than machined. They varied in size and each bore the hallmarks of time with varying levels of pitting and scratching. The crucifix was a simple cross, stained a cherry red in contrast to the beads. He wouldn't be surprised if she'd carried it throughout her life.

Placing it down on the desk in front of him, he turned to the photographs. Many of them were candid shots of a little boy, taken at different moments of his life depicting scenes of childhood joy. One was taken in a playground with a grinning child sitting on a swing. Another had him holding a balloon, the number printed on the cards in the shot behind him stated it was a fifth birthday, probably his. He assumed they were of Devon. Iriya had no other children and she never married, as far as their dive into the records could tell.

The only special person in her life appeared to have been her son. For some reason, he wasn't with her when the end came but seemingly she held no bitterness towards him, no anger, only love. Passing through the assembled pictures, he found one of the two of them. Flicking over to the reverse, he read the handwritten details on the back. It simply noted – Me & Devon 22.11.65. He knew that was Devon's birth date. Iriya looked so proud, sitting in a bed cradling her newborn son in her arms. He put the pictures down and skipped to the report Eric had compiled with all that they knew about her. She'd arrived in the country at some point in the 1960s, although no record of her arrival date could be found in official documentation.

Iriya was Jamaican and, from what her neighbour and carers told them, very proud of her heritage. She was clearly part of what became known as the Windrush generation, named after the first vessel to bring Commonwealth citizens to the country in the post-war years. So few records were kept but the timeline appeared to fit. Returning to the photographs, he found one of her alone on Sheringham's promenade. He recognised where it was taken, along the foot of the cliffs and prior to the end of the town's sea defences.

She was standing in front of a line of concrete shacks. They looked far better than when he remembered them in his youth. By then, many had been knocked down and those that remained were scrawled with graffiti from bored teenagers with a tendency towards vandalism. In this shot they looked in good condition. He judged it was in the early sixties. Fishing out the newborn shot of Devon, he compared Iriya in both. They can't have been taken too far apart. She had the same hair length, her smile youthful and warm.

How old could she have been in the promenade shot, sixteen? Not much older than that, he reckoned. It wasn't taken in summertime. She wore a heavy overcoat and a knitted woollen hat and gloves. Her hands were clasped together in front of her and he lifted it closer to his eye and could just make out the rosary in her hands. She was smiling in this shot too; but it seemed like a nervous smile, as if she was shy in front of the camera. *How did a young immigrant end up in Sheringham at that age?* That was a question he was unlikely to ever find an answer to. Anyone who knew her was either deceased or far away. Her memory all but forgotten. He stroked the image with his thumb, a thought coming to mind. *Who did know her?* A young girl in a new country, alien surroundings... who would she turn to for support?

Gathering the pictures and the rosary together, he turned off his lamp and headed out into the ops room. He gently placed the bundle into his coat pocket and slipped his arm through the first sleeve, a theory developing in his mind as he did so. He flicked the lights off as he stepped out into the corridor, glancing at his watch. It was late, or early depending on how you looked at it, but he didn't care. If he was right, then the lateness of the hour was irrelevant.

JANSSEN PULLED up at the gated entrance to the driveway. The gate was open and looked like it hadn't been used to bar access for decades. As he expected, the house was in darkness, his headlights illuminating the brick and flint construction. He hesitated before releasing the clutch and entering the grounds, proceeding up the gravel-lined driveway to the front of the house.

He got out and walked up to the front door. There wasn't a door knocker but instead there was a small brass bell and a clapper. He rang it, the clanging sound carrying in the still of the night. He waited a few moments before giving it another blast, following up by banging on the door with his fist.

He had to wait a couple of minutes before he saw signs of movement from within, a shaft of light emerging from the foot of the door and Janssen stepped back from the porch, looking to the first floor. A light was on in one of the upstairs rooms. To encourage them further, he rang the bell again.

"Who's there?" a voice asked from within.

"Detective Inspector Janssen."

The sound of a bolt being slid across and then a key turning in the lock followed before the heavy door creaked open. Reverend Ebling stood in front of him, eyes narrowed and bore a decidedly irritated expression.

"My dear inspector," he said. "I am sure you're well aware of the time."

"Who is it, Charles?" A nervous sounding female voice asked.

Charles Ebling looked back over his shoulder, lifting his tone as he spoke. "It's the police, my love. Inspector Janssen."

Louise Ebling came into view behind her husband, at the far end of the hall at the foot of the staircase. She peered past her husband to look at Janssen, her head tilted to one side as she ensured her dressing gown was pulled tight around her.

"I think we need to have a chat," Janssen said.

"At this hour? Whatever for? Have you lost your mind, Inspector?"

He reached into his pocket, withdrawing the photograph of Iriya Bailey posing on Sheringham's promenade.

"We need to talk about Iriya," he said.

Charles Ebling looked at the picture, his lips parted but his gaze remained focussed on the image. It was an expression of recognition and certainly not one of shock. His gaze lingered on the photograph for a moment longer, Louise appearing by his side.

"I knew one day someone would knock on the door," Charles said, looking from the picture to Janssen.

Louise gripped her husband's forearm, squeezing it tightly. "Be silent, Charles—"

He reached up with his left hand and placed it affectionately over the back of her hand and turned to face her.

"This day was always going to come, my love," he said softly. "Always." He patted her hand before glancing to Janssen. "I think you had better come in, Inspector."

Janssen gestured for them to lead the way and the couple turned, Louise guided by her husband with a reassuring hand placed on her shoulder, leading them into the first reception room a little way along the hall. Janssen closed the front door and followed. The room was much as one would expect from a drawing room of the period, mahogany panelling lined the walls, the sound of a grandmother clock ticking from its place in the corner of the room filling the silence. Charles Ebling offered him a seat on one of the two floral-print sofas as he sat alongside his wife who consistently averted her eyes from Janssen's.

"What was it that brought you to me, Inspector," Charles asked, nervously looking to Louise and then back to him.

"It was something that's been troubling me all along," he said, sitting forward and resting his elbows on his knees. "Why on earth would a man with such a chequered character as Devon Bailey choose to spend his time helping out at a charitable food bank? Don't get me wrong, the allure of Helen Kemp notwithstanding, it seemed like an odd decision on his part."

Charles nodded sagely, his eyes flicking to his wife although her eyes remained transfixed on the floor in front of her. "Yes, I see how that could pique one's curiosity."

"And then," Janssen continued, "we looked into his background, finding this picture of his mother taken some time around when she would have first arrived in the country." He still had the photo in his hand, his eyes drifting down to it. "When was this? I figured it was the early sixties."

"1965," Charles said with certainty.

"The year Devon was born," he said. Neither of them commented. "And I found myself wondering how a young girl like Iriya, a devout religious girl, would cope in a new country, so far from everything she knew, her home and family. Who would she turn to for support… or guidance?" Both Charles and his wife refused to meet his eye. "It must have been quite a shock for the two of you when Devon rocked up at your door."

Charles looked up, meeting his gaze. He nodded briefly. "You have no idea, Inspector. You really don't," he said, gently reaching out and placing Louise's hand in his own. "It was a shock. You see, I didn't know anything of Devon."

"But you are aware that he was your son?" Janssen asked. It was something of a reach but why else wouldn't they mention their history with Devon's mother if it were not the case?

"Iriya kept him a secret from me," Charles said, following a period of awkward silence. "Looking back, I understand why she would do so. I was married." He looked to his wife who met his eye. She was set to burst into tears at any moment but, for now, only her lower lip quivered and she maintained her composure. "I was foolish... young and quite a weak man, looking back. I can only imagine how difficult it must have been for her... a single parent with... " He looked at Louise again but she didn't acknowledge him. "With a mixed race child in the sixties. They were unforgiving times, Inspector Janssen, contrary to the whole *counter culture* thing that people speak of so fondly."

"What did Devon have to say to you?"

Charles sighed and Louise grumbled something under her breath.

"Not much that I would care to repeat," Charles said. "I can't blame him for being so angry. Growing up... with only his mother for support and having to find his way when so many people looked down on him. I would be angry too. I would have tried to make amends, to make peace with him... but he wasn't interested in that."

"Then what did he want?"

"To ruin Charles," Louise hissed. "To take away everything that we had."

She glared at Janssen and he was taken aback by the ferocity of her tone. Charles squeezed her hand, smiling at her warmly and she calmed down.

"I think you should tell me what happened on the night he died, don't you?"

Louise looked to her husband, imploring him with her eyes not to say any more. "Please, Charles, don't."

He shook his head slowly, reaching up and stroking her cheek in a caring manner.

"Louise, I cannot hide from my past any longer. More lies will only make matters worse." He turned to Janssen. Louise was crying now, tears of despair flowing down her cheeks. "It is much as Louise says, Inspector. Devon wasn't looking to learn about me or share his past. He came looking for retribution with vengeance in his heart."

"What happened?"

"He was aggressive, Inspector. I'm not going to try to claim self-defence," Charles said. "He was set on ruining me, my reputation, our good work here in the community... threatening all of it." He glanced at Louise. "I'm ashamed to say that I lost my temper. I couldn't face the consequences of my own sin... and I struck him."

"How many times?" Janssen asked, watching him intently. Charles met his eye, unblinking.

"Just the once, I swear."

"What with?"

"Excuse me?"

"What did you strike him with?" Charles looked around. "With the first thing that came to hand. I don't remember."

"Oh, Charles," Louise said, her head sagging between her shoulders and weeping openly.

"He fell... and didn't get back up," Charles said. "I must admit I was surprised. He was such a powerful man. I guess, one would say I was lucky... or unlucky, whichever way you choose to look at it."

Janssen nodded solemnly. "And afterwards?"

"I panicked," Charles said, shaking his head. "I didn't want to face up to what I did, either then or now."

His gaze drifted past him and out of the window into the darkness beyond. The whites of the knuckles on Louise's hand were visible, so tightly did she hold onto her husband's hand. Janssen stared at him. Charles held the eye contact.

"And you drove him out to the cliffs and rolled him over the edge?" he asked.

Charles looked up and to the right. "Yes, after I realised what I'd done, I had to get him as far away as possible. I know it was wrong but, like I said, I panicked. I wasn't thinking straight."

Janssen drew breath, sitting upright. "I see."

He looked at Louise. She must have felt the weight of his eyes upon her because she slowly raised her head, her tear-stained face meeting his eye before looking away.

"Now, perhaps Louise could tell me what really happened?"

Both Charles and his wife snapped to attention, glancing at one another before turning to him.

"You said no more lies, Charles and, right now, you're still lying to me."

Charles Ebling appeared ready to protest but a stern sideways look from his wife stopped him from doing so. Instead, an expression of pity crossed his face. Louise shook her head slowly.

"It's okay," she said. "You were right. We can't run from what we have done." She turned to Janssen who waited expectantly. "You are correct, Inspector. Charles wasn't at the church when Devon decided to confront me. For it was me who Devon held the most hatred for, not Charles." Janssen wanted to ask the question but he held back. He didn't have to wait long. "You see, Charles was telling you the truth. He didn't know about Devon, or the baby as he was at the time. I did... and I forced Iriya to leave. She threatened my world and..."She paused, steeling herself and drawing a deep breath. "I made her leave. I gave her all the money I could raise and I forced her out. She didn't want to go but I made her. I even drove her to the bus stop... left her there alone. I swore to her that everyone would be better off if she left. If she stayed, Charles would be ruined and where would that leave any of us? She begged me to help her, to help her unborn child… but I abandoned her with nothing but a suitcase and a pocket full of pound notes. " She glanced down to her lap before looking at her husband. "And I never spoke of it again. She was gone, and when I saw the pain that that left in my husband I felt both elation and shame. Shame because of what I had done… and joy at seeing him suffer… as I was suffering."

"Iriya told Devon," Janssen said. "She told him how she came to be raising him alone."

Louise nodded. "She blamed me, not Charles. Devon confronted me. He was positively gleeful… and couldn't wait to destroy our lives. My life. I pleaded with him, begged him… but that only made him laugh louder. I held onto him as he left the church, trying to pull him back. I was so sorry but it made no difference. He only had darkness in his soul."

"What happened?" Janssen asked quietly. Louise took a deep breath and met his eye.

"He shook me off. I fell to the floor, begging him not to do it but he laughed. I got up and ran after him, trying to pull him back inside. The things he said to me… and I got angry. I don't know where it came from but it rose from inside me like a monster and I lashed out at him."

"You struck him?"

She nodded. "I did. Not that he was hurt. He seemed to enjoy it. He laughed, walking backwards away from me, stumbling as he missed the step down to the path. He tripped and fell against one of the headstones. I screamed at him but… he didn't move, he didn't get up. He… he… was dead."

"And the two of you," Janssen said, flicking his hand between them, "decided to get rid of the problem?"

Charles nodded slowly. "That part was true, Inspector. Louise called me and… what was I to do? She told me everything. About Devon and what he planned to do as well as what had happened with Iriya all those years ago." The couple held onto one another, Louise laying her head on his shoulder. "You see, I am responsible, Inspector. I did this. *It is my fault.* Do you see?"

Janssen took a deep breath, glancing between the two of them. "That's not for me to judge," he said. "But Iriya… and Devon for that matter… deserved so much more than what they got."

———

JANSSEN SHUT the door on the patrol car. Louise Ebling didn't look at him as the car pulled away. Charles, on the other hand, watched him intently from the back of the car he was sitting in whilst waiting to depart. There was no animosity in his expression. He accepted his guilt, accepted what he had done along with the tidal wave of condemnation that was set to come his way. Tamara came to stand alongside him.

"When I said *don't spend too long on this,* I figured we'd discuss it in the morning."

He laughed. "I know. Couldn't wait."

"How did you know?" she asked.

"I didn't, not really," he said. "It just didn't sit right. I'm sorry I had to wake you but I figured you'd want to know."

"You're right. I would have been annoyed if you hadn't."

Then she laughed. He was curious.

"What's so funny?"

She turned to him, sweeping the hair, blowing in the wind, away from her face and tucking it behind her ear.

"Silly really. Eric will be on cloud nine when he comes in tomorrow, ready to recount how his heroics went down with Becca."

"And?"

"Your story will blow his out of the water."

"Well, maybe we can give him his moment before we break the news," he said with a sideways grin. Tamara smiled and agreed.

———

FREE BOOK GIVEAWAY

Visit the author's website at **www.jmdalgliesh.com** and sign up to the VIP Club and be first to receive news and previews of forthcoming works.

Here you can download a FREE eBook novella exclusive to club members;

Life & Death - A Hidden Norfolk novella

Never miss a new release.

No spam, ever, guaranteed. You can unsubscribe at any time.

Enjoy this book? You could make a real difference.

Because reviews are critical to the success of an author's career, if you have enjoyed this novel, please do me a massive favour by entering one onto Amazon.

———

Type the following link into your internet search bar to go to the Amazon page and leave a review;

http://mybook.to/Tell_No_Tales

———

If you prefer not to follow the link please visit the Amazon sales page where you purchased the title in order to leave a review.

Reviews increase visibility. Your help in leaving one would make a massive difference to this author.
Thank you for taking the time to read my work.

HEAR NO EVIL PREVIEW
HIDDEN NORFOLK - BOOK 5

SCANNING THE SURROUNDING area as he walked, the sun broke through the hazy cloud cover stinging his eyes. Cursing the decision to leave his sunglasses back in the vehicle, he squinted against the bright light.

A woman passed by him, tugging at her chador with one hand and pulling her daughter alongside her with the other. It seemed as if she deliberately avoided eye contact with him as she passed. That was common; at least it had been since his arrival. He glanced in her direction, watching her departing form as she increased her pace. The little girl looked over her shoulder, watching him with a curious expression he found hard to read. Her green eyes seemed at odds with the dark hair and olive skin.

Returning his attention to focussing on the task in hand, he surveyed the ground at his feet. It was dry and littered with loose stones. No matter where he went in this country, everywhere appeared much the same; arid, dusty... a landscape far removed from that of his home in the central belt of Scotland. He couldn't have found a starker contrast if he'd tried.

Glancing back towards the Viking, he saw his troop doing the same as he was; searching for a needle in a haystack. Next time, they should tell the Artillery to find their own stupid drone. Six went up but only five came back and now, here they were, picking over the ground on the outskirts of a village at the centre of a six-point grid reference; the best the operators had been able to provide for the searchers. What a waste of time.

This wasn't supposed to be happening.

They should be back at the Forward Operating Base getting something to eat. They'd only been back in camp for an hour before receiving the shout to head out on this little goose chase. Taking a deep breath, he scanned for the debris. If the drone came down around here then they should be able to find it unless one of the locals had already scooped up whatever was left. That was their worst nightmare, the drone finding its way into the hands of an enemy operator. Half the troop were presently on the far side of the village while they worked their way around to meet them.

A shout went up and he looked over his shoulder. His corporal was bellowing at him and frantically gesturing in the direction beyond, trying to draw his attention to something. Realising he'd drifted too far from the rest of the troop, he touched one hand to his ear piece and tapped it a couple of times. There was a crackle, followed by shouts from troopers signalling multiple contacts as small arms fire erupted all around him. The roar of mechanised armour starting their engines sounded and he looked back in the direction indicated, seeing a puff of blue smoke and a black dot racing towards him. Something whistled past and only when it struck the rocks behind did the reality hit home. The detonation of the rocket-propelled grenade sent shards of rock and shrapnel in every direction. It wasn't like in the movies but it was awesome nonetheless. The Taliban liked to tamper with the warheads, setting them to airburst at four-hundred metres to ensure they took out at least one man, usually a commander, with the resulting shrapnel. How they missed him, he didn't know. Debris rained down all around as he sprinted back to the Viking.

Both lungs and thighs burned as rounds fizzed past him in opposite directions as both sides engaged and exchanged fire.

This wasn't supposed to be happening.

Reaching the vehicle, his corporal screamed at him.

"Take your bloody time, Trooper!"

He clambered into the driver's seat as an almighty clang sounded, audible above the roar of both engine and gunfire. His ears rang. That was another RPG harmlessly striking the Viking's armour. They'd failed to get him with their second attempt. His ear's rang as they moved off in the direction of the enemy positions on the edge of the village.

They entered the village and a car appeared in front of them at the next intersection, turning in their direction. It had sheet metal cobbled together across the front with a single slit before the driver to enable him to see where he was going. It was a suicide mission. The car accelerated, bouncing its way along the uneven road surface towards them. The Viking's Browning M2 rotated and opened fire, punching through the car's makeshift armour with ease. The vehicle swerved to the right, out of control, slamming into the mud-brick perimeter wall of the village. The car exploded, a wall of flames engulfing the entire street.

HE WOKE with a start. Sweat poured from him, his heart beating like a hammer in his chest. For a second he remained confused, almost bewildered at where he was. The darkness all but encompassed him apart from a narrow shaft of moonlight passing through the rear window to penetrate the interior. The gentle breeze drifting through the cracked window, wafted the net curtain gently back and forth. He shivered; the perspiration on his bare skin and the cold night air combining to remind him he wasn't in Afghanistan anymore. His right shoulder ached. It was a familiar sensation, particularly on colder days.

Sliding out of the bed, he pulled the duvet with him and hurried outside. The hinges of the door creaked as he threw it open. The lightweight door caught on the wind and slammed against the exterior but there was no one around to disturb.

Once outside he crossed to the fire pit, the embers still visible glowing red and orange. He stoked them and added several small off cuts of timber. The wood was already beginning to smoulder as the makings of a flame began to lick at the edges of the fuel and, drawing the duvet around his shoulders, he sank into an antiquated camping chair set out before the pit. Staring into the growing fire, he watched as the flames danced before him, listening to the sound of the sea crashing upon the nearby shoreline at the foot of the hill.

It wasn't supposed to be like this.

Hear No Evil
Hidden Norfolk – Book 5

BOOKS BY J M DALGLIESH

One Lost Soul

Bury Your Past

Kill Our Sins

Tell No Tales

Hear No Evil

The Dead Call

Kill Them Cold

A Dark Sin

To Die For

Fool Me Twice

The Raven Song

Angel of Death

Dead to Me

Life and Death *FREE - visit jmdalgliesh.com

Divided House

Blacklight

The Dogs in the Street

Blood Money

Fear the Past

The Sixth Precept

Dark Yorkshire Books 1-3

Dark Yorkshire Books 4-6

Audiobooks

In the Hidden Norfolk Series
One Lost Soul
Bury Your Past
Kill Our Sins
Tell No Tales
Hear No Evil
The Dead Call
Kill Them Cold
A Dark Sin
To Die For
Fool Me Twice
The Raven Song
Angel of Death

In the Dark Yorkshire Series
Divided House
Blacklight
The Dogs in the Street
Blood Money
Fear the Past
The Sixth Precept

Dark Yorkshire Books 1-3
Dark Yorkshire Books 4-6